The Seeker

The Seeker

a novel

SUDHIR KAKAR

TRUMPETER
Boston
2008

TRUMPETER BOOKS
An imprint of Shambhala Publications, Inc.
Horticultural Hall
300 Massachusetts Avenue
Boston, Massachusetts 02115
www.shambhala.com

© 2004 by Sudhir Kakar

9 8 7 6 5 4 3 2 1

First Trumpeter Edition

Printed in the United States of America

♾ This edition is printed on acid-free paper that meets
the American National Standards Institute Z39.48 Standard.
Distributed in the United States by Random House, Inc.,
and in Canada by Random House of Canada Ltd

Designed by Lora Zorian

LIBRARY OF CONGRESS CATALOGING-IN-PUBLICATION DATA
Kakar, Sudhir.
[Mira and the Mahatma]
The seeker: a novel / Sudhir Kakar.—1st ed.
p. cm.
Originally published: Mira and the Mahatma.
New Delhi, India: Penguin Books India, 2004.
ISBN 978-1-59030-525-6 (pbk.: alk. paper)
1. Mirabehn, 1892–1982—Fiction.
2. Gandhi, Mahatma, 1869–1948—Fiction.
3. India—History—20th century—Fiction. I. Title.
PR9499.3.K273M57 2008
823'.914—dc22
2007033782

To Kamla,

whose love for Gandhi

almost equals mine for her

AUTHOR'S NOTE

THIS IS THE TRUE STORY of nine years—from 1925 to 1930, and from 1940 to 1942—in the lives of Madeleine Slade (aka Mirabehn) and Gandhi, when their lives were entwined more intimately than in any other period of their long association. She was thirty-three when she left London for his ashram in Ahmadabad; he was fifty-six. As far as possible, I have tried to tell the story in their own voices, in words preserved in their autobiographical accounts, letters, diaries and in the reminiscences of others. I have attempted to provide coherence and consistency to the narrative by filling in the gaps of the story using that peculiar amalgamation of fantasy and acts of empathic identification we call imagination. The imagination is, however, of form alone. The building blocks of this story are from life; the binding material in the interstices is fictional.

Gandhi's letters to Mira, her letters to Prithvi Singh and his to her were all written by them and can be found in the archives of the Nehru Memorial Museum Library in New Delhi. Many of the incidents that take place in the ashram, especially the ones that may seem most improbable, are based on actual events. Mira's diary entries and most of her letters to Romain Rolland, on the other hand, are fictional.

Prologue

*I*T WAS IN JUNE 1968, during the hottest part of the summer when invitations to attend conferences and seminars
in cooler climes are most welcome, that I flew to Vienna to attend
a conference on "Asian literature in the age of decolonization."
My recent book on Premchand had earned me a modest reputation in literary circles, and my conference paper was on the
influence of Premchand on modern Hindi fiction. At the reception
given to the Indian participants by our ambassador to Austria,
I casually asked one of the younger diplomats hovering around
us, anxious to ply us with a predetermined amount of food and
wine and then hurry us off the embassy's premises, whether he
knew Mirabehn.

When I had last heard from Mira, her agonizing restlessness,
no longer held in check once Gandhiji was gone, had pushed
her ever deeper into the Himalayas. In her first letter to me in
many years, written from Pakshikunj, Mira described the breath-
taking beauty of her surroundings—the patches of grasslands,
the deodar groves, and the magnificent peaks towering before
her. She would watch the sun set every evening, spreading its
golden light on the snow which rapidly turned orange and then
a brilliant pink as dusk fell. The vision filled her with peace, she
wrote, but even as she made her way back to the house from the

grassy slopes, the restlessness came creeping back, as if it had never left her. So when someone mentioned in passing in 1959 that she had left India for England and moved from there in a few months to Austria to settle down somewhere near Vienna, I was not surprised.

I had not really expected the diplomat to have heard of Mira. To the younger generation of Indians, Gandhiji is a mythical figure. They are familiar with him as an icon, as the "father of the nation." His dreams about the future of independent India, his vision of what makes for an ethical life and the people who shared this vision and accompanied him through his life, have long been forgotten. Even people who were close to him once and proudly called themselves his followers had found other gods after Gandhiji's death. Some became Marxists, others sang praises of the dynamism of a capitalist America; almost all of them turned to the worship of new idols—modern science and industry. For most, there was no sudden awakening from their infatuation with him, no kiss from a prince to transform them, just a gradual turning away of hearts that grew colder. I was quite surprised therefore when the diplomat said that he knew Mirabehn.

"She is quite a character, you know," he said, in the condescending way the young sometimes speak of the old who are no longer relevant to their generation but still occasionally intrude on their consciousness. "Anyone who visits her is immediately informed that she will not speak of Gandhi or her years with him. That chapter of her life is firmly closed, she says. All she talks about now is Beethoven. She's writing a book on him, you know. She lives just outside Vienna with an Indian servant and an old dog in a small town called Baden. Do you know her?"

"Yes," I replied. "I taught her Hindi once, some forty years ago when she first came to Gandhiji."

The young diplomat seemed interested, although in my

somewhat inebriated state I might have mistaken his polite attention for curiosity. I do not remember what all I told him as my memories of those years came rushing forth. It is possible that I exaggerated my closeness to Mirabehn, and to Gandhiji. I might even have hinted that I was privy to secrets I would reveal at an appropriate time. I had not realized that wine was, so to speak, a "nonvegetarian" grape juice which heats you from within before lighting a slow fire in the part of your brain that controls speech, that it not only loosens the tongue but also opens up the pores of a memory prone to exaggeration. I think I was boasting about how Gandhiji had regarded me as a son and how I remained wedded to his ideals to this day when the young man cut me short.

"Would you like to meet her?" he said, waving away the waiter bearing a tray of drinks just as I stretched out my hand for more of the delicious, red intoxicant.

"Yes, of course," I said hastily. "Could we go tomorrow afternoon? The conference ends at noon."

I did not know that with this casual commitment, I was embarking on a journey that would have me doubling back on the tracks of Mira's life. I would spend a good part of the next five years poring over her notes, diaries and letters, chasing eyewitnesses for their recollections besides rummaging in the chest of my own memories, as I prepared myself to tell her story, which, in a way, would also be mine.

one

O N THE MORNING of 25 October 1925, a pleasantly warm autumn day in the south of France, Madeleine Slade, a thirty-three-year-old Englishwoman, walked up the gangplank of a P&O liner docked in the port of Marseilles that was to sail for Bombay later in the day. The ship had been stoking her fires since early morning. Just before noon, she weighed her great anchor and majestically edged out of the harbor, sounding six blasts on her horn in a familiar salute to the port. Madeleine did not go up to the deck and lean against the railing to watch the shoreline of Europe recede. Unlike most other passengers, fellow Britishers going out to the colonies for the first time or returning from home leave to once again take upon their shoulders the white man's burden, Madeleine was not sailing into a parting but into pristine hope.

Madeleine's luggage consisted of two newly bought steel trunks and an old but well-preserved leather valise made from the finest cowhide, its brass clasp and the studded brass strips reinforcing its edges gleaming softly from a recent application of Brasso. The trunks were crammed with books, selected from a personal library of over four hundred volumes she had collected since she was in her teens. The ones she was taking with her were general books on philosophy and history. Repositories of impersonal knowledge, they were incapable of conjuring up and connecting her to a past she was not as much relinquishing as locking up in a secure vault of her memory. Her recent acquisitions, which she planned to dip into during the voyage, were a book on Urdu grammar, French translations of the Bhagavad Gita and the *Rigveda*, a large French-English dictionary, and two recently published biographies of Gandhi, of which one was in French—Romain Rolland's *Mahatma Gandhi*. For a while she had deliberated taking along *Jean Christophe*, Rolland's ten-volume epic novel partly based on the life of Beethoven, which she had read and reread many times over in the last few years when her involvement with the composer and his music was at its most passionate. In the end she decided against doing so, although she did slip the slim *Vie de Beethoven* into a pile in one of the trunks. Beethoven was not quite a part of the past she was depositing in the vault. True, he was no longer in full, imperial possession of her consciousness, but he was also not so irrevocably gone from her life that he was incapable of stirring any emotion in her.

The leather valise contained five new, shapeless frocks stitched from white, hand-spun khadi cloth especially ordered from India, a couple of baggy Shetland wool pullovers, a woolen scarf almost the size of a small shawl, which Madeleine had herself spun, dyed and woven during the past year, cotton underwear, two pairs of sensible walking shoes and a small box of jewelry which she planned to gift to Gandhi's commune, his ashram. All her other possessions, never many to begin with, since she had always been a young woman singularly uninterested in fashionable clothes and expensive jewelry, had been distributed among the servants of her parents' household. In fact, while she was cutting off her ties with her past life, the valise was possibly her one concession to sentiment. It was a remnant from her first trip to India eighteen years ago, when she was fifteen.

That had been a very different voyage. Her father, recently elevated to the rank of an admiral in the Royal Fleet was setting out to take command of the East Indies station in Bombay. The Slade family—Madeleine's mother, her sister Rhona, three years elder than her, and their old nurse Bertha, now promoted to lady's maid, had been the most important passengers on board the P&O liner, fawned over by the ship's captain and officers. Their luggage had consisted of more than twenty wooden crates and steel trunks of all shapes and sizes, filled with evening dresses, party frocks, fashionable hats, an admiral's gold-braided uniforms, tennis and riding clothes, saddles and bridles, double-felt hats, anti-cholera belts, bottles of medicine against all conceivable tropical maladies, and odds and ends that her mother hoped would turn the family quarters of the Admiralty House in Bombay into a passable replica of their London rooms.

Memories of that earlier voyage did not cloud Madeleine's mind. She prided herself on her ability to concentrate effortlessly on a person, a situation or a train of thought, shutting out the irrelevant and the extraneous for as long as she wanted. In other words, she could concentrate even when she was not concentrating, "a certain sign of spiritual giftedness," as Romain Rolland had told her at their last meeting. Her inner guard could always be depended upon not to let an unwanted intruder enter her consciousness unless expressly summoned. Well, almost always. Not only did she never remember her dreams but she even remained unaffected by the miasma a dream can leave upon the waking hours, subtly determining the mood for much of the day. The thoughts and feelings she dutifully wrote down during the voyage, to be mailed to Rolland in Switzerland once the ship docked in Bombay, were thus exclusively about the new life awaiting her in Mahatma Gandhi's ashram.

Each evening, the moon climbing the sky from the east laid out a lane of shimmering light on the placid surface of the Mediterranean, a lane that became wider with the passing of the days as the moon waxed. Madeleine would stay up on the deck late into night when, except for the urgent whispering of occasional lovers embarking on a shipboard romance, all was quiet, and the deep-throated hum of the engines was no longer a disturbance but had become a particular quality of the silence. Leaning against the steel railing on top of the ship's prow, she would gaze out in front of her where in the distance the band of moonlight on the water crawled into the dark horizon. Slowly, she would feel herself entering a fugue-like state, all content and form gradually leaking out of her thoughts and becoming a part of the ship as it sailed along the path of the light.

"Fugue-like state" are my words, the words of her erstwhile Hindi teacher and now would-be biographer. They are words of ignorance in search of understanding. Madeleine, in her diary, calls the state "a moment of grace." Timeless moments like these were familiar to her from childhood. Then, they would often steal up on her when she was alone with nature—while she was out for a walk in the woods on a sun-dappled summer morning, for instance, and came across a swallow's nest, fragile and leaning precariously against a sunlit stone, or when she spotted a clump of dandelions, deep yellow in the dark shade, and perceived in them "a promise of eternity." These moments of complete well-being, or rather, of a state of being that spurns all qualifiers, stands above all adjectives, became rare when she was growing into a woman. They deserted her completely for years till she encountered Gandhi in Rolland's prose and felt "the heralds of grace come whispering into my heart . . . their tendrils brush against me like the touch of eyelashes on my cheek," as she writes in her diary in her sometimes overwrought prose. It was then that she had known with utter conviction where her future path lay. "Grace," she affirms, "is the only guide I have always trusted to steer me through the shoals of an unknown fate."

To everyone's surprise but her own, Madeleine's family had not tried to stop her. After all, her father was one of the first officers of the British navy, connected to the highest officials and ministers of the land, and dedicated to the protection and continuity of the Empire. And here was his daughter setting out to join someone whom the British considered the Empire's most implacable enemy.

"Once they saw I was serious," she writes "that I was fulfilling a deep need of my spirit, both Mother and Father respected my decision. Father even helped me when I told him I needed to learn an Indian language to prepare for my life here. He wrote to Lord Birkenhead, the Secretary of State for India, who had been at Eton with him. The minister advised that I learn Urdu and even recommended an Indian student living in London as my tutor. Of course, in their quiet and gentle way they were concerned. But no one tried to stop me."

Bertha, her old nanny, had been the only one to express a little of the family's unvoiced apprehensions. "How lonely you'll be, lost among all those Indians," she said.

"It will be the first time in my life when I shall not be alone, Bertha," Madeleine replied. Indeed, the exile was returning home, although her destination was the man, Gandhi, rather than the country.

Madeleine was to travel to India via Paris where her father had gone for some official work. "Be careful," was all he said when he came to see his daughter off at the Gare de Lyon from where she took the train to Marseilles. He had come straight from a function at the French defense ministry. The white ostrich feather plume in his admiral's hat was visible for a long time from the window of her compartment, bobbing above the heads of the people on the platform, as the evening train steamed out.

Unlike the preceding years which were considerably tumultuous, the year Madeleine arrived in India had been unusually uneventful. Completely unaware of the social and political context for events in far-off India, her interest in what was happening in the country channeled solely through her fascination with the Mahatma, Madeleine could not know that 1925 had been a quiet year only because the British believed that Gandhiji (as an Indian I would feel extremely uneasy if I did not add the respectful suffix "ji" to his name) was a spent political force. They were convinced that he was pursuing vague social programs which were sufficiently far removed from actions that constituted a threat to their empire. As we came to know later, Lord Birkenhead had commented with evident satisfaction, "Poor Gandhi has indeed perished! As pathetic a figure with his spinning wheel as the last minstrel with his harp, and not able to secure so charming an audience."

It had been five years since Gandhiji's call for noncooperation with the Raj had electrified the country. The movement had given birth to unprecedented enthusiasm and hope among the masses that self-rule, swaraj, freedom of the country from the British colonial masters, would be theirs in a matter of months. The hope had been dampened but not extinguished by the violence in Bombay and Madras, and especially the incident at Chauri Chaura where twenty-one policemen were burnt to death by a mob which set fire to the police station. In characteristic protest Gandhiji had gone on a five-day fast of penance. Then, declaring that the violent incidents had convinced him that the country was not yet ready for self-rule, he had called off the civil disobedience movement.

Four years had passed since the political ferment of those days, and two years since his release from Yervada jail. The British might have written him off, but we knew better. We watched and waited for his next move, not quite ready to believe that he had retired from the political stage for good. Although he repeatedly affirmed that the movement for self-rule now had a different form—a moral politics which emphasized spinning, eradication of untouchablity in Hindu society and the fostering of Hindu-Muslim unity—most people remained unconvinced. How could such mundane activities replace the heady excitement of the earlier civil disobedience movement when crowds had taken to the streets all over the country to protest British rule? The students were especially incensed by his decision to stop the mass agitation. Instead, he was now asking them to participate in campaigns whose purpose they could not comprehend. What if there had been some violence in 1921? These things happened. There could be no omelet without breaking eggs. Even a vegetarian like him should know that. All this talk about India not being ready for swaraj! How was spinning yarn from cotton supposed to prepare the country for swaraj? And what about the campaigns against untouchability and for Hindu-Muslim unity? These problems went back hundreds, if not thousands, of years and were not going to be solved in a few. Was it not enough that a beginning had been made, that all of us were now aware of these evils? And if the Hindu-Muslim problem had to be solved first, before India was ready for swaraj, then the country may well have to wait another hundred years for freedom! Some, quietly agreeing with Lord Birkenhead's assessment of Gandhiji's growing irrelevance in the political scenario, were looking with increasing favor upon the young revolutionaries in Punjab and Bengal who advocated violent means for the overthrow of British rule.

However, though politically uneventful, 1925 had not lacked in the normal catastrophes: floods in Bengal and Assam, drought in some districts of the Madras Presidency and in most of the princely states of Rajputana, caste atrocities in a dozen villages of Travancore and, of course, Hindu-Muslim riots throughout British India had ravaged the country claiming the lives, property and livelihoods of thousands. Madeleine avidly followed the reports of the riots in London newspapers in which Gandhiji's name often cropped up in connection with efforts at restoring peace between the two communities. In the beginning of the year there was a report about him being refused permission to visit Rawalpindi where Hindu refugees from Kohat had taken shelter after their Muslim neighbors had attacked their homes and places of worship. In July he was in Calcutta, setting up peace committees after riots disrupted Bakr-Id festivities. In August, the newspapers printed a short version of his appeal for calm after Titagarh was engulfed by religious strife and killings. Madeleine had been especially alarmed by a small item on an inside page of the *Guardian* which said that Mr. Gandhi was considering going on another prolonged fast for the cause of Hindu-Muslim unity, like the one he had undertaken the previous year after riots broke out in Delhi. To her relief, the report proved to be unfounded.

It had been the ending of the Delhi fast, which many people had not expected Gandhiji to survive—after all, he was fifty-five years old, and exhausted from the strain of incessant work and travel—that had finally prompted Madeleine to write to him. The twenty-one days of the fast had been agonizing. The thought that she might lose him even before they met, that he might forever remain a sacred image in her mind, enveloped in the aura of her devotion, but never acquire the density of flesh, never become a living person, was unbearable. Each day, as she went about her studies and preparations for her life in India, she silently prayed for his survival. When the news finally came that the fast was over, her joy was so great that her strong sense of self-discipline deserted her. She threw the newspaper down on the floor of the morning room of their Bedford Gardens house where she had just finished breakfast and rushed to the kitchen. Without uttering a word, she threw her arms around her astonished mother who was giving instructions to the cook for the special dinner to which Winston Churchill and two of her father's colleagues from the Admiralty had been invited. Madeleine did not remember hugging her mother with such fierce abandon since her tenth birthday when her parents had given her a pony as a birthday present.

In her relief she decided that her thankfulness to God for sparing the Mahatma's life needed a more concrete expression. Not wishing to ask her parents for money, she sold the only valuable item she possessed, her grandmother's diamond brooch, for twenty pounds in a jewelry shop in Kensington. She sent a check for this amount to Gandhiji at the ashram together with the first of many letters she was to write to him. The letter was both shy and determined. She was thankful that the fast had ended successfully, she wrote, and hoped he did not mind her writing to him. Six months ago, she had read Romain Rolland's book about him and had been so moved that she had wanted to leave immediately for India. But on further reflection she had realized that she should prepare herself through a year of rigorous training, in which she was now engaged. She hoped he would accept her check as a contribution to his work in which she wanted to participate one day.

Madeleine had not really expected a reply, and was both surprised and quietly happy—it was not in her nature to be deliriously so, at least not openly—when she got one on a worn and creased postcard. Written in a spidery handwriting and in cheap black ink that was already beginning to fade unevenly, some letters demanding attention while others seemed content to remain in the background, the letter read,

Dear Friend,

I must apologize to you for not writing earlier. I have been continuously travelling. I thank you for the twenty pounds sent by you. The amount will be used for popularizing the spinning wheel.

I am glad indeed that instead of obeying your first impulse you decided to fit yourself for the life here and to take time. If a year's test still impels you to come, you will probably be right in coming to India.

> *On the train,*
> *Yours sincerely,*
> *31.12.24*
> *M. K. Gandhi*

Madeleine had not given Gandhiji the details of her training. Reading books about India, studying some of its sacred literature and learning Urdu were only a part of the exacting regimen she had set up for herself. The language sessions with the Indian student were particularly difficult. Both teacher and student spent many frustrating hours trying to cut through the nets of mutual incomprehension: he struggling to recognize his language in her upper-class English pronunciation of Urdu words, she occasionally glimpsing familiar landmarks through the heavy Punjabi accent that befogged his English.

Madeleine was also learning to spin and weave, since spinning was an obligatory daily activity in the ashram. She had read that spinning was essential to Mahatma Gandhi's constructive program for the masses which he had been zealously pursuing ever since his release from prison in 1922. An activity that would involve every house in every village, spinning, he believed, could make a perceptible dent in India's desperate poverty by making the poor economically self-reliant. Apart from its economic benefits, he saw daily spinning as the most efficient aid to mass discipline without which a nonviolent people's movement of civil disobedience against British rule was impossible. In a recent issue of the weekly *Young India*, which Madeleine now read regularly in the periodical reading room of the British Museum, Gandhiji had written that the spinning wheel stood for the greatest good of the greatest number.

"The whole trend is to think of the privileged few and neglect the poor," the article stated. "I have no quarrel with those who conceived the system. They could not do otherwise. How is an elephant to think of an ant? I do not wish the educated classes to do anything else except to spin for a limited time every day to represent in a living way their sympathy with the poor and the oppressed, their brotherhood of man." The spinning wheel had thus become a symbol of many things: India's poor, the nation's fight for freedom, universal brotherhood.

No one spins cotton in England, or indeed in Europe, Madeleine was told when she began to look for a teacher who would initiate her into the craft. She had to learn to spin with wool from a friend of her mother's who ran a small school called the Kensington Weavers. Madeleine bought a spinning wheel and carding brushes and began to spin wool at home while going to the school for weaving lessons. The spinning wheel may have been a symbol invested with multiple meanings and high ideals, but Madeleine soon learnt that the the actual act of spinning was hard work and it stretched her patience. Ever so often the thread would snap, requiring the difficult effort of repair. Her eyesight was strained and her arms and shoulder muscles throbbed with a dull ache long after the daily hour of practice was over.

Madeleine's intensive preparations for the life ahead of her extended to her personal habits as well. Learning to sit cross-legged on the floor caused much less difficulty (the protests of unused thigh muscles and ligaments in the knee relatively muted) than practicing to sleep on the floor. In the beginning, it was less a matter of stiffness in her neck and back when she woke up in the mornings and more a realization that this part of her training was making the other members of the household decidedly uncomfortable. Again, no one tried to stop her or even voiced any disapproval, but she could hardly miss Bertha's incredulous expression or the pained look on her mother's face when Madeleine wanted the bed to be removed from her room. A week later, when she wanted even the carpet to be taken away, her mother went so far as to ask, "Are you sure, dear?" Madeleine was insistent, she wanted to get used to sleeping on the bare floor because that's what the inmates did at the ashram.

Her father, absorbed in his work at the Admiralty and often away on tours of inspection, did not seem to notice when Madeleine gave up her evening glass of sherry and the occasional glass of wine with dinner. But Madeleine did not miss the quick exchange of looks between her parents when she refused the roast for the first time. "They don't eat meat there. I must get used to being a vegetarian," she felt impelled to explain. From her parents' subsequent reactions, she realized that though they understood her reasons, they mistook her intent for compulsion. At the dining table, her mother was overly solicitous, as with a child not sick but also not quite healthy, pressing her to eat more of the vegetable stew that was becoming a regular item on the dinner menu. Even her father occasionally engaged her in such discussions as why the cauliflower soup could be regarded as vegetarian although the cook had used chicken stock to make it, or whether she could be coaxed into eating eggs. Yes, an egg was not a vegetable, but it was also not quite meat. One could say eggs lay in food's gray zone, which was subject to more than one interpretation.

After eight months of training, which included a six-week stint at the beginning of summer working on a farm in Switzerland to toughen her physically, Madeleine again wrote to Mahatma Gandhi. "By September, I expect to be mentally and physically ready for ashram life. Some months ago, I had an experience which I can only tell you in person when we meet. It revealed to me that my life was to be joined to yours, that all I want is to come to India and live with you, assisting in your work in any way I can. When can I come? I enclose samples of wool that I have spun on my wheel."

This time the reply came within two months. Its tone was perceptibly warmer, although it still ended with a formal "Yours sincerely, M. K. Gandhi."

I was pleased to receive your letter which has touched me deeply . . . The samples of wool you have sent are excellent. You are welcome whenever you choose to come. If I have advice of the steamer that brings you, there will be someone receiving you at the steamer and guiding you to the train that will take you to Sabarmati. Only please remember that the life at the Ashram is not all rosy. It is strenuous. Bodily labour is given by every inmate. The climate of this country is also not a small consideration. I mention these things not to frighten you but merely to warn you.

That very afternoon, Madeleine went to the P&O office in London to book her passage to India.

two

MADELEINE'S SHIP DOCKED in Bombay's Princess Docks late in the morning on 6 November. The profound feeling of calm she had experienced during the voyage, many of its nights spent in solitary communion with the sea and the stars, had left Madeleine unprepared for the sheer exuberance of life lying in wait for her. Around her in the harbor the brightly painted funnels of steamers loomed above the native dhows, their patched canvas riggings hanging limply from sloping masts, bobbing on the light swell. The hooting of sirens, the cries of seagulls and the loud whines of leprous beggars mingled in a most disagreeable melange of sounds. Along the quay, Europeans and Indians—the latter with garlands of flowers—who had come to receive friends and relatives, customs officials in spotless white uniforms and pith helmets, coolies in dirty red turbans and crumpled uniforms, milled around the ship's berth, looking up expectantly towards its deck. Overwhelmed by the sensual overload, Madeleine was overcome first by dizziness and then an eerie detachment as she stood on the deck waiting to disembark. Squinting against the reflected glare of the midday sun, perspiration gathering in beads on her forehead and upper lip, seeping into the roots of her hair under the solar topi the ship's captain had insisted she wear, Madeleine hesitated for a fraction of a second before she walked down the gangway. By the time she stepped on land, her frock was sticking to her shoulders, but her step was firm.

Impatient to reach the ashram, she politely declined the invitation from her host, a rich Parsi lawyer with nationalist leanings deputed by Gandhiji to meet the ship, to spend a couple of days in Bombay, where she could rest for a while and do some sightseeing. Instead, Madeleine insisted on taking the train to Ahmadabad the same evening.

Driving from Apollo Bunder to the lawyer's bungalow on Malabar Hill, their Victoria passed through narrow streets lined with tall color-washed houses. The streets were crowded with people—mostly men—oxen carts, stately Victorias and a surprising number of mangy dogs. Madeleine was as blind to the visual excesses of the city as she was deaf to the din made by the cries of hawkers, the jingling of bells around the necks of the oxen, the clattering hooves of the horses, the shouted warnings of coachmen and the squawking of black crows that, unlike the parrots, seemed to feel safer on parapets and on the ground than on trees. More than anything else, Madeleine was acutely aware of a peculiar smell—a mingled odor of totally unfamiliar spices, the sea, and of fish drying in the sun. Her expression of courteous interest masked her indifference to the monuments of Bombay to which her host drew her attention with a fervor this most cosmopolitan of Indian cities sometimes inspired in its inhabitants. She did not tell him that she had lived here with her family between the ages of fifteen and seventeen. She felt embarrassed to betray how little she knew of Bombay, in spite of the two-year stay, and dreaded the curiosity that was certain to follow such an admission.

Madeleine had never really "lived" in Bombay except in a strictly geographic sense. What she now remembered was how insulated her life had been from its Indian surroundings. The isolation had not been total, of course. Loud, garish and smelly, Bombay did not insinuate as much as it tried to batter down the doors of a sensibility that struggled to keep it out. Hindus, Muslims and Christians, further subdivided according to their linguistic and regional origins, populated this overcrowded city. Each community had its characteristic dress, headgear, music and cadences of speech, its distinct food and cooking smells that gave the city its unique aroma which seeped through the walls the British had erected over the two hundred years they had been in India. The walls were not only the red and orange bougainvillea-covered brick walls which enclosed their spacious bungalows, but also those of rigid formality and social distance which the colonial rulers had erected to keep India and Indians out. The isolation was such that their women and children were aware of the country that was their temporary home chiefly through its tropical climate and vegetation. The rest of their Indian experience remained indistinct, a colorful but unobtrusive backdrop to the dramatic production of British expatriate life. The higher one was placed on the social pyramid of this life, the greater the isolation and less the seepage, and Madeleine's father, Sir Edmond Slade, the commander-in-chief of the East Indies Station, along with the governor of the Bombay Presidency, Sir George Clerk, was perched at its apex.

Except the household staff, Madeleine could not recall close contact with any Indians during those two years. Here, too, her memory was selective. The images of some servants were still sharp—the lushly bearded and turbaned coachman, for instance, who drove the family in a closed carriage to the houses of the few highly placed British officials the Slades regarded as socially acceptable, the Goan butler, dark as polished rosewood and with crinkly black hair beginning to be flecked with gray, who waited at the dinner table and spoke a lilting English in a fusion of Indian and Portuguese accents, and the balding Muslim syce with rheumy eyes and an orange-brown, henna-dyed beard who looked after her horse and ran behind it when she rode, crying "Missy! Missy!" in alarm whenever he felt she was going too fast. There were also some out-of-focus images, indistinguishable brown faces silently going about obscure tasks she had not bothered to comprehend: the skeletally thin Muslim tailor with wire-rimmed spectacles slipping down his nose, sitting in the veranda hunched over his Singer machine, making shirts, pajamas and silk suits for her father and copying the London tailor-made frocks for the memsahibs; the masal, who roamed about the grounds in the evening, singing to himself, filling the innumerable oil lamps and hurricane lanterns all over the bungalow, even in the horse stalls; the cook's nephew and assistant, a shy young boy who stuck close to his uncle and accompanied him on his early morning visits to the market to carry back meat, fish, ice, bottles of soda water, vegetables and fruit, and the assistant grooms to the head syce, as well as the sweepers, and the pattadars from her father's office who lounged about the garden and the verandas, unwilling to lend a hand to the household servants.

Madeleine's life in Bombay followed a routine most girls of her age would have envied. Each day, she rode her horse, a gigantic black Waler no less than sixteen hands, around the Back Bay, returning to Admiral House when the early morning gray of the Arabian Sea changed to a pale, milky blue as the sun rose higher and patches of water began to glint on the gently rolling surface of the sea.

Admiral House itself was a palatial bungalow, with dozens of rooms, quarters for servants and stables for horses. It had a large garden, tended to by four or five gardeners engaged in a daily struggle to keep its English character intact. Madeleine had a dim memory of the head gardener, a small, wizened man who always wore a shirt reddened from the soil, his thin, bare arms and skinny legs gleaming with sweat like polished bronze. The number of gardeners increased during the monsoon, constantly weeding and pruning, as the garden threatened to snap the strings of its English corset and reveal its elemental Indian lushness.

Madeleine's daily horse rides were usually gentle canters on the hard sand left behind on the beach by retreating breakers; except on one particular day when there was a break in the monsoon. For more than a week, Madeleine had been confined to the musty smelling rooms of the Admiral House, unable to concentrate on whichever book she picked up to read. The days had been dark and damp, the sun remaining hidden behind a mass of pewter-colored clouds. For two days the rain had been pouring down in a steady torrent, as if someone had opened and then forgotten to shut the sluice gates of the heavens. When the rain finally stopped one evening and the sky cleared, Madeleine could barely sleep through the night in anticipation of taking her horse out to Back Bay in the morning. The dawn was just breaking when she reached the beach in time to welcome the reappearance of the long-lost sun. The familiar orange globe, though, had a menacing reddish rim. The sea, too, had a heavy, oily swell to it. Before long, the light breeze had become a whipping wind that blew foaming spume at the rider and the horse. The clouds in the sky, pale gray puffs when she had started out, soon became thick, dark streamers. In less than fifteen minutes, a turgid mass of leaden clouds, luminous with a violet light in the east where it was illuminated from within by the rising sun, covered the sky fully.

"Let's turn back, Missy," the syce said, looking up worriedly at the sky. "A storm is coming. It looks bad."

Madeleine would never be quite sure about what happened

next. Perhaps it was the sudden dying down of the wind, the final exhalation of a heavy, moist breath in a low whistle. Far out on the sea, flashes of lightning zigzagged around the sky, the attendant claps of thunder not discrete but merging into each other in low rumbles. Instead of turning back, Madeleine found herself loosening the reins and bending low, urging the horse forward. The rain was whipping into her face as the horse broke into a gallop. Madeleine felt the power and the speed of the Waler flow into her body through her legs that were pressing tightly against its flanks. For a while, she was no longer the rider but an appendage of the horse, flying across the sand, wrapped in a rare exhilaration. When they were returning to the Admiral House, the horse again tightly reined in, the syce mumbling to himself as he walked behind them rehearsing the complaints he would make to her mother, she could feel the memory of the incredible energy that had surged through her still alive within her body.

The horse rides at dawn were followed by piano lessons later in the morning, given by the musically proficient widow of a British merchant who had decided to make Bombay her home. But, as in England, Madeleine struggled with the scales and exercises, her fingers refusing to move as nimbly as they did in her mind's eye.

Madeleine would spend the rest of the morning reading or accompanying her mother on her rounds as she struggled to make work for herself in a household that seemed to run very well without a mistress. It was the Goan butler who engaged and dismissed the servants, parceled out their duties and settled their disputes. Since Mrs. Slade had no idea of either the prices or the quantities of all that was consumed in the household, her weekly inspection of the accounts was a sheer ritual. All she had to do was to check whether the gutters were free from mosquito larvae, compliment the head gardener on the success of his flowers and vegetable patch, dole out quinine tablets to sick servants and find something for the tailor to stitch and sew. Bertha was luckier. She had appropriated for herself the task of looking after the family's clothes. This absorbed much of her energy and most of her time since the task involved preventing the clothes from rotting in the damp and protecting them from the insidious assaults of cockroaches and white ants. Madeleine often found Bertha lifting out dresses from the tin-lined boxes to give them a vigorous shaking, or filling up the steel saucers holding the feet of the teak almirahs with water to prevent white ants from climbing up and feasting on the silk and wool inside their darkly gleaming shutters.

On winter afternoons, there was tennis, either at the Government House or the Admiral House where Rhona joined her, doubtless because of the prospect of playing mixed doubles with the governor's or her father's handsome young ADCs. With the frequent exchange of looks between the partners and across the net, light pats of appreciation or encouragement on bare arms, the brush of fingers as a ball was handed over for a serve, tennis offered more avenues of flirtation than golf which Rhona had recently taken up. Rhona also loved the dinner parties at the Government House, which alternated with those hosted at the Admiral House. She particularly looked forward to the dances and balls that were held frequently during Bombay's mild winter season. To Madeleine, dancing was unrelieved torture. She found Rhona's attempts to teach her the steps of the waltz, the pointless exercise of going round and round in their bedroom, agonizing enough. The actual dancing in the ballroom, where she was dragged around the floor by perspiring young men with damp hands, uncomfortably aware of their bodies and smells, she found simply repulsive; she much preferred the sweaty odor of horses to that of men. Yet, as the commander-in-chief's daughter, not only was she expected to be present at these parties, but she had to graciously, even smilingly, accept the invitations to dance. And this, irrespective of what she felt about her partner (almost always boredom or indifference) and the ridiculous activity in which they were about to engage themselves.

However, Madeleine's distaste for social gatherings did not extend to one Government House party, which stood out in her memory because of its combination of sheer spectacle and boredom. This was the "purdah party" hosted each year for the wives of Indian princes and Bombay's leading Indian citizens who were in the city for the winter races. The Ranis and Maharanis looked forward to the party—actually an afternoon tea—and began preparing for it weeks in advance. The Government House was the only place where they could meet on neutral territory, where the various cross-currents of old family feuds, recent slights and hardened jealousies could be set aside for a couple of hours while the women warily circled around each other, full of apparent good cheer and mutual compliments. Since almost all the women were in purdah, to be shielded from the gaze of any man who was not a family member, the governor and his male staff could not be present. Normally it was the governor's wife, assisted by the wives of other senior British officials, who played hostess. But since Sir George had lost both his wife and his only daughter in an outbreak of cholera a few years ago, Madeleine's mother was asked to host the traditional party assisted by her daughters.

As the carriages drove into the porch one by one and stopped at the entrance, the coachmen, attired in the uniform of the state, its splendor reflecting the much greater glory of the prince, jumped down. Each coachman fastened one end of a long piece of dark silk to the carriage and handed the other to Madeleine and Rhona. The two girls then ran up the three red-carpeted steps, and held the silk aloft to make a covered passageway that was safe from any male eyes peeping down from the upper floors of the Government House. As soon as the coachmen disappeared to a side of the house, the princesses alighted. Dressed in their gorgeous silk saris embroidered with gold and laden with their best jewelry, they walked under the silk awning and climbed up the steps, where Madeleine's mother greeted them. The constant running up and down the steps, to the coach and back, holding up the silken veil, supervising the serving of refreshments, attending to the orchestra that was screened from view so that its musicians could not look at the purdah ladies, was as tiring as it was exhilarating. In fact, this party had an additional attraction for her—a chance to admire the wonderful horses, both Indian and others, which the princes imported from all over the world and were rarely seen in England. There were the local, sturdy Marwaris, no longer bred for war, powerful Australian Walers, versatile Gulf Arabs, even a couple of New England Morgans. But, best of all, were the Shagya Arabian stallions with their muscular bodies and flowing manes and tails whose noble bearing and beauty left Madeleine transfixed. All her running around, the pointless, polite exchanges with the guests, the cajoling with the Sicilian bandmaster for the orchestra to play something other than the polkas favored by the governor's housekeeper whom he was currently wooing, were redeemed by that single moment when she stood next to those magnificent horses.

———

Next to the Punjab Mail which covered the 2,500 miles from Bombay to Peshawar in forty-seven hours, the Gujarat Mail to Ahmadabad was one of the fastest on the Bombay, Baroda & Central India railway network. As it sped through Gujarat's countryside, its features concealed by an impenetrable darkness, Madeleine willed the train to go even faster. Tossing and turning on the lower berth of a first-class compartment of which she was the sole occupant, sleep eluded her. The steadily mounting but firmly restrained excitement, the unaccustomed, yielding softness of the bed, the cries of hawkers in strange tongues whenever the train stopped at wayside stations ensured that she lay awake most of the night. Yet, she did not feel tired in the least when the train pulled into Ahmadabad station the next morning. The anticipation of coming face to face with Mahatma Gandhi, of a quest approaching its end, energized her. It transformed any heaviness she might have felt in her limbs into a lightness of the head that sharpened all her perceptions while slightly distorting them. The platform outside the window of her compartment was a swirl of unfamiliar movements, colors and sounds. Madeleine felt a brief flash of apprehension before it was anaesthetized by another rush of exaltation. Looking up she saw a young man with thinning hair, his eyes magnified by the thick lenses of black horn-rimmed spectacles peering through the window, a wide smile of welcome spread across his face. An older man stood behind him looking over his shoulder, his smile more restrained, softening a craggy face that she imagined would be dignified, almost stern in repose, while a third head which left no other impression except of frenetic movement bobbed up and down in the background. Gandhiji's personal secretary Mahadev Desai, his trusted political lieutenant Sardar Patel whose stature in the Congress Party was rivaled only by Jawaharlal Nehru, and Swami Anand, the manager of the weekly *Young India*, had come to receive her.

In the ashram, where there were no secrets, or rather, nothing remained secret for long, everyone was aware of Madeleine's impending arrival. All of us knew that she was a former British commander-in-chief's daughter who had decided to cast her lot with Bapu. (That's what the ashram inmates called Gandhiji, the Gujarati word for "father." According to Gujarati custom, everyone else in the ashram had either a "bhai," brother, or "behen," sister, attached to their names as suffix—except, of course Kasturba, "mother," to Bapu's "father.") We also knew that she came with an introduction from Romain Rolland, the great French writer and Bapu's admirer. A month before her arrival, Bapu had received a letter from Rolland, which he read out at the morning prayer meeting a day before her arrival.

My dear brother,

You will soon be receiving at Sabarmati Miss Madeleine Slade, whom you have been kind enough to admit to your Ashram. She is a dear friend of my sister and myself and I look upon her as a spiritual daughter. She has recently undergone a violent and passionate disturbance and I am delighted that she is coming to put herself under your direction. I am sure you will find in her a most staunch and faithful disciple. Her soul is full of admirable energy and ardent devotion; she is straightforward and upright. Europe cannot offer a nobler or more disinterested heart to your cause. May she bear with her the love of thousands of Europeans, and my veneration.

There had been a good deal of curiosity about Madeleine's person and some speculation, especially among the women, on how she would adjust to the way we lived. In the kitchen, presided over by Kasturba, the misgivings were expressed openly. Some grumbled that Bapu seemed to be giving her a special status. A corner room in the first building to the right as one entered the ashram, opposite a well, had been assigned to her. The room was light and airy, with two windows, a door at each end and a small, private veranda. More important, she would be provided with the ashram's ultimate luxury, a separate bathroom for her exclusive use, and would not have to wait in a queue with other women for the morning bath. Ba, sitting on a low stool—her knees had been giving her trouble—and supervising the preparation of dough, the cleaning and cutting of vegetables, and all the other chores that went into cooking meals for the hundred-and-fifty-odd people who ate from the kitchen, looked on grimly without intervening to stop the discussion.

After the car carrying Madeleine and her reception committee drove into the ashram, Madeleine refused to accept her bespectacled companion's suggestion that she first wash up and rest before meeting Bapu. Politely but firmly, she insisted on being led straightaway into his presence. There are two versions of their first meeting. In one, after entering Bapu's hut, Madeleine prostrated herself on the floor and Bapu, quickly getting up from his cushion and coming around the desk, helped her up on her feet. Holding both her hands in his, he then said, "You shall be my daughter!" In the other version, Madeleine fainted as soon as she saw Bapu. When she came to, she was lying on the floor. Bapu's worried face was peering over hers. His lips were moving but she could not make out what he was saying.

Decades later, Richard Attenborough, while researching for a movie on Gandhi, asked her which version was true. "Both," she answered cryptically. Then added, "The moment I saw his slight figure sitting on his cushion on the floor, I felt a strong sensation of light coming from his direction. It was a light I felt rather than saw . . . till it exploded behind my eyes."

three

$\mathcal{I}$N 1925, THE ASHRAM had been in existence for almost six years. Gandhiji had chosen its site carefully: the ashram of the legendary sage Dadhichi was said to be located at the same spot on the bank of the Sabarmati, or at least close enough not to make a difference. The saintly sage (of Hindu mythology, not modern Indian history) was famed for giving Indra, the king of gods, a rib from his own body. With this rib, Indra had forged his mighty weapon, the thunderbolt, with which he annihilated the legions of the asuras on the battlefield.

The buildings on the ashram grounds were simple structures of mud, brick and wood, their tiled roofs thickly coated with tar to seal them off from rain. Gandhiji's cottage, adjacent to the rise of the riverbank, had three rooms, a small kitchen and a storeroom. Kasturba lived in one of the two rooms at the back of the house, the other was meant for guests. Gandhiji himself used the room in front, which had a small veranda facing the river. It was from this small space, an area barely measuring two hundred square feet, that he supervised the ashram's affairs even as he directed India's freedom struggle. As far as he was concerned, the development of a community of men and women who would adhere to the highest standards of nonviolence and truth and strive to achieve their greatest spiritual potential was just as crucial as the attainment of political independence for the country. It was in this room that he sat spinning on his wheel for at least an hour every day, where he edited *Navajivan* and *Young India*, attended to his voluminous correspondence, advised his nephew, also the administrator of the ashram, Maganlal Gandhi, on the problems that cropped up in the day-to-day running of the ashram, and discussed political strategy with senior Congress leaders. This was also the place where he received a regular stream of visitors, many of whom wanted to spend just a few minutes in his presence, to come face to face with the Mahatma and absorb some of his spiritual energy, his "mana."

The daily routine of the ashram followed an austere regimen and Madeleine embraced it with the fervor of a newly ordained Carmelite nun. She would wake up at 4:00 a.m. and join the other ashram dwellers for the morning prayer half an hour later. The day's work in the fields, orchard, dairy or the workshops was interrupted only by the community meals in the dining hall. Breakfast was served at 6:30 a.m. and was followed by the main meal of the day, comprising rice, vegetables, milk and slices of bread, at 10:30 a.m. The evening meal was served at 6:30 p.m. or 7 p.m., depending on whether it was winter or summer. This was a lighter meal, without milk, which Gandhiji believed was difficult to digest and hence made for disturbed sleep. By 9 p.m., everyone was expected to be back in their rooms and to have extinguished the lamps by 9:30 p.m. Gandhiji's own punctuality was legendary. He hated to waste time. Even in the lavatory, sitting on the commode, he read the Gita, learning it by heart. "As god is present everywhere, his work can also be done everywhere," he said.

The ashram's daily activities were closely regulated by a bell that seemed to wield an authority second only to his own. At mealtimes, for instance, the bell rang thrice: the first ring was a summons to the dining hall, the second a prelude to the closing of its doors and the third a signal for the meal to begin. Madeleine counted that the ashram bell rang fifty-six times during the day.

If the vegetable garden, orchard and fields, the dairy, carpentry, tannery and weaving sheds constituted the body of the ashram—its limbs and organs, its bones, muscles and sinews—and the common kitchen and dining hall its stomach, then the terraced piece of ground on the bank of the river facing Gandhiji's hut was its heart; the ashram's soul was movable, to be found wherever Gandhiji happened to be at a given moment. Punctually at 4:30 a.m., at a signal from the ubiquitous bell, the morning prayer began with a recitation of Sanskrit verses. This was followed by the singing of devotional songs conducted by the ashram's resident musician, Pandit Khare, a large man with a large mustache upturned at the ends and whose voice seemed to Madeleine's European ear more stentorian than musical. The songs were not exclusively Hindu; Madeleine was surprised when on the third day after her arrival Gandhiji asked her to lead the singing of his favorite Christian hymn, "When I survey the wondrous cross." The singing was followed by readings from the Bhagavad Gita, which Gandhiji was translating into Gujarati at the time. After that, he spoke for fifteen to twenty minutes on a spiritual subject before the prayer meeting ended and the ashram inmates began their day's work.

The evening prayer always began with a roll call. Gandhiji would sit in his usual place under the neem tree, often with a small child in his lap. Sometimes, there would be a struggle for this honor between two children, which he normally resolved by letting them share his knees. The men and women sat separately, in two distinct groups, facing him. When their names were called, the inmates reported the amount of yarn they had spun during the day. After the devotional songs and the recitations from the Gita, the Granth Sahib, the Koran or the Bible were over, Gandhiji invited questions, even the most personal, which someone in the audience needed him to answer: Why am I a late riser? Why do I ejaculate in my sleep? How does one conquer anger? Does someone living in the ashram need jewelry? How does one's diet affect the mind? Often Gandhiji himself brought up issues that had a bearing on the ashram's communal life. These informal exchanges between Gandhiji and the ashram dwellers were not unfailingly earnest, but accomodated a fair share of lighthearted banter. A fortnight after Madeleine's arrival, when the weather was turning cooler and there was a definite nip in the early morning air, one of the men asked whether the time to wake up could not be delayed by half an hour.

"That is true, Bapu," another man said. "Sometimes we sleep so soundly that we don't hear the sound of the bell."

"What do you want then? That the bell be rung next to your ear?" Gandhiji tried to laugh off the question.

"No, Bapu. I am only looking for a way out of this difficulty."

"If we look at this small matter as a "difficulty," then we should forget about getting freedom from the British," Gandhiji commented, his smile masking the seriousness of his words. "Anyone who wants to wake up will always find someone to awaken him. If you want, you can come and sleep next to me. I will wake you up at three."

Everyone laughed and Gandhiji joined in.

"If you find a fellow inmate sleeping after the bell has rung, you have my full permission to splash drops of cold water on the person's face," he said.

An elderly woman complained that the bell could not always be heard since in winter we slept wrapped up in a quilt and the bell was quite far from some of the rooms. There were murmurs of assent from different parts of the assembly.

"We must have more bells, then," Gandhiji said. "And I know how to get more bells without buying new ones. Everyone should sleep with their steel thalis and spoons next to their pillows. Those who wake up with the ashram bell should start striking the thali with the spoon."

There was another burst of loud laughter. Gandhiji too laughed, and said, "This is not a laughing matter. From tomorrow, I will also strike my thali. From now on, we will have scores of bells, not just the one."

———

Madeleine's first impressions of Gandhiji are to be found in the two letters to Romain Rolland that she wrote within three days of her arrival. The first is a short note, dated 9 November 1925.

Ah, my dear Father, I could never have imagined how divine he is. I had been prepared for a Prophet and I have found an Angel. Thank you, thank you! Oh! That I may become worthy!

This is followed by a longer letter in which, to my surprise, I too find a mention as her Hindi teacher, though in terms I would have preferred to be more flattering.

10 November 1925

My dear, dear Father,

Yesterday, I was too full of feelings to write words. And I know how eagerly you must be awaiting my description of him. Forgive me for my selfishness.

What is he like? I have to step back from myself to

look at him as others would. To see him with the eyes of a stranger, or the eyes of a writer who records without participating.

He is small, even by Indian standards, but well-built. He is quite broad and strong in the chest and upper arms. But his legs are skinny, perhaps because of the Indian habit of sitting cross-legged. The first impression he gives, that of fragility, is deceptive, for his constitution is strong. He does not sleep for more than five to six hours at night, works all through the day, and yet on his evening walk his pace is so brisk that much younger men struggle to keep up with him.

His head is well-shaped; not bald, but shaven bare. His ears stick out. I like to think of them as the ears of a leprechaun. He has a broad but well-formed brow, a large, straight nose with broad nostrils. His cheeks and face are firm and show no sign of the network of wrinkles that mark the faces of European men of his age. His complexion is weathered rather than dark, bronzed by the sun. A wispy gray moustache shades his upper lip; the lower lip is full and protruding. When he laughs, which is often, he shows a gap in his front teeth, which makes his laughter all the more irresistible. He wears broad spectacles whose lenses consist of two half-moons framed together for distant and close vision at the same time. But, Father, his eyes! They look you full in the face and see right through you. Often, they are full of mischief and humour, immediately followed by great seriousness and concentration. He has a calm, tenor voice that he keeps on an even keel, without inflexions. He speaks English with purity and perfection, without ever correcting himself and without stumbling; each of his sentences says exactly what it wants to say. But it is not simply a matter of what he says; one must live near him because it is his life and his actions (from the most important to the smallest) that are more eloquent than his words.

I must add that his outer appearance of calm is deceptive. There is a controlled tension in his body. It is evident in the twitching of his refined hands, and in the constant tapping of his feet when they are not tucked under him. One senses that his is a hyperactive body, kept on a tight leash by a strong mind and an iron will.

But, Father, what do you or I have to do with the body? For myself I can say, I have been fortunate enough to be confronted with the spirit of God. In our very first meeting, as I rushed into his room straight from the railway station, I saw him encircled by light. It appears rarely, and only when he is deeply moved. And when he raised me from his feet, I felt through his hands that mysterious touch of the Eternal that is just under the surface of all that is living.

I cannot talk of this to anyone else except you, dear, dear Father. For the most part, the people here in the Ashram are gentle and simple. Some are like my Hindi teacher, who is highly educated yet curiously naïve in so many ways. They are incapable of comprehending the European mind. They know nothing of the ferment produced by an awareness of the ambiguities and contradictions in our minds, nothing of the exultation of creativity or the depths of nihilistic despair. He is the only one I feel I can talk to, to whom I can pour out my heart, who I can welcome into the depth of my soul.

Madeleine

It could not have been more than a couple of days after Madeleine's arrival when Gandhiji became aware that the women in the ashram were grumbling (sooner or later he came to know everything that happened in the ashram) about what some of them felt were marks of favor he was showing towards the Englishwoman. No one remembered a potential ashram inmate ever being received at the railway station by three men of such high status as Mahadevbhai, Sardar Patel and Swami Anand. Since Madeleine's skill in spinning wool was of little use in the carding and spinning of cotton, Surendrabhai, the best spinner in the ashram was assigned to be her teacher. And that afternoon, Mahadevbhai personally told me that it was Gandhiji's wish that she should learn Hindi as quickly as possible so that she could integrate herself in our life and help him in his work—I was to be her Hindi teacher.

Gandhiji's solution to squelch any loose talk on Madeleine's special status was typical. The very next day, around noon, when most of the men were working outside in the ashram's orchard, vegetable garden or the dairy, and the women were chatting in the verandas in the little free time they had between the morning's household chores and tending to the children once they came back from the ashram school, we saw an unusual sight. A broom in one hand and a bucket in another, Gandhiji strode briskly towards the common latrines, closely followed by Madeleine, who in spite of being taller, had to hurry to keep pace with him. Both seemed to be in high spirits, oblivious of the stench the latrines gave off by midday, as Gandhiji began to instruct her in the proper way of sweeping and washing the latrine floors. We soon came to know that Gandhiji had given Madeleine the task of the daily cleaning of latrines after the group of young men and women responsible for removing the buckets and emptying them in the compost pits in the morning had scrubbed them clean with coconut-leaf brooms. Hers was a task that everywhere else in the country was considered the lowest of the low, to be performed only by the untouchable scavenger.

This was the first time I saw Madeleine from close quarters. On the day she arrived, she had stayed in her room, unpacking and settling down. Her meals had been sent to her from the kitchen. She had sent back the table and the chair provided for her, as she did with the bed and the heavily darned mosquito net curtains. She said she was used to sleeping on a mat on the floor and was willing to take her chances with mosquitoes or any other specimen of insect-life India could throw at her.

On the morning Gandhiji assigned her the task of cleaning the latrines, Madeleine was wearing a full-sleeved khadi frock stitched for her in London. Hanging loosely from her wide shoulders, it came down to her ankles. She had long, glossy, chestnut-brown hair which was pulled back and tied in a thick plait. Her skin glowed ember pink from the heat of the midday sun, with splotches of a darker shade of red sprayed across her throat. By our canons of beauty, Madeleine was not a beautiful woman. She was too tall, her shoulders too powerful, her nose too long and her eyebrows too thick. Even her skin was much darker than that of an upper-class Englishwoman. One felt the full impact of her personality, overriding all musings on the nature of female beauty, when one came into closer contact with her. Not that she was a scintillating conversationalist who charmed with words. Quite the opposite, in fact: her personality expressed itself more through silence than speech and therefore spoke only to those who were receptive to the nuances of stillness. Only then did one realize that her apparent impassivity was but an exquisitely poised balance between obscure but vital passions, that Madeleine's attractiveness lay not in what she revealed through her face or figure but what she concealed within her soul. Today, I flatter myself that apart from Gandhiji I was the only other person who really *saw* her. Here, I am not excepting even Prithvi Singh. He was too close to her, and for too short a period of time, to be able to really know her. It took me many years, though, to remove my cultural cataracts which would not let me look at an Englishwoman except through the cloudiness of stereotypes, before I was granted that clarity of sight.

———

Madeleine's experience of the ashram was quite different from what she had expected.

With almost two hundred men, women and children, the ashram was less a monastic community living a life of manual labor, silence and prayer than a noisy, often squabbling, village. Most of the women and the children did not live this life out of choice. They were here because their husbands and fathers had decided to live with Gandhiji and follow his social, political or ascetic ideals. For the men, the ashram, with its connotations of ancient forest hermitages, was a place of refuge where they imagined living a life that was not dissimilar to one lived thousands of years ago. When I was leaving the college where I taught to join Gandhiji's ashram, my friend Aman, a lecturer in philosophy who had written his doctoral thesis on Rousseau, tried to dissuade me. The Sabarmati ashram, he said, like all such experiments, was ultimately based on an illusion. It was an attempt to create an imaginary past for those who found the present unbearable. He was willing to wager that Gandhi himself was gripped by an intense nostalgia (I noticed that he did not add the respectful "ji" after Gandhi).

For what? I asked.

Who knows? For a pristine, unspoiled nature that is vital, soothing, for a childhood that was never really as idyllic as it remained in memory, for a lost freshness of vision wherein every experience is not only startlingly new but also comes garbed in purity and innocence. Your own hero Premchand is swayed by a similar sense of heightened loss. His illusion is the memory of a village community that has never existed, the imaginary community of strong emotional bonds and shared values, united by a common purpose. This nostalgia, the mourning for an imagined loss, animates Gandhi's ashram as much as it does Premchand's novels. He could understand my attraction to both, of course; they were two sides of the same coin. But illusions are always dangerous, irrespective of their worth for the creation of culture or utopian communities. Moral values need nostalgia, but also realism.

The reading of Western philosophers had damaged him, I said. Western thought had clouded his vision, doubts had dulled his mind. He had become a cynic.

I admire Gandhi, he said, but I do not idealize him. Indians cannot admire, only idealize or, worse, revere.

I confess, the distinction escaped me. I also believe Aman underestimated Gandhiji's realism, which was often overlaid by the stubbornness with which he pursued his ideals.

If Madeleine possessed any illusion of entering an ideal community, she was soon disabused. The ashram was not free of the inevitable discord, petty jealousy and envy among a people who shared a community life because they either had no choice in the matter or because they were attracted to Gandhiji for very different reasons and, wishing to stay with him, discovered that they also had to live with each other. She marveled at the amount of energy Gandhiji expended in keeping life on an even keel in a community where people were close but not intimate. Their bickering was thus not quickly washed away by the demands and pleasures of intimacy but kept rankling after what had occasioned it was long over. In spite of the huge demands made on Gandhiji's time by his frequent travels, voluminous correspondence, the planning of a constructive program for the ashram community, and Congress politics, he still found enough time to lecture, exhort and cajole ashram inmates to pursue his vision for the community, a vision he termed as the most important experiment he had ever undertaken. Setbacks did not discourage him or sap his strength, for as a visionary he looked beyond what people were like and focused on what he knew they could become.

And the vision? A physical life close to the rhythms of nature—a simple vegetarian diet, with an emphasis on natural foods, and traditional medicines derived from healing nature; a life of utter simplicity, with a good dose of manual labor, the use of hand-spun and hand-woven cloth and other handmade articles; and a moral life dictated by the strictest standards of truth, honesty and rectitude. These realms were not distinct from each other but integrated, each affecting the others. Spinning, for instance, was as much a moral as a physical or economic activity. "I regard the four hours I spend spinning the most profitable part of my day," he said to Madeleine one evening. "The fruit of my labor is visible before me, and not one impure thought enters my mind during the four hours. The mind wanders when I read the Gita, the Koran, the Ramayana, but it is fixed while I turn the wheel." And prayer, which he regarded more essential than food, was indispensable to his running the ashram, or leading the freedom struggle. It constituted a daily purification of the heart so that God could light his way when he was in doubt, whether in decisions regarding the ashram or finding the right path in the maze of national politics.

Within the ashram, Madeleine soon discovered, the faith in Gandhiji's vision varied from the frank skepticism of most women who longed to be back in the web of family life in their villages and towns, savoring its small pleasures and sharing its travails, to the fanaticism of a few men who pushed the ideal of simplicity to extremes of asceticism. For most men, though, it was not the vision that had drawn them to the banks of the Sabarmati but the visionary. Madeleine realized that there were very few inmates whom she could respect as strong men and women marching shoulder to shoulder towards the creation of the communal life Gandhiji envisaged as essential for the awakening of a person's spiritual potential. It was preeminently the weak, the hapless and the depressed, for whom Madeleine had little tolerance, who were drawn to Bapu as if to a magnet. And he welcomed them! To fall ill in the ashram was a boon, rewarded by two daily visits from him. Not only did he inquire about the sick person's well-being but took over the major role of prescribing the diet, the nursing regimen and the medical treatment, which had lately transformed into a reliance on mud packs around the abdomen and head as panacea for most minor ailments.

Madeleine had embraced the vision wholeheartedly two years ago when she read about Gandhiji in Romain Rolland's book. Now it was only a question of translating it into her daily life, a task that she approached with what Gandhiji initially regarded as an excess of ascetic zeal. He had not made any comment, only looked at her quizzically when she first took to wearing Indian clothes, exchanging khadi frocks for khadi saris. But after a week, when she asked his permission to take a vow of celibacy and to cut off her hair, he objected.

"I am not the Buddha, and you are not my nun," he said with a smile that was both teasing and protective. "These vows are a serious matter, not to be undertaken lightly or in a hurry."

You inspire in me the same holy passion that Jesus inspired in St. Teresa, she wanted to say, but kept her answer matter-of-fact.

"You know that I never take lightly anything that has to do with you. And I have fully grasped that your concept of brahmacharya is not only celibacy but all forms of self-discipline and self-restraint. The ascetic atmosphere of the ashram attracts me and I want to help in making it even more so."

"If you crop your hair, you would stand out from the other women. It will isolate you further. Think it over tonight. Let's talk again tomorrow," he said.

That night, Madeleine lay awake for a long time. She had never thought of herself as a nun but suddenly it seemed clear that cropping her hair and taking the vow of celibacy were the signposts on the path she had been destined to travel. From tomorrow, she would no longer think of him as Mahatma Gandhi but simply as "Bapu." "Bapu!" she said out aloud. The Indian word for father tasted strange on her tongue. It troubled her to share the word with the rest of the ashram. The only solution was to call him Bapu, but in her own voice. She would not use the word as a term of address, but as one of endearment. Only she would know how personal and private her "Bapu" was, and with how much love she spoke the word.

Gradually the orchestra of night sounds—the whistling of hundreds of crickets that struck the ear as a single high-pitched drone punctuated by the croaking of river frogs and the occasional hooting of an owl—subsided into silence. By the time Madeleine fell asleep, sometime after midnight, she felt calm, peacefully empty, as if she had been delivered of a heavy weight pressing on her heart.

The next evening, after the prayers were over, Madeleine went to Gandhiji's hut. He was standing in the courtyard in front of Kasturba's room, talking to her through the open door. He seemed pleased to see Madeleine and asked her to wait in his room. When he came back, he went up to her and took both of her hands in his own. Looking deep into her eyes, holding them with his piercing glance, he nodded.

"I am pleased for you . . . and for myself," he said. He then called out to Ba for a pair of scissors. Madeleine closed her eyes as she knelt on the mat in front of him. She felt the heat of his body on her face, the tug on her hair as he lifted up the end of her long braid and began to cut off her hair. After it was over, he stepped back.

"I am a pretty good barber," he said, nodding with satisfaction as he regarded his handiwork.

Madeleine bowed down her cropped head to get his blessings. He patted her affectionately on the shoulder and said, "I know there is no one else in the ashram who will make as great an effort as you to realize the ideals for which it was established. And now I have a present for you—a new name, Mira. She was a princess blessed with great devotion and perseverance. Mira's songs are still sung all over the country. Ask Navin, your Hindi teacher, about her."

As she left the hut, Madeleine could have sworn that behind the broad glasses of his spectacles she saw Gandhiji's eyes glisten with tears. The very next morning, when she was returning from the prayer ground, Maganlalbhai informed her that she had been allotted new accommodation: a one-room hut on the high riverbank. Along with Maganlalbhai's own house, which also served as the ashram's storeroom, hers was the only other building in Gandhiji's close vicinity, no more than fifty yards away from his living quarters.

four

*W*ithin a few weeks of her arrival, the other residents of the ashram began to regard Madeleine, now Mirabehn, as someone who was aloof, but no longer mysterious. Her tall figure, striding purposefully in a white khadi sari, a garment actually meant for graceful gliding rather than purposeful striding, was now a familiar sight as she made her way to the common kitchen where she supervised the cutting of vegetables, or on the prayer ground where she invariably arrived ten minutes before Bapu did, or when she accompanied him on his evening walk to the Sabarmati jail. The rest of the time, after her duties were over, she stayed by herself in her hut on the riverbank, spinning or reading. Ba, Mahadevbhai, Tulsi Mahar, her spinning teacher, and I were the only people in the ashram with whom she initiated an exchange of greetings. Her response when addressed, though, was friendly enough, even if it was marked by a reserve that discouraged any further presumption of intimacy. She still stood out among the Indian women, but with her cropped head covered by the pallu of her sari and a complexion tanned enough by the sun to pass for that of a Pathan woman from the

Northwest Frontier Provinces, it was only her large gray eyes, now even more startling against the darker skin, that reminded one of her European origins.

A London newspaper had published a sensationalist news report about the circumstances under which she had joined Gandhiji and it had been reprinted in many Indian newspapers. In her response to the story in a February issue of *Navajivan*, Mira had clarified, "I have renounced neither my family nor my religion. My religion, which lay hidden within me for thirty-three years, has now become manifest.

"I have not sold my books. I brought them with me to the ashram so that others can read them. My friends did not try to stop me from coming here. They knew that my resolve was firm. Gandhiji did not immediately say 'Come' when I told him of my wish to join him. He asked me to wait and think about it for at least a year. When he accepted me, he neither made me promise that I will never deviate from the path I have chosen nor did he demand that I give up all that I had. On the contrary, he always warned me not to take any vow in a hurry and agreed to keep my belongings in trust only for a year.

"When I first arrived, people here were neither 'overjoyed,' nor did I receive a 'grand' welcome. I joined the community simply and without fuss.

"I do not listen to 'speeches' nor am I engaged in a 'study of the situation' here. I am only learning to card, spin and speak Hindi."

Her statement had the simultaneous effect of squelching the strong rumor that had been circulating in the ashram after Gandhiji had renamed her Mira. Her sixteenth century namesake, the Rajput princess Mirabai, had dedicated herself to Lord Krishna since childhood. Married off at the age of thirteen into the ruling family of Mewar, Mira had refused to carry out the duties of a wife. It was impossible for her to be married to the king, she insisted, since she was already married to the lord. In her passionate devotion to Krishna, Mira broke some of the strongest taboos that governed the lives of Rajput women of nobility of her time. After the premature death of her husband, when her in-laws began to harass Mira, she fled from the palace and wandered around the land as a minstrel, composing and singing mystical love songs to the dark god that are still regarded as some of the finest in Hindi poetry. To this day, Mira continues to be disliked and disparaged by the Rajput nobility, even as she occupies an honored place in the hearts of the people as a beloved saint. Bapu had named the Englishwoman Mira, the ashram gossip went, because her story paralleled that of the legendary Rajput princess, with Bapu replacing Krishna in the modern Mira's heart.

———

Mira now felt at home in India. When she went out of the ashram, she did not observe the life around her with the eyes of a tourist, of someone who is simultaneously excited and apprehensive and strives to retain a sense of control by relating the starkly unfamiliar to things he is accustomed to at home. For Mira, the ride to the city, lurching on the back seat of a low, flimsy looking tonga, pulled by a small but wiry Kathiawari horse, no longer evoked memories of her rides in the front seat on top of a London omnibus. As a young girl, she had sat next to a coachman who was wrapped in a great overcoat and muffler, a thick rug folded across his lap, looking down as if from a great height, on the shop fronts, on innumerable hats on the heads of the people hurrying along on the sidewalks, and on a variety of hansoms clattering along the streets. Unlike a tourist, but like a resident foreigner, any comparisons she now made were based on differences rather than similarities. For instance, in the winter months, the Indian men wore some kind of headgear or wrapped woolen mufflers around their heads but walked around in open sandals without socks. Not for them the thick wool socks and heavy boots of the British with their European belief in the importance of keeping the feet warm. For Indians, heat did not seep away from the feet but from the head.

The street scenes of Ahmadabad were now almost as familiar as those of London. The hawkers standing behind their bicycles and hand carts, selling everything from colored glass bangles to deep-fried Gujarati street food, carts loaded with gunny bags and construction material pulled by oxen or camels, men wearing white dhotis, kurtas, round-collar coats and black boat-shaped caps, had become a part of the background and no longer tugged at the hem of her attention. Only the rare sight of a group of Rabari women on the street, birds of paradise among the drably clad Ahmadabadis, had the power to throw her back to an awareness of her European origins, make her feel alien in this exotic land. Dressed in long black skirts, their lithe torsos encased in blouses heavily embroidered in yellow, maroon and green thread and studded with mica fragments, their kohl-lined eyes and foreheads tattooed with curving garlands of black dots, heavy silver neck bands and anklets and thick silver earrings hanging from liberally pierced earlobes, the Rabari women, in fact, did more than remind Mira of her Englishness. Disturbingly, even if fleetingly, these striking women, walking beside tall, mustachioed men with small children in tow, also made her aware, although never questioningly, of the life she had chosen for herself.

Within the ashram, too, Mira's gaze had become more acute, more discerning. From an undifferentiated mass of small, brown men and women, individuals had begun to stand out. She soon discovered that some of them were prone to eccentricities which even the upper-class Englishmen of her acquaintance would be hard-pressed to match. Like Harenbhai, who ate exactly fifty-five chapattis at meals, a goodly number considering that each chapatti was equivalent to a thick slice of bread. If he was served fifty-four he would shout, "Why are you so stingy? Do you want me to starve to death?" If by accident he was given fifty-six, he would complain, "Do you take me for a ravenous demon?"

Above all, there was Bhansali. An ex-professor of English at the local college, he had been Bapu's close associate for many years. Gandhiji had great respect for the strength of Bhansali's ascetic convictions and the perseverance with which he put them into practice. On a journey from the ashram to the Himalayas, Bhansali had decided to take a twelve years' vow of silence. Who knows what terrible sin he was atoning for. One night, on his way back to the plains, he was sleeping in a cattle shed in a village when he was suddenly awoken by the sound of moving cattle. "Who's there?" Bhansali shouted before realizing that he was breaking his vow. Determined to prevent such mistakes from occuring again, he found a goldsmith who was willing to stitch his lips together with a copper wire so that he could keep the vow of silence even when he was sleeping. Since at that time he was on a diet of wheat flour and bitter neem leaves mixed with water to make a thick gruel, the goldsmith also made him a copper tube through which he could suck in the gruel from one side of his mouth.

Bhansali's first meeting with Bapu after his return had become a part of the ashram lore. In spite of his long beard and hair, unkempt and uncut for many months, Bhansali was recognized as soon as he walked in through the gate and the news spread fast, "Bhansalibhai is back! Bhansalibhai is back!" By the time he reached Bapu's room, a good dozen of the ashram people were following him. Naked to the waist, Bhansali looked healthy and fit in spite of his odd diet. His eyes, though, were dull and lifeless, devoid of all expression. Everyone sat in Bapu's room, waiting for Bapu who was out visiting a sick inmate.

When Bapu returned, his joy at seeing Bhansali was apparent in the way his face lit up. Every line on his face seemed to spread out in a broad smile. After the two friends had embraced, they sat down. As it happened, it was Bapu's day of silence. He could not talk, but kept smiling and nodding his head vigorously to show how pleased he was at seeing Bhansali again. Bhansali couldn't smile back because his lips were stitched together, but he too nodded back as vigorously as Bapu. His eyes, though, remained as empty as ever.

The next day Bapu ordered that the wire be removed from Bhansali's lips. It took him a few days more to persuade Bhansali to break his vow of silence. At first, Bhansali insisted on communicating with Bapu using scribbled notes. Then Bapu convinced him to make an exception by saying God's name out aloud. Ultimately, Bhansali agreed that he would talk only to Bapu. Someone who had overheard one of their conversations, reported that after so many months of disuse, Bhansali's voice sounded as if it was deeply rusted.

Bapu then tried to get Bhansali to engage himself in ashram activities but Bhansali's stubborn response to each of Bapu's suggestions was the same question—"Why?" Why should he spin? Why should he work in the orchard? Why should he eat with the others? Finally, Bapu hit on the solution to his obduracy. "For me," he said. "Won't you spin enough cotton for a lungi for me?" Bhansali, utterly devoted to Bapu, his only remaining connection to his fellow human beings, agreed. However, he firmly put his foot down when Bapu spoke to him about changing his diet and even convinced Bapu to experiment on his own food with neem leaves. Bapu drew a line on the consumption of gruel of wheat flour and water, though. He was convinced it was harmful and persuaded Bhansali to eat thin rotis from the dough made of flour and water and dried in the sun instead of being baked on fire. Whenever Mira happened to walk past his hut, she saw Bhansali sitting at the same spot, in the same, unchanging posture, spinning. He never looked up, not even at the flat, round rotis drying on the stone steps of his hut, and she never found out if his eyes were as empty as people claimed they were.

five

$\mathcal{A}$T FIRST, when I began to notice that Mira preferred to keep to herself in the ashram, I thought it was because of the utter strangeness of her surroundings, that the loss of all familiar landmarks had made her gather the memsahib's usual cape of reserve even more tightly around her. As I got to know her better I realized that her reluctance to engage with anyone other than Bapu in the ashram was deliberate. It was much later, when I began to work on the story of her life, that I discovered that Mira's need for solitude was a part of her character, not a mask which she could take off at will.

In Schopenhauer's imagery human relationships resemble hedgehogs on a cold night. They creep closer to each other for warmth, then pricked by quills they move away till their freezing bodies compel them to seek each other out once again. This carries on till they find the perfect distance from each other, where their bodies are warm and the pain inflicted by the quills is also bearable. Mira's interaction with those around her was much like this. If closeness to others brings warmth but also causes occasional pain, then Mira's choice was the coldness of distance, the ice rather than the fire.

Even as a child, Mira, Madeleine then, had been lonely. Her loneliness though, she writes in her diary, was not isolation. Solitude was what she had chosen, it was not something that was imposed on her.

Madeleine's childhood recollections centered on Milton Heath, her grandfather's sprawling country house amid the rolling hills and farmlands of Surrey where she spent most of the first ten years of her life. Whenever her father, who was often away at sea for two years or more at a stretch, returned to England, the family would live in London while her father went to work at the Admiralty. The London years, however, were almost erased from Madeleine's memory, whereas those spent at Milton Heath, where her family lived during her father's absence, remained fresh and alive in her mind, teeming with images that possessed a peculiar vitality. Standing on twenty acres of land on the high ground, the three-story Tudor house had a beautiful view of the Dorking Valley, with the North Downs to the left and the Leith Hill to the right. Well laid out gardens with a rich collection of trees, shrubs and flowers, stables for the riding, hunting and carriage horses, paddocks for cows, a carriage house, chicken coops and pigsties, fulfilled the specifications for the country estate of a well-to-do gentleman farmer. With a little effort, Madeleine could see her beloved grandfather, a quiet, thickset man, tranquil-eyed, and with a white beard that curled like a sea horse, puttering around among the flowerbeds in his mud-spattered thongless boots. In her mind's eye, she saw him walking around the unkempt lawn, sunned by dandelions in the summer, while she, still a little girl, followed in his broad shadow, neither of them exchanging a word.

Sweeping the garden paths with a long besom broom, grafting roses and doing other odd jobs in the garden were her grandfather's hobbies. They were more important to him than his work in London as a director of a company importing spices from the East Indies.

Ever since she could remember, Madeleine had preferred the company of plants, trees and animals to that of humans. When Rhona went away to boarding school, Madeleine was more relieved than sad that she would no longer have to join Rhona in all her silly games in which she was condemned to immobility. Madeleine was always the wild bear in the cave (underneath the nursery table with a bedcover hanging all around it), the slave who was not supposed to move a finger without a command from the queen, the robber imprisoned in a dungeon (under the bed) in the game of police and robbers, or the paleface tied to the stake (the stairs at the top of the landing) while Rhona Apaches danced around the fire.

Madeleine and Rhona had never been emotionally attached to each other; in fact, they did not even look like sisters. Temperamentally too, they were very different from each other. Rhona's complexion was fairer, her hair softer and lighter, her nose pert and upturned as compared to Madeleine's sharply aquiline one. While Rhona's correct and conventional ways belonged to their father's side of the family, Madeleine took more after their mother's. Their mother's great-great-grandfather had married a gypsy woman while serving in Hungary (or perhaps Romania). Madeleine believed that a wild and unpredictable strain had passed through her mother's family, manifesting itself in a propensity for unusual behavior in the succeeding generations. It may have lain dormant in most of her cousins, uncles and aunts, but was pronounced in both her mother and herself.

Her father's family, on the other hand, was decidedly conventional. Her grandfather was an Anglican bishop, her great-grandfather was a general and her grand-uncle was the Provost of Eton. Naturally, the family had a touch of the aristocratic about it, a trait Madeleine did not recognize in herself and disliked in others. Her parents' varying temperaments, too, were reflected in their appearance: in contrast to her thin mother with her quick birdlike movements, her father was solidly built and moved with gravity and deliberation.

Soon after Rhona left, their mother gave up her halfhearted attempts at inviting other girls of Madeleine's age to the house. Madeleine simply ignored them. She was content to play by herself under the trees in the garden or, when the weather was bad, in her day-nursery on the top floor that looked out on the Dorking Valley, its features now obscured by fog or swirling flurries of snow. Except for Bertha, her nanny, and her mother, Madeleine's interaction with others was occasional, her meetings with the elders living in the house regulated. She preferred it this way. Besides the Sunday lunch, which she ate downstairs, sitting next to her mother, all her other meals were served in the day-nursery or the night-nursery on the middle floor that overlooked the stable yard. Every evening, after tea in the nursery, Bertha would dress Madeleine in a freshly laundered smock and take her downstairs to the drawing room where her Scottish grandmother sat silently, knitting, while Madeleine played with picture puzzles on the floor. The only pleasant part of this evening ritual was the time she spent with her grandfather when he got down on the floor with her to help with the puzzles. But this too was only if she asked.

When the time came for her to go to school, Madeleine was horrified. To be surrounded by noisy children, to have her life regimented by others, her time no longer her own, was an unbearable thought. Luckily, her mother, less a flouter than an innocent of all convention, understood. She decided that her younger daughter need not go to school. Instead, she would take lessons at home. "I have always felt close to my mother," Madeleine writes in her diary. "She was a beautiful woman but an unknown spirit, to herself as much as to others. She loved me, I know, and in her deep affection watched over me, but she let me go my own way."

Lucy Saunders, a young and impoverished cousin without marriage prospects, was employed as Madeleine's governess. She taught Madeleine to read and write, and the rudiments of arithmetic, and stayed on with the family till its departure for India. Although a quick learner with a decided flair for history, Madeleine never progressed beyond the basics in arithmetic.

Madeleine's father, who might have objected to her being educated at home, was away at sea, although in the end he too would have deferred to his wife. Over the years, he had gradually abdicated all decision-making over family and household affairs to her. She closely monitored his personal appearance and guided every detail of his grooming. She selected his shirts, socks, ties and civilian suits. His rather unkempt beard of the early years of their marriage was now neatly trimmed, his mustache short and nattily waxed at the tips.

In her grandfather's estate, Madeleine spent much of her time with animals, especially the horses. Seeing how fond she was of them, her grandfather's head coachman taught her how to saddle and bridle riding horses and how to harness the carriage horses. Madeleine was ecstatic when she was given a Welsh pony for her tenth birthday. Her happiness, though, was short-lived, for the pony lived only for six months. During those six months, Madeleine did not let anyone else take care of it. Every day, morning and evening, she went into the paddock to feed it its meal of hay and a handful of grain. She trimmed its feet every month and regularly brushed its coat which became sleek and shiny in the summer months.

One night, in the beginning of November, the pony escaped from the paddock and got into the grain bin where it merrily ate grain till it was sick. The next morning, the pony seemed listless, its eyes dull and utterly disinterested in the feed. It was pacing around, trying to kick at its belly. "He's got the colic, Miss," one of the stable hands who was passing by offered his diagnosis. "He needs to be walked so he won't roll and twist his intestines." Madeleine walked him around the field but the pony seemed to be in deep distress. Ever so often, it would stop, paw the ground and twist its head to look at its belly. The vet was summoned but the disease had progressed too fast, perhaps also due to the change in weather. The colic would kill the pony within twelve hours, the vet pronounced before leaving. Madeleine sat with it through the cold night. After thrashing around and trying to roll, the pony lay still as the end approached. Huddled against the animal's fevered flanks, stroking its hot forehead, Madeleine was deaf to her mother's entreaties and her grandfather's muttered command to leave the paddock and come back inside. And when she felt Bertha forcefully tug at her arm in an effort to drag her away from the dying pony, Madeleine found herself screaming, unable to stop, suddenly as unrecognizable to herself as she was to the others.

Madeleine was twelve when she was finally allowed to ride full-grown hunters. She could vividly recall the sound of the hunting horn, the baying of the hounds and the thrill of galloping across the open country. If she closed her eyes, she could see herself dismounting from the horse when they returned home in the evening, mud splashed all over her riding clothes, reeking of the heady mixture of animal and human sweat, hungry and delightfully tired.

When she was little, what Madeleine most looked forward to were the long afternoon walks through the Downs. Past farmhouses and wisteria-covered cottages, past rolling meadows sprinkled with cowslips and cow parsley, towards the distant Surrey hills, the hilltops lined with thick-crested oaks, a spreading green stain in the spring. These were almost always solitary outings. At her express wish, Bertha, her nanny, followed some paces behind her. Walking up the lane that led past a pond with swans, fields, and a coppice full of sweet-smelling primroses in spring, Madeleine discovered within herself an overwhelming affinity with the trees, plants and flowers. In her busy life at the Sabarmati ashram where she was surrounded by people at all times during the day, where privacy was not only at a premium but looked at askance as an expression of egotism and a lack of fellow-feeling (unless it was part of one's spiritual regimen), it was only at night that she could be alone in her hut. As she lay on her bed in the dark, the orchestra of night sounds—the whistling of hundreds of crickets that struck the ear as a single high-pitched drone punctuated by the croaking of river frogs and the occasional hooting of an owl—gradually subsiding into silence, Madeleine would often take that walk through the open wrought iron gates of Milton Heath, along the cobbled path leading to the Downs, past hollows of sweet grass and pale clover and the dog rose shining in the hedge of woven beech. Her memory would accelerate the blooming and wilting of the whitethorns and the dangling fingers of the foxgloves. Weak waves of their dying fragrance would reach her through the passage of almost thirty years.

Madeleine's intimate connection with nature grew stronger with the years. Whenever they came to live in London, the first thing she did after settling down in a new house was to seek out the nearest park. Afternoon walks in Battersea Park with Lucy or Bertha were among her best memories of London which otherwise made her feel shut in. Not that she was a hermit. She went shopping with her mother but never enjoyed it, she participated in the family's social life but never really felt a part of it. In London, she also discovered theater. (She wished it had been music, but that had to wait till she entered youth.) She vividly remembered the first play she was ever taken to by her parents—Shakespeare's *The Tempest*—but had no memory of seeing other plays. The crowds and the stuffy air that almost always gave her a sickening headache soon put a stop to the theater visits.

The Slade family did not always live in Madeleine's grandfather's house when her father went back to sea. Among the other houses they lived in, the one which occupied a special place in her heart and in the memories of her late childhood was the farmhouse on the highland above Great Bookham, a village in Surrey. By an extraordinary coincidence, the house had the same name that Gandhiji had given to his first ashram in South Africa—Phoenix Farm.

"Early youth," she writes in her diary, "was to bring with it restlessness and a vague, inexplicable feeling of dissatisfaction with myself and everything around me, although I was surrounded by the greatest affection . . . Phoenix Farm had rolling open fields to its north and a mix of fields and woodland to the south. On weekends, early in the morning, Mother, Lucy and I went for long rambles through the glorious down and the sweet-smelling woods. My memory compresses all those walks into one: a day at the end of July, a week before my thirteenth birthday. We leave the house at dawn, walking up the partly cobbled lane that leads to the woods. Shrugging off the last remnants of sleep, my eyes begin to make out the shapes of the hedges bordering the damp fields, alive and breathing around us. Gradually, the light becomes stronger, revealing the speckled sphere of the sky. Ferns stick out of the gaps between the old flagstones. Blades of grass lining the path are bending under the weight of translucent beads of moisture. Reaching the woods, the lane breaks into pioneering paths that twist in the undergrowth before they disappear into deep shadows. Once inside the woods, the shadows begin to lighten as the sun climbs higher. Spotted butterflies are all around us. At mid-day, we break for a snack of cucumber and watercress sandwiches Lucy has packed for lunch. We sit on a carpet of bluebells under a giant oak tree.

Next to us is a patch of ripening blackberries, glossy purple clots studded with red and green beads, as hard as knots. Bluebottles weave a gauze of sound around us. In another month, the ripe berries will be lying in a sticky mush on the earth, fermenting, their sweet smell turned sour . . . Both Mother and Lucy were passionate botanists and I soon learnt to look at the plants and flowers in the fields with a trained eye. It was the same with birds. I began to recognize different bird cries and to hear the song of an unknown bird was always a special thrill. If I came across a bird's nest and looked closely at the eggs, the shells freckled with colour, cradled in the warmth of feathers, twigs and earth, I could distinguish a robin's nest from that of a wren's, a plover's from that of a lapwing. We would return home late in the afternoon when the dying sun had stained the colours of the heather on the downs to crimson, the voices of hermit thrush far in the darkening wood behind us."

Next to this diary entry is the draft of a letter to Gandhiji, dated 20 November 1925. I am not sure whether Mira finished writing this letter or, if she did, that she ever gave it to him.

Bapu, when I look back at myself as a girl, every now and then there were moments when something would take me away from the world in which I lived and for a while I would not know who or where I was. Sometimes this dislocation would fill me with terror. When I overheard my elders talk of stars, galaxies and the infinite space between them, for instance, a cold dread would seize me as my mind desperately scampered to put images to their words. I would hurriedly try to think of something mundane and very ordinary—one of Lucy's blue slippers which was getting frayed in the front, a missing button on my father's uniform that Bertha had not yet sewn back—to try and keep away the horror of which I could not speak to anyone else, even my mother. In the same way, I could not bring myself to imagine eternity without breaking into a cold sweat. I used to dread going to church where I might have to listen to the prayer that ends: "As it was in the beginning, is now, and ever shall be, world without end—Amen."

But sometimes infinity and eternity came in another garb to which I was exquisitely receptive. This was the garb of grace and exaltation rather than of dread and dislocation. The grace came through the voice of Nature and it came at quiet moments. It could come through the song of a bird, waft in on the scent of a flower petal, or come with the rustling of the wind in the leaves of a tree. I did not speak of this to anyone. I hear this voice again, though this time it comes through the medium of a human soul—yours. Do I embarrass you, Bapu, when I say that? Did you expect greater reserve from an Englishwoman?

Once before, many years ago, the voice of nature came to me through another human soul. I was twenty-one, Bapu. I long to tell you about it. I want to tell you about the joy, but also the anguish it caused me then. That was the only time I ever kneeled down on the floor in the seclusion of my room and prayed, really prayed, for the first time in my life. I prayed to God to rid me of the anguished joy but also to let me savour it again and again. To you, I must pour out all that is in my heart. I shall go out of my mind if I try to suppress it. A tinny voice of doubt, a feeble flapping of intellect's wings whispers, "Will you accept the pouring out of all that I have held back for so many years? Will you hold me, contain me, so that I do not scatter into millions of tiny pieces—cold stars forever condemned to populate a cold universe?" And the heart thunders back, "Of course, he will!"

But, Bapu, I am English. You cannot know how difficult it has been for me to hold myself back, not to intrude on your privacy, when I long to be with you every single moment of the day. But one day it will happen, an inner voice tells me. I shall be as your shadow and you will accept my nearness as unthinkingly as you do it with the shadow. *That* vision is my hope. It keeps me glued together. It . . .

six

THE GENESIS of the "violent and passionate disturbance," about which Romain Rolland wrote to Gandhiji in his letter introducing Madeleine, went back twelve years, to the year Madeleine turned twenty-one.

In November 1913 the Slade family had been back in England for almost two years and were living in Milton Heath, Madeleine's grandfather's country house. Because of his long hours of work at the Admiralty, her father spent most of his time in London. Rhona, too, no longer lived at home. She had moved to India after her marriage to an officer of the Indian Civil Service. They had met during the festivities on the occasion of the visit of the King and Queen and the durbar of 1911 in Delhi, the new capital of British India, where the Indian princes had gathered to pledge their allegiance to the British crown.

Madeleine was content to be left on her own. She went riding across the downs in the morning, played a game of bezique with her grandfather in the evening, and took long walks in the cool high shade of the woods with her mother on Sunday mornings. The rest of the time she spent in her room upstairs, reading and listening to music. A new mechanical pianola that gave a player some freedom since the music could be played as loud or as fast as desired had been attached to the upright piano in the room next to hers. Angleus Company, the makers of the pianola, had a good selection of rolls of classical music in their library. From them Madeleine procured all of Beethoven's sonatas and played them one after the other all through the day, day after day.

In Beethoven's music, though distorted and unclear because of the limitations of the mechanical player, Madeleine perceived unmistakably the "heralds of grace" she had fleetingly encountered during her walks through the woods and the downs when she was a child. One day, she believed, such grace would once again storm into her soul, submerging it and altering the contours of its landscape.

Her infrequent excursions to London were solely for the purpose of attending concerts in which Beethoven's music predominated. Thus when she saw the announcement for a Beethoven recital in *The Times*, she immediately set off for the city. She had not heard of the pianist, Frederic Lamond, before but a further item in the newspaper informed her that he was well known on the Continent for his interpretation of Beethoven's sonatas. A native of Glasgow where he was regarded as a wunderkind in the music circles, Lamond was only sixteen when he studied with Max Schwarz in Frankfurt and then with Bulow, the greatest contemporary authority on Beethoven. Married to an Austrian actress, he had now made Berlin his home.

The moment Lamond stepped onto the concert platform, took his seat in front of the darkly gleaming grand piano and struck the first chords of the Apassionata Sonata, Madeleine knew that at last she was going to *hear* the music she had listened to with such unbearable longing over the years. What she had heard on the unsatisfactory pianola, or even in concerts by lesser pianists, was but an intimation of the musical treasures contained in Beethoven. This evening, though, an old promise was going to be kept. More than the thickset Scotsman's strength of rendering, the fullness of his tone or the directness of his expression, it was Madeleine's conviction that she was, at last, hearing Beethoven's music as the composer himself must have heard it as he put it down on paper. Unlike other pianists, Lamond did not impose his own personality between Beethoven's music and her. The communion was especially intense in the slow movements during which she felt the fearlessness, strength and purity of the music lift her into regions of the spirit that can be felt but not expressed in words. Since the age of thirteen, Madeleine had been aware of a core of yearning that often expressed itself in an inexplicable restlessness or in sudden stabs of anguish, even dread. As Lamond's rendition of *The Tempest* rolled over her, with its contrasts and its passion, Madeleine had a strong physical sensation of time slowing down, a feeling similar to moments that precede the loss of consciousness, but free of the dread and disorientation that such a loss entails. The music reverberated in her head, prolonged now, growing suddenly, stretching without a pause. And then it was as if her soul was convulsively released from its long incarceration in flesh. For the first time since her days in Phoenix Farms, Madeleine felt completely at home in her body even as she stepped out of its boundaries. She did not join in the standing ovation when the recital ended but continued to sit in her seat, her head bowed, the hall emptying around her. Many years later, she would rediscover the same purity and strength in Gandhiji, in moments when Bapu was most himself.

———

Eight years were to pass before Madeleine would hear Lamond play again.

The World War had intervened. Madeleine had not been immune to the surge of enthusiasm that greeted the outbreak of war with Germany. On the day the war was declared, the whole family—with the exception of her father who had been camping at the Admiralty for many days—trooped into the street to join the gathering crowd. As if in a single wave, thousands all over London spontaneously converged at the Buckingham Palace. When the King and Queen appeared on the balcony, Madeleine too joined in the singing of the hymn "Oh, God, our help in ages past" followed by "God save the King." Almost half a million voices had mysteriously united in the selection and singing of the songs without being led by anyone.

The declaration of war had come after a long period of tense waiting. It was marked by a sense of relief, like a shower of rain at the end of a long, hot summer day. Everyone Madeleine knew had welcomed the war. In the public arena, artists, writers, journalists and university dons made ringing statements in support of the war. Clergymen preached war as a sacred duty, and two million men volunteered for active service within the first six months. Most people thought the war would be over within a year; four years later, they began to think it would never end.

In those four years, the horrors of the war had begun to penetrate even the thickest of armors crafted by propaganda and patriotism. People realized that this was a different kind of war. It was a war employing a vast amount of new technology for killing—machine guns, gas, submarines, tanks, airplanes—which, feeding on itself, spawned ever newer technologies for ever greater slaughter. Madeleine could rightfully claim that she saw through the war and what it would really accomplish much earlier than most. The grim news of some of the young men she had danced with in Bombay going down with their ships (the Slade family often received the news earlier than the families of the men since her father's job at the Admiralty was to organize the protection of England's trade routes from German submarines), and the sight of young soldiers returning from the war with missing arms or legs, leaning against a wall or a door, smoking their woodbine cigarettes as they helplessly dragged out their maimed years was bad enough. But, for Madeleine, the corrosion of people's souls was even worse. The kindest and sweetest people talked of the Germans as if they were not human beings but just so many vermin to be exterminated. She could hardly bear to carry out her work as a volunteer, preparing bandages, when day in and day out she had to listen to hate-talk that at first shocked and then sickened her. At home, Madeleine withdrew to her small sitting room on the top floor. Here, she would be alone with her piano and her books, coming down only at mealtimes so as to avoid listening to her family's revolting discussions about the war. How could she ever forget that Beethoven was German, that the music for which she lived had come out of Germany and Austria?

There was no joy, no gaiety when the war ended, just a mood of simple thankfulness that the guns had fallen silent, the killings had stopped and the survivors would soon be returning home. The sense of emptiness and disillusionment that such a great sacrifice had brought so little gain, the general mood all over Europe that Madeleine shared in as little as she had the Continent's fervor at the start of the war, was to come later. With rare exceptions, Madeleine had always kept herself inviolate from the ebb and flow of popular moods that swirled around her. The stars that lit her way belonged to a very private and personal galaxy.

Immediately after the war ended, when feelings against Germany and all things German were running high, concerts of what was regarded as German music were not in demand. At least this is what Lamond's agent, a prissy, unresponsive and unimaginative little man with a liberal sprinkling of dandruff on the shoulders of his worn-out tweed jacket, told her. Besides, he said, although a Scot by birth and someone who had spent the war years in Holland, Lamond had lived too long in Germany to be welcome in England. The man's final declaration that in any case Beethoven's music was too dark and heavy, quintessentially Teutonic, to appeal to a postwar English audience looking for a lighter, gayer fare, convinced Madeleine to go into the concert agency business herself.

Madeleine took Lamond's address from the agent and wrote a shy, spare letter to the pianist, its tone not unlike that of her first letter to Gandhi, offering to arrange three concerts in England. Lamond was hesitant at first, but impressed by the young woman's obvious sincerity and enthusiasm both for Beethoven's music and for himself as its interpreter, he agreed. The first concert was to be held in the Town Hall in Dorking. Since an evening consisting solely of Beethoven's sonatas would probably be too demanding of Surrey's rural gentry, Lamond suggested that the program be lightened by the inclusion of Chopin's Valse op. 34, no. 3 in F, Liszt's Hungarian Rhapsody no. 14 and Ravel's *Jeux d'Eau*.

On the day of the concert, Madeleine was so agitated that she drove poor Bertha crazy with a barrage of instructions on getting the guest room ready for Lamond's impending arrival. Flowers and flower vases were chosen and discarded, the bed cover had to match the curtains and then the curtains changed to be in harmony with the new bed cover. In spite of doing the work required for the evening's concert all by herself—seeing to the printing of the tickets and programs, putting up the posters, making sure the piano was tuned and the seating satisfactory—Madeleine showed no signs of being tired. She went up and down the stairs, from one room to another, forgetting why she had entered a particular room, till her mother persuaded her to go for a walk to calm her nerves. She thus missed Lamond's arrival.

When Madeleine came back to the house, shortly before 3 p.m., glorious sound was pouring out of the little piano upstairs. Entranced, she stood outside the room for a few minutes, soaking in the music, loath to interrupt. But since the time for the recital at the Town Hall was drawing near, she picked up enough courage to knock on the door, first gently and then more firmly. The music stopped. A voice, gravelly and warm, called out from inside, "Come in."

Lamond was standing next to the piano. In her excitement and nervousness, Madeleine could barely manage a few words of welcome. But Lamond's own shyness and halting speech, with its pleasing Scottish accent, calmed her. He had grown thinner but still exuded a quiet strength. A dark blue serge suit, evidently stitched by a good London tailor in the years before the war, hung loosely from his frame. The effect, though, was not one of dishevelment but of an odd elegance, heightened by a still thick head of hair where salt was marching victoriously through pepper country. Lamond's hands, she noticed, were perfectly still while he talked. They were strong hands, their backs dusted with a down of fine black hair, darkly brooding against the pale skin. In her mind's eye, she could see them glide over the ivory keys, pound them to a crescendo, before caressing them again as the music faded away.

The two remaining concerts were to be in London, the second after an interval of four days, and the pianist had agreed to be put up in the Slades' Church Street flat. No longer shy in his presence, Madeleine sought out Lamond's company, seizing every opportunity to spend time with him, a prospect that the pianist, flattered by the young woman's attention, did not find disagreeable. In the morning, they took long walks, exploring London's many parks, Lamond's feeling for nature not much less than her own. In the afternoons, she sat in one corner of the living room listening, enraptured, to Lamond play on a rented piano as he prepared for his concerts. There were certain moments in Opus 106, which was on the program for both recitals, when she had the odd feeling that the man and the music were coalescing together, that it was becoming increasingly difficult to hold them apart.

Madeleine had never felt as fiercely alive as she did during those five days. It was like being on a continuous high, quite distinct from the quick, short bursts of childhood elation. And they talked, not during the quiet walks but later, after the concert was over and they had eaten dinner and returned to the flat. Actually, he talked and she listened, hanging on to his every word, aware of each inflection in his voice. The middle-aged pianist did not miss the glow in the young woman's large gray eyes that spurred him on to narrate his adventures when he was a young man starting out in the musical world. He saw her eyes widen in admiration at his triumphs, moisten in commiseration at his rare defeats, as when Clara Schumann had refused to accept him in her classes. And when it came to the stories about his initiation into the universe of Beethoven's music, Madeleine was no longer a listener but a participant; more, she was an identical twin who could intimately share every feeling, every experience.

"At my first lesson with Bulow, he asked me 'What are you going to play?'

"'Opus 106,' I answered, which is the longest and most difficult of Beethoven's pianoforte works.

"'Impertinent boy!' Bulow said angrily. 'Wait five years before you attempt such a work.'

"'In the next lesson,' Bulow again asked, 'What are you going to play for me?'

"'Opus 106,' I said again.

"Bulow's face turned beetroot-red. He stamped his foot and just spluttered. He didn't ask me again till near the end of the course. When I again answered, 'Sonata, Opus 106,' he laughed.

70

"'All right. I will hear the scherzo.'

"I played the scherzo. When I finished, he came up to me and clapped me on my shoulders. 'Bravo. We will commence with the opening allegro,' he said, smiling in delight.'"

Lamond's account of his meeting with Liszt, the pianist he admired above all, brought tears to Madeleine's eyes, for as a boy, Liszt had received the dedicatory kiss from the sublime Beethoven himself. He was an old man when Lamond met him, wearing the apparel of a priest, his white hair hanging in long locks, his face covered with warts. "But when he sat at the piano and began playing . . ." Lamond said, shaking his head from side to side, his voice heavy. "I particularly remember his performance of a variation in Schumann's Symphonic Studies—a magical fascination emanated from him. No other pianist, and I have heard them all, ever got that sighing, wailing, murmuring accompaniment in the left hand and certainly no other pianist played the melody in the right hand with such indescribable pathos as Liszt did."

When the time came for Lamond's departure, Madeleine realized that her magical fascination was no longer confined to Lamond's music but had begun to inhabit his person. To put it plainly, she had fallen in love with the fifty-six-year-old pianist who lived in Holland, had a wife and a daughter, and who enjoyed her admiration but was oblivious of her infatuation.

The first few days, wrung from November's damp gray skies, were the worst. Madeleine continued to stay at the London flat, unable to part from the places where his presence still lingered. She fought against her feelings for Lamond with the same intensity with which she had organized his concerts. She was fully aware that these feelings had no resolution, no natural evolution that led to a desired goal. Although overcome by passion, Madeleine was still strong enough to resist the onslaught of her fevered imaginings. Not for her the lying awake in bed at night, conjuring behind closed eyes his face bending down on her own, his warm breath on her mouth, his hand sliding down to her breasts, his fingernails lightly raking her flank, or hearing the murmur of words of love and longing again and again. Her suffering was truly silent; not only did she not breathe a word about the state of her mind to anyone, but she also succeeded in resisting the temptation of those obsessive internal conversations with the object of her desire. What finally helped was prayer. Time and again she would enter a church or a cathedral if she found it empty, or with only a few others scattered in its cavernous darkness, and seek silent communion with God. For almost a year, even after she returned to Milton Heath, Madeleine could not bear to listen to the rolls of Beethoven's music, a privation that was even greater than the absence of the music's interpreter. Two years later, when she first met Romain Rolland, a meeting she had sought after reading his fictionalized biography of Beethoven, the penetrating gaze of the writer had no difficulty in detecting the traces of the "violent and passionate disturbance" she had been through.

A year after Lamond's departure from London, Madeleine's despair had subsided but not disappeared. That summer, at her mother's quiet urging, Madeleine decided to take a trip to Europe. She had always wanted to follow Beethoven's trail, which started in Bonn, a sleepy little town on the Rhine in the heart of Germany, where Beethoven was born and spent the first years of childhood and where he occasionally returned in his later years. Wandering around the rooms of the small house, looking at the portraits of the composer, Madeleine marveled at the contrast between the musician's lofty spirit and the small, thin body in which it had dwelt. Beethoven had certainly not been handsome, though he was not positively ugly (a description that would also fit Gandhiji). Of all the relics treasured in his birthplace, she was most moved by the piano, its yellowing keys worn out by the continual touch of Beethoven's fingers. Madeleine could well imagine him as a small boy, practicing on this piano for hours at a stretch, forever fearful of being boxed on his ears by his ambitious and strict father whenever he struck a wrong note.

From Bonn, Madeleine took the train to Vienna, the once glittering capital of the Hapsburg Empire, where Beethoven had spent most of his adult life. Her pilgrimage did not go so far as to search out and visit each of the scores of sites where Beethoven had lived at various times during his thirty-five years in the city. She was aware that his mercurial temperament and unpredictable temper had led him to change apartments ever so often. His had been the untamed personality of a genius, not to be judged by ordinary standards. Beethoven (and in this Madeleine shyly claimed to be a kindred spirit) had found the commerce of daily life unbearable.

Of all the places on the Beethoven trail, the valley of Helenental near Baden, south of Vienna, especially attracted Madeleine. Beethoven had spent the last summers of his life here, seeking a cure for some of his many ailments in Baden's natural mineral baths. She stayed here for a week, at the Zum Goldenen Schwan, a small inn at the edge of the spa where Beethoven had lived for one summer. Each morning, Madeleine walked up the little valley which the composer, who had by this time lost his hearing, had passed through on his long solitary walks across the fields and into the forest, composing music in his head he would never hear with his ears. One day, before her departure for England, Madeleine sat down on a grassy bank in a small clearing in the forest, the afternoon sunlight filtering softly through the thinning autumn foliage. She imagined Beethoven sitting at the same secluded spot, the glory and enchantment of the silent forest around him, trying to put into musical language all that stirred and swelled in his spirit. She remembered his words, scribbled in the margin of his Helenental musical notebook in the Bonn house, "The Almighty in the Forest! I am blessed, happy in the

forest: every tree speaks through Thee. Oh God! What glory!"
She could see the ailing composer reach for his notebook and attempt to put his feelings into music and then, failing, throw the besmirched paper on the ground, convinced that no mortal being would ever be able to represent through sound, word, color or chisel, the divine vision which had unfolded before him.

The images dimmed as Madeleine felt herself being overtaken by a trancelike calm, an old familiar feeling from her childhood walks in the Surrey woods. In the total clarity of an unaccustomed inner silence, Madeleine heard the Tempest as Lamond had played it that evening in London. No, this was not an auditory hallucination. She *knew*, with the utter conviction that such a knowing produces, that the music had been there all along even if she had never heard it before. It was like a dreaming which is continual, which goes on night and day, whether we're asleep or awake; only our consciousness in its waking state makes such a noise that we no longer "hear" the dream.

Madeleine sat there for a long time, absorbed in the music, coming back to the ordinary world with a start when it was over. Before leaving, she picked up a newly fallen leaf. The leaf, now dry and discolored, dotted with black spots, its veins brittle, had remained with her ever since, tucked safely inside the pages of Rolland's biography.

Before leaving Vienna, Madeleine bought the first volume of Romain Rolland's *Jean Christophe* and his *Vie de Beethoven* from a bookshop in Graben that also stocked books in foreign languages. Someone had told her that *Jean Christophe*, Rolland's epic novel, which had won him the Nobel Prize for Literature in 1915, was based on Beethoven's life. She struggled hard to read the book with the help of a French-English dictionary, but her French was too rudimentary for her to fully understand what she was reading. She laid the book aside, but had grasped enough of it to conclude that Rolland's was a rare spirit, fully attuned to that of his subject. She made up her mind to learn French, both to be able to read the book and to meet its author and speak with him in his own language.

London soon began to gnaw at the feelings of serenity and composure Madeleine had carried back from Austria, and she became restless again. Since there was little to hold her back in London, Madeleine left for Paris. Her plan was to stay in Paris for six months for an intensive study of French, read the ten volumes of *Jean Christophe*, and then write to Rolland requesting a meeting. Nothing if not persistent, Madeleine achieved each of the goals she had set herself. The response to her request for a meeting was warm and gracious; Rolland invited her to visit him at his home in Villeneuve, a village on the Swiss-French border, high above Lake Geneva.

Madeleine's account of her first meeting with Rolland sounds oddly familiar. "I bicycled around the end of the lake, and arrived on time in a state of intense inner suspense. *It is all or nothing* was the only sensation I had. I rang the bell, the door was opened by a maid who showed me into a small sitting room and said that M. Rolland would be there in a minute or two. I sat down mechanically. I heard steps and a hand on the door handle. I stood up. Romain Rolland entered—tall and pale and clad in black. He greeted me gently, almost shyly, and sat down on a small chair by the door. As I sat opposite him I could think only of the quiet, all-embracing penetration of his blue eyes, holding me in their gaze. I tried to express myself, but my words were halting and awkward. He listened and replied patiently, but it was as if an invisible veil separated me from him."

During all the time I was Madeleine's Hindi teacher and well after, I never asked myself why Rolland and Gandhiji found the "it's all or nothing" attitude with which Madeleine approached them so irresistible, why her determination to raze the barrier separating her from them met with such a heartfelt response. I do not pretend to know the answers even now. Perhaps their own natures resonated with hers in ways that remain mysterious to outsiders. Perhaps they sensed in her deeper truths about themselves—a concealed and tightly reined in passion that, in the men, could only be expressed in their work. Perhaps they admired, and shared, her capacity for committing to an ideal (though for Madeleine the ideal had to always be embodied in a person), a commitment that did not shy away from any hardship or balk at any obstacle met on the way. And, in following their star, all three of them would cheerfully swim against the current without agonizing about the rest of the world hurrying in the opposite direction.

By their third meeting, Romain Rolland had adopted Madeleine as his "spiritual daughter." "The former embarrassment had disappeared, the veil separating us lifted, and I could speak freely," she writes of her subsequent meetings with Rolland. "He sat opposite me at the table and we talked on and on. It seemed we had always known one another."

In their fourth and last meeting before Madeleine was to leave for Paris and then go on to London, Rolland casually mentioned Mahatma Gandhi whose biography he had just published.

"Who is he?" Madeleine asked.

"He is another Christ," Rolland said simply. "Certainly, Gandhi is not inferior to Christ in goodness and sanctity, and he surpasses him in touching humility. Gandhi is the prophet of hope in this age of pessimism and disillusionment. He is a promise of sanity in the madness induced by our world's heedless drinking at the fount of war."

Smoothening down his moustache with the thumb and forefinger of his right hand, he stood up from his chair and went into his study from where he soon emerged holding a slim volume in his hand. "Here," he said, "if you would like to read about him. It would pass your time on the train journey to Paris."

seven

IN CONTRAST TO Madeleine's careful preparations before joining Gandhiji at Sabarmati ashram, my own decision to become his disciple was a matter of impulse, or so it seemed at the time. To even call it a decision is to claim too much on behalf of my will; it will be more correct to say that it just happened, that I strayed into my future.

I was an MA student of Hindi literature at the time, writing my thesis on the novels of Premchand. The day after I received my BA results—which I had passed with a first division—and announced that I did not intend to appear for the provincial civil service exam remains etched in my mind to this day. Ever since I was a little boy it had been taken for granted by the family—my grandparents, uncles, aunts and cousins—and especially by my father, that I was destined for a high position in the administration of British India. Nothing so exalted as being in the Indian Civil Service, of course, but prestigious enough to make the family proud that Mahabir Prasad's son was headed for the upper echelons of the sarkar. My father was furious when I told him that I intended to join MA classes in Hindi literature. He started by calling me an ungrateful wretch and threatened to turn me out of the house, before directing his wrath at my mother and accusing her of spoiling me; it was her fault I had turned out to be so willful. He wished he had had more sons to make up for the distress I was causing him. He cursed Gandhiji, whose call for civil disobedience and noncooperation with the government early that year had had such a pernicious effect on the country's youth. He then became tearful and pleaded with me to change my mind: I should not waste my intelligence by ending up as a mere college teacher, that too in a subject universally held in low esteem. My intellect may be god-given, but it was also inherited from him and my forefathers; I owed a debt to my ancestors. He became angry again as I kept my eyes firmly downcast and went on shaking my head in refusal. I did not answer him for the fear of adding the sin of disrespect to the charge of stubbornness. I did not tell him that not only did I admire Gandhiji, but I also planned to live a celibate life according to his principles and example. That would have broken his heart. After loudly pro-claiming his intention of henceforth only talking to me through my mother— "Navin's mother, tell that son of yours . . ."—he stormed out of the house to seek consolation from his friends on being one of those unfortunate modern fathers who have no control over the actions of their sons.

My mother was gentler in her reproaches. Each was pref-aced by the remark that her sole consideration was my future happiness, when I knew (for she had often repeated it as I was growing up) how much she had looked forward to being the mother of a magistrate, the envy of her older sister whose most successful offspring was a mere civil engineer. For many days, the disappointment I had caused her was on open display. At mealtimes, she would peck at her food or altogether refuse to eat even while she piled food on my plate. Her eyes were full of silent reproof, her voice punctuated by involuntary sighs whenever she spoke to me. And there was Mira's mother, helping her pack for a long and indefinite stay in a far-off land, and her father gravely shaking his daughter's hand, perhaps holding it for a shade longer than usual, but only saying "Be careful" as he saw her off on a journey that would pit her against all he had believed in and stood for in his own life. "Be careful!" I confess I will never understand the British.

I must, however, admit to a sneaking admiration for her parents. For despite the total intellectual disagreement between them and Mira, they accepted her decision—even her father, the admiral. No doubt they regretted it, unable to understand why she was doing what she was doing, but they did recognize the nobility of her action. Few Indian parents, I fear, would have been capable of this self-abnegation and respect for their child's liberty.

———

Gujarat College, where I was in the final year of my MA classes, prided itself on training the "elite" of Ahmadabad, (which meant, the most affluent). Many of its students would eventually take over the running of their family's textile mills or other businesses that served the city's dominant textile industry. Some of them, sons of spinning, weaving and carding masters of the mills, would go for further training in textile technology after finishing college. A few, and here the business-minded Gujaratis differed from the people in the northern provinces, would take the civil service examination to enter the higher rungs of the Raj's bureaucracy.

In college, I had a reputation of being a nationalist, although I was mindful not to overstep the boundary between nationalist leanings and what could be construed as seditious talk against the British Empire. When I started wearing khadi, I had to face the not-so-subtle expressions of disapproval from the college administration. The principal pointedly ignored me whenever our paths crossed. Messages were conveyed through other students that I was being watched and that I needed to be careful about what I said in class. I was good at skirting the edge of open insubordination but still hesitated to make the short trip to Sabarmati ashram and meet my idol in person. Then I heard that Gandhiji was coming to our college to give a talk at the invitation of the students; there was no way I was going to miss the chance of hearing him speak.

For a few days it was uncertain whether Gandhiji's visit would take place at all, whether the college administration would not make an issue of the invitation to Gandhiji to address the students. Fortunately, the principal was a coward and an opportunist whose main concern was to avoid trouble at all costs. Afraid of offending the British but also fearful of the students going on a strike, he hesitated before reaching one of his usual compromises: he would not allow the meeting in the college auditorium but would also not raise any objection to a private meeting the students might wish to hold with Gandhiji—for whom he had the highest regard—in their hostel. When Gandhiji arrived, he came to receive him at the hostel gate. Hands folded in a greeting of welcome, a wide, obsequious smile in place, he pleaded a previous engagement in the city which would not allow him to attend the afternoon's talk.

The dining hall of the hostel was packed with students, teachers and college staff, the crowd overflowing into the verandas, when Gandhiji began his talk one warm April evening. This was the first time I was seeing Gandhiji from close quarters. He was bare-chested, clad as always in a short dhoti that ended well above his bony knees. I was surprised at how small and thin he was. His shoulder blades and ribcage were prominent against a walnut-brown skin. He could not have weighed more than a hundred pounds. True, he was recovering from a long fast (once again for the cause of Hindu-Muslim unity, this time after the Delhi riots), but my surprise was more due to the incongruity of his physical appearance with the stature he held in my mind's eye. In the last couple of years, I had often sneaked away without my father's knowledge to attend Gandhiji's occasional public meetings in Ahmadabad. At these large gatherings he had always sat on an elevated stage with a microphone in front of him. From where I stood, usually in the middle of the densely-packed crowd, from time to time standing on the tip of my toes to catch a glimpse of him, the impression of his stature was not only distorted by his elevation and the distance but also by the waves of awe and reverence sent out by the crowd. As I watched him now, from just a few feet away, I realized that these waves had flowed through my unresisting mind, overwhelmed my perceptions, and made him appear much larger than his physical reality.

There was a hushed, expectant silence as Gandhiji began to speak. He spoke in Gujarati, his tone conversational, without the rhetorical flourishes and the overwrought declamatory style favored by most of the other leaders. After a few minutes, however, restlessness began to sweep through the hall. It was signaled by a loud clearing of throats, coughing spells and shuffling of feet as the students first looked at each other questioningly and then, in growing disbelief, at the Mahatma. For Gandhiji was saying that the way to attain swaraj was for the students to begin their day by cleaning their lavatories and removing the feces themselves rather than waiting for the untouchable sweeper to do the job. If they really wanted independence for the country, they should go into the crowded, old part of the city every day and clear the garbage littering the streets. This was the way to show their solidarity with the untouchables who performed these mean tasks and thus remove the evil of untouchability without which any talk of self-rule was meaningless.

"Why should the removal of untouchability be a precondition for swaraj?" came an incensed interruption.

"We can set it right after getting independence."

"Yes, by passing the needed legislation."

"Do not look down on the panchama and his work," Gandhiji was saying. "Sweeping is an art in itself. If I had my way, I would be out there sweeping those roads myself. Not only that, I would plant flowers by the roadside and water them daily. Where there are dungheaps today, and they are all over our villages and towns, I would make gardens."

The decibel level in the room was mounting. Gandhiji stopped speaking. Sitting still and immovable like a rock, he let the noisy protests wash over him. After a couple of minutes, he raised his right hand. The shouting subsided to a murmur.

"I abhor with my whole soul the system which has reduced a large number of Hindus to a level less than that of beasts," he began again, his voice calm, its concealed passion betrayed only by each "s" that hissed through his missing front teeth as a "sh." "Swaraj for me means the freedom for the meanest of our countrymen. If the lot of the panchama is not improved when we are all suffering, it is not likely to be better under the intoxication of swaraj. I am not interested in freeing India merely from the English yoke. I am bent upon freeing India from any yoke whatsoever."

There was scattered, perfunctory applause. Gandhiji consulted his pocket watch and stood up. Followed by Mahadevbhai, he briskly walked out of the college to the waiting car, his raised hands folded in greeting. We all knew that next to cleanliness it was punctuality that he considered godly, and that he had never been late for the evening prayers at the ashram.

The talk did not go down well with the students. Perhaps I was the only one who agreed with all he had said. His words reflected the greatness of a man who thought deeply even about small matters—who could think of individual cleanliness on the same level as political freedom, to whom clean lavatories were as vital as spiritual salvation. Looking back, I recognize that it was less an agreement with the words he spoke that day than their virtual ingestion, their collective impact conveying Gandhiji's essence, which seemed to affect my physical being. I was prepared to give myself up to his care, to walk on any path he chose for me, hoping to absorb his calmness and strength (that I so woefully lacked) through some kind of osmosis. That very evening, writing feverishly late into the night, I poured out the secrets of my heart in a letter to Gandhiji.

I have little doubt that it was this letter that prompted him to accept me as a member of the ashram and thus as a part of his family. He could never resist the appeal of sickness, of the body or mind. It was impossible for him to close his ears to the cry of a lost soul, especially if that particular cry resonated with a conflict of his own, as mine so obviously did.

Even after the passage of fifty odd years, I can feel a shiver of shame slice through my body like a mild electric shock whenever I think of the letter I wrote him after his talk at our college, elaborating on what I called my "difficulty." Actually, the "difficulty" that I found so embarrassing at the time, which loomed so large in my mind as a momentous lapse from some unattainable ideal of purity if not as an unforgivable sin, was quite unremarkable. It was not even *my* "difficulty," in the sense that it was not uniquely personal to me but something that was common to the condition of being young, celibate and a man. I know that now, and yet I still hesitate; perhaps because Bapu, although protecting my identity, made what I wrote to him public at the time. Striving to live his private life publicly, Bapu was not particularly understanding about the intense embarrassment such disclosures about personal matters caused others.

In an issue of *Young India*, he published his response to my letter under the title "How to Conquer Desire." It read:

A young man who is trying to conquer passion has written me a heart-rending letter. There are many people in the position of this reader. It is difficult to conquer passion but it is not impossible. This young man is particularly troubled by his semen discharges at night. He is right to be worried. One *should* feel worried and ashamed even if there is involuntary discharge only once. It is certain that such discharge is the result of impure desires. I was told recently that a person who suffers from constipation might also get it. This is true, but constipation is also the result of impure desires. A man or woman who is free from such desires will not eat even a grain too much of food. Such persons never suffer from constipation.

But, then, there are two kinds of worry, one necessary and uplifting and another unnecessary and tending to draw us down. Despite worry and shame, we would remain cheerful if our lapse was not intentional or if we did not take pleasure in it. Such worry may also be called vigilance. The second kind of worry is the remorse one feels afterwards though one had taken pleasure in the lapse when it occurred. Such worry preys upon one's mind and yet one sinks even deeper into the vice. You will perhaps understand now that a man who gets involuntary discharges cannot afford to remain unconcerned. If he can remain free from them during waking hours, he should not be frightened by the emissions but should take them as a warning that impure desires are secretly eating him up from within, and he should ceaselessly struggle to save himself from them. I am myself not completely free from involuntary discharges. There was a period in my life when I remember to have remained free from them for many years but after I came to India and started taking milk they became more frequent. There are other causes besides milk. The atmosphere here revived memories of early life.

There are many steps one can take to weaken sexual desire. Fasting is the best remedy but if you cannot fast then try to live on uncooked food as much as possible. Sweets and spices should be totally avoided and milk taken in minimum quantity. But, above all, this struggle will need patience for the god of desire is strong, and man, weak.

To me, he wrote a short note.

10-7-25

Chi. Navin,

You can read the answer to your problem in the latest issue of *Young India*. The Ashram will be a good place for you to carry out your struggle against sexual desire and perhaps even emerge victorious. I have talked to Maganlalbhai. You may come whenever you are ready. As for your decision to take a vow of celibacy, I will not advise you to take such a vow lightly. The whole world may perish, but a vow once taken ought never to be given up.

I appreciate your wish to be of service to the poor. Remember, it is easy to serve the poor but difficult to live like them as we do here.

Bapu's blessings.

The letter came by the late afternoon post. Afraid that he might change his mind, that on further reflection he might find me unworthy, I rushed off to the Sabarmati ashram. I wanted to thank Gandhiji, reassure him that he had not made a mistake, that he would never regret his decision to let me spend the rest of my life with him.

The unmanned gate of the ashram was next to the biggest tamarind tree I had ever seen. It was just after sunset. The din made by hordes of starlings and pigeons settling in for the night in the foliage muffled the creaking of the gate and the sound of my own hesitant steps as I pushed open the wooden shutters. I had never imagined it would be so easy to enter the ashram. As I walked up the narrow brick path that passed through an orchard of custard apples, I tried to slow my hurried gait into a stroll. My heart was racing madly and it was difficult to quieten the jangling of my unruly nerves. Small groups of men and women returning from the prayers, deep in conversation about Gandhiji's evening talk passed by me. A few looked up as I stood there, hesitating, uncertain in which direction to turn, but my inquiring look bounced off incurious eyes. Finally, I picked up enough courage to ask an elderly woman—I have always felt more comfortable with older women—the way to Gandhiji's cottage.

"Can I meet him?" I added.

"Yes," she said, and pointed to a hut inside a small garden, next to the prayer ground. "He is inside."

I walked up to the wicker garden gate at the back of the hut and stood in front of it but did not push it ajar. I needed time to compose myself. The simplicity of the thatched, whitewashed brick hut, its veranda awash with a dim yellow light leaking through the open door of the room, only increased my anxiety. After all, this was an emperor I was approaching. He may not have been George VI of Britain, who ruled over Indian lands, but he was the unquestioned emperor of three hundred million Indian hearts.

I must have waited outside that garden gate for at least ten minutes, looking for someone whom I could ask for permission to enter, all the while apprehensive of an unpleasant scene if someone seeing me standing outside Gandhiji's hut doing nothing became suspicious and decided to question my intentions. No, I needed a little more time. Feigning self-assurance, pretending that I knew exactly what I wanted and where I was going, I walked past the hut towards the end of the ashram grounds where the land sloped away gently for about a hundred yards to meet the almost dry river bed.

The monsoon was late that year and by now, in July, the Sabarmati was a narrow stretch of barely moving water. In many places it was no more than a random collection of small pools, doomed to shrink still further into sandy puddles till the monsoon restored the river to the full flow of its youthful exuberance. The still evening, the calmness of the river bed and the quiet of the ashram grounds combined in a potent draught that slowly spread through my veins, washing away the last remnants of anxiety. For a while, I sat on the ground watching the men on the opposite bank move as if in slow motion, folding the saris they had spread out to dry during the day. The brilliant yellow, green, vermilion and indigo blue colors in which the saris had been dyed were now muted, distinguishable from each other only in the darkness of their shades. Further away, beyond the hovels of the dyers and washermen on the riverbank, the chimneys of Ahmadabad's textile mills loomed above the old part of the city. In the absence of any breeze, the smoke from the chimneys appeared to stand still, a wavy extension of the stacks, sooty black pillars holding up a rapidly darkening sky. Night was swiftly lowering its cover on the surface of the river and across the far bank, now perforated by dots of light as lamps began to be lit in the city. Calmer now, better prepared for the meeting that had brought me to the ashram, I stood up and walked back towards the hut.

Gandhiji was sitting on a round, white cushion on the floor, his feet tucked under him at an angle. In front of him was a low wooden desk with a pile of papers, a reed pen, a squat bottle of black ink and a blotting pad arranged neatly on its flat top. Otherwise, the room was largely bare. Its floor was covered with woven reed mats. An earthen pitcher of water with a baked clay plate covering its mouth and a glass tumbler overturned on the plate stood in one corner of the room. A spinning wheel, which had occupied a prominent place in recent newspaper photographs, took up most of the space in another corner. Next to it lay a wicker basket containing the day's spun yarn and unused fluffy balls of cotton. A young man with thinning hair and black horn-rimmed glasses, wearing a loose fitting kurta and pajamas, stood beside the desk taking notes in a diary while Gandhiji talked. The man's body bent and straightened at the waist in jerky, awkward movements in the effort to show deference to Gandhiji and avoid being disrespectful by looking down at him at the same time. Used to people coming into his room without knocking at the door, which was always open, Gandhiji did not look up as I entered. I stood near the door, waiting.

After Mahadevbhai (for that's who the bespectacled man was) left, Gandhiji looked up, peering through his wire-rimmed glasses.

"Yes?" he said in inquiry, his voice friendly but not overly welcoming.

As I began to explain who I was and why I had come, the expression on his face changed. It was no longer distant but perceptibly warm. When I knelt down on the floor and touched his feet to show my gratitude and get his blessings for the life ahead of me, he said, "What will you give me in return? You know that I am a bania who does not give anything for free."

"Bapu, I'll edit your Hindi correspondence."

"You do not think my Hindi is good enough?" he asked, with what I hoped was mock sternness.

"I don't know. I am sure it is. But everything can be improved."

"Yes," this time the seriousness of his tone was not in doubt. "There is no perfection except in god. Each of us can always improve if only the necessary effort is made."

Actually, except for the use of some Gujarati expressions, his written Hindi was excellent. Bapu wrote as he spoke—with minimum fuss. He used short, clear sentences that proceeded straight to the heart of the matter. No going off on a tangent, no meandering; he did not have time for all that. This does not mean that his letters were terse and uncaring. Concern was their primary sentiment, even if it was sometimes expressed in a scolding.

Many, many years later, when a selection of his letters to Mira was published, we discovered the hidden poetry in his soul that occasionally found expression when he described nature. One began, "In front of me are the Himalayan peaks wrapped in snow and shining brilliantly in sunlight. Below are hills clad with greenery, as though, feeling shy, they had covered their bodies with it."

Granted that Bapu was not a poet, that his metaphors were sometimes limited by his enduring concern for chastity. Yet it would be false to maintain, as a British writer of Indian descent has recently done, that preoccupied with his inner mental states, Bapu paid no attention to nature or was indifferent to the physical world around him.

eight

SOON AFTER Mira's arrival in the ashram my knowledge of Hindi was put to another use when, in November 1926, I was appointed her Hindi teacher.

Our lessons began well; I wish my former students at Gujarat College had been as committed and hardworking as she. However, I soon found that it wasn't much fun teaching Mira. I was too much in awe of her being a mem, and one close to Gandhiji at that, to think of indulging in the normal teacher-student banter. As for Mira, she remained as formal as ever, unfailingly polite, and never less than serious.

Even though Bapu was never present during Madeleine's Hindi lessons, he was aware of everything that transpired between Mira and me. At the end of our second lesson, I had expressed to Madeleine my desire to learn French and she agreed. That very evening, after the prayers were over and Bapu had retired to his hut, I was summoned to his presence.

It was an early December evening. There was a nip in the air, although this seldom translated into a winter-bite in our part of the country. I was nervous as I climbed up the three steps to the veranda and entered his room, the doors, as always, yawning wide open. I sensed the summons had something to do with Madeleine but was uncertain whether it was praise or censure that awaited me. I felt reassured when Bapu, who was sitting on the floor with a beige shawl, a mixture of hand-spun cotton and wool, wrapped around his bare shoulders, his spinning wheel in front of him, smiled as he motioned to me to sit down. After inquiring whether the new diet of raw vegetables, fruit and milk he had prescribed for my mysterious stomach cramps was agreeing with me, he came to the reason for this meeting.

"So you want to learn French, Navin?" he asked, his tone neutral, his eyes and hands concentrating on the task of spinning yarn. I made an affirmative sound, wondering what was to come.

"Why? Because Miss Slade is a scholar of French and she is here, or because you want to read Romain Rolland in the original? Or do you want to help me with our French correspondence?"

"I thought I'd enjoy learning a European language, and people say French is not that difficult to learn."

"Well, do you know that even most Englishmen do not know French? And much of the best French literature is translated into English as soon as it is published?"

There was a small pause as Bapu pushed the spinning wheel aside to give me his full attention.

"Do you know that in coming here Miss Slade has left everything behind her? Do you know that her sacrifice for our cause is greater than any of ours? That she is here to learn and study and serve and give all her time to the service of our people and thereby her own people? Every minute of her time is thus doubly precious and it is for us to give her as much as we can. Since she wants to know everything about us, she must master Hindi. How is she to do it unless we help her make the best of her time? She may be willing to oblige us, but our duty is to give her as much as we can. Our own time is sacred enough, hers is an even more sacred trust."

I bowed my head, my silence a confession of my blunder. Bapu's voice was kind, already forgiving my error, as he suggested my penance.

"So when you meet her tomorrow, tell her of your mistake and devote yourself compeletely to her Hindi lessons. Learning French is a luxury we can only afford once we have achieved swaraj, but until then we have to struggle against our wishes and choose to do only what we must."

"Yes, Bapu," I said, getting up to leave. But he was not finished yet.

"And your own difficulty? Did my suggestions help?"

I felt a hot flush start from my chest and streak up my face. If I had Madeleine's complexion, I would have turned crimson.

"Yes, Bapu. All is well."

He nodded. His eyes were alert and concerned but he respected my wish not to pursue this particular subject further. I left.

I may have reproduced the conversation as a succession of rapid-fire questions and hesitant replies, but, except for the last interchange, it was not like that at all. Bapu's questions were not like arrows that needed to be deflected. They were his side of a profoundly engaged dialogue, the purpose of which was to help me arrive at a correct understanding of the situation. I felt Bapu was gently guiding me towards a truth that would rid me of false beliefs and thus make me happier. His words were infused with a deep concern for—and I must say this at the risk of exposing myself to the ridicule of our cynical times—the virtue of my soul.

A week later, I was called to his hut again, this time in the afternoon. Bapu was sitting on the mat behind his low desk, the small of his back supported by a thick, round pillow. His knees were drawn up. A wooden takhti rested on his knees, an unfinished letter lying on top of it—this is how he did his writing. The day's mail was stacked beside the desk. He was examining the nib of his pen, which seemed to have bent. Bapu had once possessed a fountain pen an American admirer had presented him. It was stolen on a train journey and he had vowed never to use an article that was so attractive as to tempt anyone to steal it.

"Ah, Navin," he said. "How are the Hindi lessons progressing?"

"As well as can be expected, Bapu. Miss Slade tries very hard but it's not easy for her."

"And what have you given her to use for writing purposes?"

"Slate and chalk, Bapu," I replied.

"Why not the kitta and takhti?" he said. "They are much better for learning good penmanship."

He was right, of course. The simple pen made from easily available reeds and the rectangular wooden tablet coated with a thin layer of pale yellow clay were superior writing implements. One end of the reed pen was sharpened to a desired thickness, and the thickness of the lines that it produced could be varied further by the amount of pressure one applied. It was thus far superior to chalk, which only made uniform gray-white lines on the slate. The slate was easier to use, though. A simple swipe with a moist cloth would wipe out whatever was written on it and it would be ready for use again. The takhti, on the other hand, had to be first washed and scrubbed. Then the clay, prepared to the right viscosity with the addition of water would be applied in a thin, smooth coat on the surface of the wood and left to dry in the sun for a couple of hours or longer, especially during the monsoon when the humidity was high. The reed had to be cut to a proper length, its edge shaved with a sharp knife till it was of the required thickness, not to speak of mixing water with the gob of black resin to prepare the ink, an operation that always left the fingertips stained black.

More than the consideration of superior aesthetics, Bapu's objections to chalk and slate derived from their higher cost. Paper and pencil were, of course, completely out of the question; they were far too expensive. Bapu himself used all the pieces of paper he could get his hands on. Backs of envelopes, letters, circulars which had writing only on one side, were cut into different sizes and shapes to leave him maximum writing space. He reminded us time and again that the Sabarmati ashram was his most important experiment in search for truth, an experiment supported by donations from the people of a very poor country, and it was the duty of each one of us to ensure that not a single pie was wasted. Everything—money, time, even our minds and bodies—was held in a "sacred trust." They were not our own that we could decide what to do with them. "Sacred trust" was one of his favorite expressions.

"To serve the poor we must live as the poorest among them," he said. "What people listen to is your life, not your ideas." His eyes began to gleam through his glasses. A faint smile hovered around his mouth, a sure sign that a witticism was on the way. "After all we are not like the leader of the communist party they have just formed in France that Miss Slade was telling me about, are we? When asked how he reconciled his luxurious lifestyle with his communist convictions, the man replied, 'I am a socialist, not an idiot!' Here, we strive hard to be idiots."

As I laughed out aloud, his smile widened into a delighted grin. Bapu was often like that, lightening the weight of his remarks by a jest whenever he felt them becoming too heavy for the listener to bear. Carry only what you can, take from me only what you agree with after reflection, was a refrain in his letters to those close to him.

nine

*M*IRA WORKED HARD at learning Hindi, just as she did
on her carding and spinning lessons with Tulsi Mahar.
She had never been someone who took her undertakings lightly.
She threw herself into ashram life with the same zeal with
which she had organized Lamond's concerts in England. In
the mornings, she awoke before the bell rang. Invariably, she
was one of the first to reach the prayer ground where she sat in
the front row of the women's section, directly facing Bapu. She
lavished the same care on the cleaning of lavatories as she did
on the washing of pots in the kitchen after the main meal of the
day was over. The little free time she had in the late evenings was
occupied by her studies, not only in preparing for the next day's
Hindi lesson but learning more about the country she had made
her home. She wore Indian clothes, ate vegetarian meals, avidly
read about India and Indians but had no intention of becoming
Indian, of "going native." Her sense of her own identity was
much too strong for that. She strived to become the ideal ashram
inmate, someone Bapu could take pride in and point out to others
as his foremost disciple.

Her need for solitude and silence, though, had become even more pressing in the noisy, bustling community where she was expected to work eight hours a day in close contact with other men and women. She generally kept her distance from other inmates, gently rebuffing their overtures with a cool courtesy, deflecting their curiosity with monosyllabic replies. Not that too many of them tried. They were in awe of her, of her background as much as of her special relationship with Bapu. Barely a week after her arrival, she had been given the unheard of privilege of spending an hour every evening with him before he went to sleep. She would sit on the ground at his side while he lay on his bed in the veranda of his hut. No one disturbed them while she talked in her grave and warm voice, pouring out all that had over the years retreated into the silence of her heart. Bapu would listen, occasionally nudge her along with a question, giving Mira his complete attention, while Kasturba silently rubbed coconut oil on his head, unable to follow their conversation because it was in English. Once in a while, though, Ba would look up whenever she registered the play of intense emotions in the Englishwoman's voice or animation in Bapu's own when he spoke to her.

This hour was the most precious part of Mira's day, a time when she was most herself, when she felt intensely alive. Sitting next to Bapu, Ba's presence a soothing backdrop rather than an intrusion, Mira felt that she could drape her cloak of solitude around the two of them, that she and Bapu had become a two-person universe. Naturally, she was devastated when their evenings together were suddenly called off by Bapu in the beginning of December.

The signs had been there but as a newcomer whose command over Hindi was rudimentary, Mira could not have deciphered them. For two days almost everyone in the ashram roamed about with drawn faces. They gathered in small groups and spoke in low voices. When Mira returned to her room after the prayer one morning she saw Maganlalbhai, Surendrabhai and two other senior inmates whose names she did not know walk into Bapu's hut. They looked grim when they emerged from what turned out to be a long conference. That evening the feel of the prayer meeting was more like that of a wake. Even the children were subdued. At the end of the meeting, Bapu did not invite questions but spoke himself, his voice measured and thoughtful. A groan of protest arose from the audience when he ended his speech. Bapu raised his hand, commanding silence. Mira did not understand what he was saying but the steely resolve behind the words did not escape her. As people streamed out of the prayer grounds, I saw Mira frantically looking around for me. She needed someone to explain to her what had just happened.

"Bapu has decided to go on a week's fast from tomorrow," I told her.

"But why?"

"Because of what happened in the ashram school," I said, sounding evasive, even to myself. I was uncomfortable and wanted to get away from any further questioning.

"What happened?" Mira persisted.

"Something bad."

I heard myself give a bark of that peculiar laughter, a reflexive response that many Indians have when caught in a situation of profound embarrassment, that Mira found most irritating.

"Three boys were caught doing dirty things with each other. Bapu is going on a fast to atone for their misconduct," I said, and quickly made my escape.

When Mira went to Bapu's hut in the evening, he looked composed, at peace with himself and the world. Once he had reached a decision, all the doubts and agonizing simply melted away, leaving behind a calm certainty about his chosen course of action. He smiled at Mira who stood next to his bed, refusing to take her usual seat on the ground.

"Why? Why do you have to go on a fast?" she burst out, barely able to control her angry tears.

"You know what happened?"

"Yes, three boys were caught engaging in homosexual acts. So what? At that age it happens, all the time, everywhere."

"But it happened in this ashram. People from all over India contribute to the upkeep of this ashram in the hope that I am building a new man here, that I am building up character. The character of those boys is a sacred trust to me."

"And you are going on a fast? Endangering your health, your life?"

"What else can I do? Punishing them is out of the question. As their teacher, I must try to enter their lives, their innermost thoughts and desires and help them eradicate their impurities. Mira, inner cleanliness is the first thing that must be taught to children. Other things will follow only after the first and most important lesson has gone home. Punishing myself by fasting will make these boys turn inwards. That is my hope. It will make them realize their error. It will make them aware that purity and truthfulness in the little things of life are the only secrets of building up character."

"To take such an extreme step? To fast for a week in your condition?" Mira was unconvinced.

"Come closer," he said. "Sit down." His eyes, usually soft and often gleaming with unspent laughter were now opaque. He said something in Gujarati to Ba. Mira thought Ba was on the verge of tears even as her hands continued to mechanically rub ghee on Bapu's head.

"The fasts are a part of my being. I can do as well without my eyes as I can do without fasts. What the eyes are for the outer world, the fasts are for the inner. A still, small, inner voice tells me that the impurity within the boys is also within me. That I must purify myself through the fast."

"But what if you are wrong?"

"Then, if I die, in this fast or in some other such ordeal that lies ahead of me, the world will be able to write an epitaph over my ashes: 'Well deserved, you old fool.'" His smile invited Mira to join him in the self-mockery, but this evening Mira was immune to his charm.

"Bapu, is there nothing that will make you give up this fast?" she was pleading. She looked imploringly at Ba whose eyes were downcast, her attention absorbed by her task.

"I shall lose all my usefulness if I try to stifle my inner voice, Mira," he said. "For the time being my error, if it be one, must sustain me. Is it not better that I satisfy my conscience, even though it may be misguided? That is still better than listening to every voice, be it ever so friendly but by no means infallible. If I had a guru I would surrender my body and soul to him. I would accept his guidance in all my actions. But there are no perfect gurus we can turn to in our imperfect times. It is better to grope in the dark and wade through a million errors to reach the Truth than to entrust oneself to someone who knows not that he knows not. Has a man ever learnt swimming by tying a stone to his neck? So let me go my own way even if it is the wrong one."

For the first three days of the fast, Bapu walked to the prayer meetings. On the third, he needed to be supported. On the last four days, he was carried to the prayer ground on a cot. During the whole week, he was able to sit up for just over half an hour every day to spin with a pillow to support his back. He overcame the occasional bouts of nausea by sipping water, and drank copious quantities of water mixed with salt and bicarbonate of soda during the entire period of the fast. By the time the week ended, he had lost seven pounds. His weight fell to ninety-six pounds, sixteen pounds less than the most he had ever weighed in the last three years since his release from prison. On the seventh day he broke the fast by drinking a glass of orange juice mixed with grape juice and sucking on the pulp of an orange. Later in the day, he drank goat's milk diluted with water. He increased the quantity of his milk intake each day but did not eat any solid food for twelve days during which he regained the seven pounds he had lost.

A fortnight after the fast ended, Bapu resumed his brisk morning and evening walks from the ashram to the gate of the Sabarmati prison one and a half miles away. On the first morning, Bapu chose two of the boys involved in the homosexual acts to be his companions as he took his morning walk. They were his human walking sticks, his hands resting on their shoulders as they treaded slowly on either side of him. He seemed to be in high spirits, laughing and joking all the way. For the last fifty yards, he lifted his feet off the ground and putting his full weight on the shoulders of the two boys, shouted, "Come on boys, let's see how fast you can run!" There were renewed shouts of laughter as the boys, bearing a hundred-odd pounds of Mahatma-weight, scampered towards the prison gate.

Bapu had not spoken during the seven days of the fast. The silence was to help in expelling the impurity he had sensed within his mind, just as the daily enema expelled the physical impurities from his body. On the very first day of the fast, when Mira came to his hut in the evening, he handed her a short note.

Mira,

I shall not see you for a week. I shall miss our evenings together but I must not get attached to them. I await the answer of my inner voice on the nature of my obscure passion that has polluted the ashram, and the minds of those boys. I do not know when the answer will come. Or if it ever will.

I hope you will accompany me to this year's Congress session. It takes place in Kanpur at the end of the month.

Bapu's blessings.

He looked calm, the faint lines of tension that had begun to appear around his mouth now erased. His right foot, which had lately discovered a life of its own, abruptly tapping on the ground without the consent or even knowledge of its master, remained demurely still. Mira was about to speak when Gandhiji raised his index finger to his lips, reminding her of his vow of silence.

"Now go, behen," Ba, who was sitting beside him, said to her in Hindi, her voice kind but firm. Bapu was already bent over his desk, writing.

ten

*T*HAT YEAR, the annual session of the Indian National
Congress was held at the end of December in Kanpur,
a particularly cold time of the year in that part of the country.
Gandhiji and Mira were away from the ashram for almost three
weeks. On their way to Kanpur, they stayed for a week in Wardha,
a small town in the Central Provinces where Vinoba Bhave, one
of Gandhiji's most devoted disciples, had his own ashram.

Mira calculated that she must have spent at least a hundred
hours in third-class train compartments in the course of their
travels. Of course, each time, Gandhiji's party—a group of ten
people from the ashram accompanied Bapu—had the compartment to itself. Mira was glad that her hair was cropped so
short, otherwise it would have taken days to wash out the coal
dust and grit which the engine's steamy smoke carried into the
compartment through the open windows. Nostrils and ears were
easier to clean.

In her letter of 20 January 1926 to Romain Rolland, written
after their return to Sabarmati ashram, Mira penned down her
impressions of the trip.

. . . I have now seen a very different face of the man I call Bapu, and you, "my friend Gandhi." In the intimate setting of the ashram, I had forgotten that my familiar Bapu is the revered Mahatma to the nation, that the object of my adoration is an object of veneration for the country. His hold on the Indian masses must be seen to be believed! At each station, large or small, where the train stopped, we were met with full-throated cries of "Mahatma Gandhi ki jai"—"Victory to Mahatma Gandhi." The time of the day or night did not matter. The crowds on the platform would press forward, straining to catch a glimpse of the man who for them is something between a saint and a god. Indians call it darshan, which, my Hindi teacher tells me, is infinitely more than its literal translation, "sighting." It is an ingestion of the sacred person or image through the eyes. And those Indian eyes transfixed me! Especially of the peasants who had often waited for hours at the smaller stations in the countryside. Theirs were the eager, thirsting eyes of devotees, gazing at their saviour with a faith they could not have expressed or explained in so many words. I watched in wonder, deeply moved by the sight, repeated again and again at so many stations where the train stopped—hundreds of emaciated brown bodies pressing towards Bapu's carriage window with folded hands, the glow of hope in their eyes obliterating the poverty of their raiment.

Father, how strange that on those cemented platforms along the railway tracks that disappear in the dusty Indian countryside, I kept seeing a painting that hangs in London's National Gallery! Have you seen Sebastiano del Piambo's "The Raising of Lazarus," the faces looking up at Christ in expressions combining different proportions of awe, wonder and adoration? *Those* are the faces I saw on the platforms.

And Bapu? He sat by the window in the compartment, perfectly quiet and still, his hands folded in acknowledgement of the salutations, his face without expression, perhaps even a little stern. The stark contrast between the surging humanity, aglow with deep and sublime emotions, needs a Michelangelo, or at least a del Piambo to be conveyed. It is a task beyond my meagre capacities of description. All through the train journey but also at the Congress session where ordinary Congress workers mobbed him whenever he ventured out of his tent, I saw that this was his invariable reaction to excessive expressions of emotion, especially those of admiration and devotion directed towards him. As if he needed to keep his innermost self inviolate, be on guard against being carried away by all the veneration and not begin to believe in his own greatness. I now understand what he means when he says that he could never be a guru.

He would relax a little when the train was moving but those eyes full of hope weighed upon him throughout the journey. Most of the time, he sat on his seat in the far corner next to the window. Once in a while he would stretch out on the berth above his seat, a berth no one used out of respect for him. But he did not get much rest. The crowds would not allow him that. At station after station, Mahadevbhai would plead with the people.

"Gandhiji is sleeping now. Won't you keep quiet?"

"He is a god. He needs no sleep," they would answer. Mahadev would get angry.

"The gods you know are the ones you see in the temple. Even they sleep during the afternoon and at night. This god has to travel. He works for your sake, day and night. Won't you let him rest?"

Neither his pleading nor his anger was of any avail.

And like offerings to a god, snacks, baskets of fruit, even full meals would be passed into the compartment from the crowd.

Bapu had little rest during the long journey to Kanpur. Yet his energy during the Congress session and the many conferences organized around it where he was the featured speaker was amazing. If there is something wherein this most truthful of all men practices deception, it is in his looks. Under that frail appearance he is as hard as nails. His skinny heron-like legs run like the wind, and his calm voice can go on speaking for twenty-four hours without a trace of fatigue. Yet his talk is so different from the flights of eloquence aspired to by our European statesmen. He not only avoids saying things he does not put into practice, he also invariably surpasses the measured prudence of his words by the boldness of his actions. Used to keeping promises even before making them, he laughs at people who are merely full of brave words.

I now know why you gave me your little book on him and why it affected me so strongly. You wanted me to encounter a man whose inner forces are realized in action, not a savant whose inner life is found in his thoughts. Men of pure thought, pure in an intellectual sense—dare I say it to you?—have no more than a weak effect on our lives. Bapu, as a man of *active* faith, is a direct intermediary between the forces of Eternity and the present movement of history. Oh, I hope I may continue to be worthy of him!

And now there is not a moment to write anything more, but you can easily guess all that is in my heart without my putting it into words.

Mira

The Kanpur session, in which Sarojini Naidu succeeded Gandhiji as president of the Indian National Congress, continued the period of lull in India's freedom struggle. No new challenges to British rule were mounted. In his many speeches, interviews and interventions during the Congress deliberations, Gandhiji continued to reiterate his conviction that the energies of the party workers and of the country needed to be directed to the constructive programs of the spinning of khadi, eradication of untouchability and Hindu-Muslim unity. These were indispensable to his vision of India's swaraj. Freedom from British rule was only one aspect of swaraj. Not all Congress workers, especially the educated, urban youth, who had begun to gather around the charismatic Jawaharlal Nehru, agreed with his ideas on what needed to be done. As he said to Mira on the train journey back to Ahmadabad, "I am not really made to attract educated India to myself. I do not mind. It is my limitation." However, his authority over the party and the country was so complete that the opposition did not express itself in more than scattered grumbling.

To our great delight, Bapu also announced that he planned to cancel all his speaking and travel engagements for the coming year and stay put at the ashram. Some recent events had led him to believe that he had been neglecting the affairs of what was after all his most important experiment: to raise a disparate group of ordinary individuals, normal men and women, to the highest levels of truth and nonviolence.

After their return from the Congress session, many people in the ashram began to remark on the intimacy that had ripened between Bapu and Mirabehn. Now "promoted" to being her general-purpose assistant, besides her Hindi teacher, I could observe their burgeoning intimacy from close quarters. After the obligatory eight hours of attending to ashram activities, Mira spent much of her free time looking after Bapu's personal well-being. She hovered around his hut like a watchful sentinel, conveying through a stern, searching look at all those who came to see him that they were either wasting his time or making unreasonable demands on his health. She also told Bapu that she would like to perform other acts of service for him, such as rubbing with ghee the soles of his feet, which chapped and cracked during winter, in the evening while he lay in bed and they talked. For a long time Bapu resisted her plea; the physical care of his body was still Ba's prerogative. With the approach of summer however, he agreed to let Mira prepare his daily "head cooler," a moist towel wrapped around wet mud which needed to be moistened with water every couple of hours.

At the beginning of May, when Ahmadabad had begun to bake in the summer temperatures that stayed consistently above 100 degrees Fahrenheit in the shade, dropping no more than 10 degrees at night, Mira was entrusted with an additional task—the preparation of Bapu's food now became a part of her duties and, as her assistant, also of mine. This meant that two meals had to be prepared every day for about ten people who constituted the core group that took the lead in putting Bapu's ascetic ideals into a sometimes fanatical practice. The group did not include Ba. Mira felt her new responsibility was Bapu's way of rewarding her for cheerfully carrying out her duties without grumbling about the tropical heat; he had often expressed the fear that she would find it unbearable, and long for the cooler climate of the hill stations.

Now, to be in charge of Bapu's kitchen, that too across Ba's room as she impassively watched our daily preparation of his food without comment (a comment in itself), was an exacting task. Ever since he had set up his first ashram in South Africa, Bapu continued to experiment with a strictly vegetarian regimen in order to find that elusive combination of foods which not only tamed the palate and protected celibacy, his primary goals, but was also cheap enough to be affordable to the masses and, finally, required as little time as possible to prepare. This was typical; Bapu always demanded a moral, social and practical underpinning to his actions. In South Africa, there had been months of cooking food without salt or condiments. Another period had witnessed the absence of sugar, dates and currants being added to sweeten food when required. This was followed by a period of "unfired" food served with oil. For some time a dish of raw, chopped onions as a blood purifier had formed a regular part of the dinner meal till Gandhiji came to the conclusion that onions, like spices and milk, were bad for the control of passions. With the possible exceptions of prescribing natural methods of healing and the proper nursing of the sick, nothing animated Bapu as much as a discussion on the moral qualities inherent in various foods and their effect on the human body. "We talk about food quite as much as gourmands do, except that he really is a gourmand of tasteless food!" Mira grumbled to me good-naturedly. It was apparent in her tone that she welcomed these discussions as another chance to be close to Bapu, and she went about her assigned task in his dietary experiments with a characteristic zeal that caused me a good deal of trouble.

I remember, because of the time and labor involved in the preparation, that the particular experiment at the time demanded that bread be replaced by sprouted wheat, milk by ground coconut, and all vegetables be eaten raw. My work involved the spreading of thick, damp cloths on grass mats in the storeroom behind the kitchen, with wheat grains laid between the folds, which sprouted in twenty-four hours. In addition, I had to grate the coconut and cut the vegetables. Because of his missing teeth Bapu, more than the others, found the sprouted wheat difficult to chew in sufficient quantities to satisfy his hunger. I was then asked to grind the sprouted wheat for him. Soon, the others also demanded ground sprouted wheat. This had to be done using a chakki, a stone roller on a stone slab, that was kept in the veranda outside Ba's room. It was my job to roughly grind the sprouted wheat while Mira would further grind Bapu's portion to a finer consistency. Grinding dry grain in a chakki is hard enough, but to grind sticky sprouted grain that keeps escaping from the sides of the roller in a glutinous mass presents an entirely different challenge which I could not quite master, especially since I was always in a hurry to finish—I was convinced that the harsh noise of stone grating against stone would disturb Ba. Mira must have thought so too because one day she asked me to bring the chakki to the kitchen. She noticed my hesitation and said, "It's all right. I have talked to Bapu. What use is the chakki to Ba? Bapu says that if she needs it she can always go to the kitchen and use it there." I followed her instructions, although not without a sense of foreboding.

The next morning the grinding stones had disappeared from the kitchen. I found them in their original place outside Ba's room and was busy grinding the sprouted wheat for the morning meal when Bapu came out of his room. He frowned when he saw me.

"I thought you had taken the grinding mill to the kitchen," he said.

"It would be troublesome for Ba to go across the courtyard into the kitchen if she ever needed to grind something, Bapu," I said. "Let it stay here."

"Then should we buy another one?" he asked with a hint of sarcasm in his voice intended to remind me of my profligate ways with writing materials. "Take it back to the kitchen. Why should it remain with Ba? Actually, it is partly my fault. I forgot to tell her yesterday. Take it away. I will tell Ba now."

As I staggered across the courtyard, my arms wrapped around the heavy stones, I could hear the sounds of an argument from Ba's room and then Bapu's raised voice. He was scolding Ba. As I was soon to discover, although Bapu was invariably gentle and calm in public, tranquil in even the most trying circumstances, he could get very angry, furiously so, with those who were closest to him.

For a while after this incident, Ba's manner towards me was perceptibly colder. I knew that I was not at fault and that Ba, with her basic sense of fairness, would soon realize that her anger was misplaced. She continued to supervise the main kitchen and ate with the others in the common dining hall. With her fondness for fried Gujarati farsan, she had always been reluctant to take part in Bapu's experiments with food.

Luckily, the experimental diet proved difficult to digest. I was the first to go down with diarrhea, followed by Surendrabhai and Bapu. It had the opposite effect on Mira who suffered a stubborn bout of constipation. Bapu immediately abandoned the experiment and we returned to cooked food.

Mira was now not only Bapu's eyes and ears as far as ashram life was concerned but also his nose. And when I say nose, I mean it literally. Mira's aquiline nose, too long for her broad face to be considered shapely, was an exquisite instrument of smell. I imagined the walls of its tunnels to be richly lined with olfactory nerves, sensors that picked up the faintest scent and conveyed it to the brain for a quick and accurate identification. Bapu, who was known to lack all sense of smell, his nose dedicated exclusively to breathing and to holding his spectacles in place, depended on Mira's assistance in all matters that involved the exercise of the olfactory sense. At the Kanpur Congress session, Bapu had suggested the digging of trench latrines for the camp which was to house thousands of delegates and volunteers attending the annual meet. A day before the start of the session, when Bapu was asked to inspect the facilities, he had taken Mira with him to carry out the "smelling part" of the inspection. Being Mira's assistant in such ventures involved me in a particular activity which demanded that I jump over my own shadow, that I violate one of the strictest taboos of my upper-caste upbringing. My nature revolted each time I did so, balking at being dragged over what it considered to be its boundaries. I could not convince myself that the response of nausea and disgust at any contact with bodily wastes was not rational, that my unconcious belief that the body was a dirt-factory was merely the result of a childhood conditioning that needed to be left behind together with many other senseless convictions from that period.

My first experience was the worst. I did not know what awaited me when Mira came into the kitchen that morning. She seemed to be in a hurry, still adjusting the pallu of her sari over her shorn hair, damp from the bath. I had finished peeling the potatoes and was about to turn my cutting knife on the pile of brinjals heaped in front of me, their purple silky skins darkly aglow with the rays of the sun streaming in through the window. The hint of a warm breeze, dying down even as it struggled up the riverbank, promised another scorcher of a day.

"We must be there before Bapu arrives. You know how he hates being late for anything."

"Where are we going?" I said, getting up.

"Just follow me," she said, as she turned to walk out, bending her large, stately frame to avoid bumping against the doorjamb.

In the garden at the back of the ashram, we found Shyam already waiting in front of the men's lavatory. He was an untouchable youth, the second untouchable to join the ashram after Bapu took in and adopted the ten-year-old Lakshmi as his daughter. Looking older than his twenty-five years, his dark face ravaged by small pox scars, Shyam was Bapu's special joy, not only because he was an outcaste but because of his susceptibility to mysterious ailments. These brought out Bapu's favored persona, that of the doctor who goes against established modes of treatment to experiment with regimens of his own devising. I remember one of Bapu's letters, I think it was to Hakim Amjad Ali, in which he said that these experiments were as dear to him as the struggle for the country's independence, that he found in them as much joy as he did in the latter. Bapu seldom seemed as happy and relaxed as when he was examining a sick inmate and prescribing a treatment.

Bapu joined us immediately after finishing his morning's correspondence. Pride, shame and embarrassment washed across Shyam's face as he found himself, or at least his product, at the center of such exalted attention. With Bapu's arrival, the examination of Shyam's slushy feces, spread on a thin muslin cloth on the ground in front of him, commenced.

Bapu's enthusiasm about the enterprise in which Shyam played the main supporting role was infectious. "Just think, Mira, how many of our poor countrymen suffer from chronic indigestion and dysentery. Like Shyam. Education in hygiene and sanitation is one part of the solution. The other is to find a diet of cheap and easily available vegetables and lentils the poor can afford and which are easy to digest." Since a couple of weeks, Shyam had been the subject of his experiments in determining what this diet could be, and Mira was his indispensable assistant.

Peering through his round, wire-rimmed glasses that had slid down to the tip of his nose, Bapu poked around in the yellow slush with a thin twig. "It needs to be cleaned more," he gave his considered evaluation. He took off his glasses and wiped them with the edge of his dhoti. Mira nodded towards me and pointed to an earthen pitcher of water outside the lavatory door. A tin ladle with a long handle curved at one end was hanging down from its lip. As I ladled the water onto the cloth, Mira carefully stirred the thinning slush with a spoon, washing it slowly, the yellowish liquid draining away through the muslin cloth, leaving behind solid particles of indeterminate origin. I soon gathered that the task was to identify the food source that had not been properly digested and needed to be eliminated from the diet. Whenever the matter appeared to be in some doubt, Bapu's visual examination of the particles was augmented by Mira's olfactory expertise.

The sun shone, the birds sang, and Shyam's shit stank, the horrendous stench increasing as it became heated by the sun. My eyes watered from the effort not to gag at the stench. The others were oblivious. Particularly Shyam, because the smell was his own. For him, the sense of ownership and creation of the drying excreta spread out before him overlay the stench with an intriguing pungency bearing within it a hint of his deepest essence, however disgusting it was for others.

Mira's olfactory gift was not only a natural endowment but had been honed throughout her childhood on her grandfather's country estate. An abandoned well, covered with a rotting board top and with its rusting pump, bucket and windlass, was an old friend that demanded a daily visit and greeted her with a distinct mixture of the smells of waterweed, fungus and dark moss. Then there was the barn, with its smell of baled hay and dry harvest days. Her nose had breathed in the various animal odors as she learnt to brush and rub down the horses, feed the chickens and the pigs, milk the Jersey cows, reveling in the hiss of milk squirting into the pail. She had helped in cleaning out the stables, the coops, the pigsties and the cowsheds, each with its characteristic odor that changed with the time of the day as well as with the season, becoming faint to the point of disappearance on cold winter days. On her walks through the Downs, she had often stopped on the way to inhale the scents of flowering shrubs and bushes, sniffing them to get to know them better. Her favorites were the rhododendrons that grew outside the wrought iron gate of Milton Heath and a dying oak tree a hundred yards down the lane. On the way back from the walk, she would sometimes throw her arms around its trunk and bury her nose in the rough bark to inhale the tree's emanations of decay. It was a faint, dark smell, unlike any other—the smell of desiccation, of the imminent, inexorable dryness after the last remnants of sap had been expelled. Not only could she pick out a single smell from a harmonic background of accompanying odors but, in some of her more meditative moments, inhale several smells at the same time. As each smell contended for exclusive attention, they often negated each other, with the result that for some time she would not be consciously aware of any odor at all. During such an experience she would sense within herself an abundance of olfactory information, unlike anything she had experienced even in her active forays into smelling. "It is like the difference between horizontal and vertical listening in music," she said. I had never quite understood what she meant by that but assumed that at such times she was like an enlightened yogi dwelling in the highest realms of aroma.

Unfortunately, this was not such a time, either because she was distracted or because the powerful stench had overwhelmed the individual odors of the food particles.

"Let it dry out in the sun for a while till the fecal smell evaporates," Bapu commanded. "Mira's nose can then ferret out the fainter odors of different foods."

He patted Shyam's shoulder and smiled at him. "Just sit here and guard it from the crows."

My final image of the scene is of a forlorn-looking Shyam squatting on the ground with a stick in his right hand, keeping watch over the dun-colored layer of feces drying out on the cloth spread next to him. His eyes are following Bapu with a mute devotion as he strides away towards his hut, deeply absorbed in conversation with Mira who does not seem to have any difficulty keeping pace with him.

eleven

*B*ETWEEN JANUARY AND JULY of that year, Gandhiji left the ashram only once for a week in May when he was invited by the Governor of Bombay to meet the members of the Agricultural Commission set up by the Government of India under the chairmanship of Lord Linlithgow. The meeting, held at the hill station of Mahabaleshwar, lasted for a day. Gandhiji used this opportunity to visit some ailing family members and friends: his son Devdas, who was recovering from an appendicitis operation in Bombay, a sick Mathuradas in Deolali, Kaka Kalelkar in Poona, and Behram Khambatta, who had been Mira's host, in Bombay.

All over the country, people who wanted Gandhiji to give speeches at various political and apolitical functions were surprised that he declined every invitation, even to events promoting causes dear to his heart. There was much speculation, even among British Government officials (as we came to know later when the official documents were unsealed after Independence), about what kept him bound to his ashram. Was it because India's freedom struggle was in a state of suspension? Or had he decided that it was more important to first bridge the divide within the Congress party between those who wanted to continue on the path of noncooperation with the government and those who advocated entering the legislative assemblies of the states through the electoral process to fight the British from the inside? This state of confusion and inactivity led some to wonder whether Gandhiji was considering retirement from public life.

During these months, Gandhiji took classes in the ashram school, discussed passages from the Gita at the prayer meetings, and attended to ashram affairs and to his extensive correspondence. Above all, he immersed himself in writing his autobiography in Gujarati. Chapter by chapter, it was published in serial form in *Navajivan*. Mahadevbhai was given the job of translating each chapter into English for publication in *Young India*, a task in which he found Mira's assistance invaluable. The writing of the autobiography, unique in the annals of Indian autobiographical writing as Gandhiji attempts in it an honest self-examination by laying bare his inner conflicts and motivations, seemed to preoccupy him more and more. It also made him moody.

Then there was the endless stream of visitors. Mira had been forbidden to deny anyone access to Gandhiji's room but was permitted to enter and cut a conversation or interview short if she thought it had gone on for too long and Bapu needed to be rescued. Of course, there were some visitors, his close political associates among them, whose meetings could not be thus regulated. In such cases, Mira made it a point to take up a seat in the veranda outside the room, clearly visible to the visitor inside, a silent, accusing presence. Once, when Mahadevbhai was sick, she was called in to act as Bapu's secretary at a meeting of his chief political lieutenants. Bored by Congress politics—by the debates between the "no-changers" and the "pro-changers" on whether to continue or change the party's policy towards the British, and the discussion on the merits of Gandhiji's constructive program versus the need to take immediate and direct political action—her attention wandered. The words of the four men came in snatches as visuals of their faces, especially their noses, playfully vied for her attention. Sardar Patel's nose was broad, with wide nostrils and large pores. Nehru's nose was thin and slightly curved and turned pink at the tip when he was excited. By far the most impressive was that of Abdul Ghaffar Khan, the leader of the Pathans in the Northwest Frontier Province bordering Afghanistan, known to most as "Frontier Gandhi." It was an alarmingly hooked appendage, almost as long as the face it graced.

In their evening conversations, when no one else was present except the silent Ba, Bapu would sometimes talk about the day's visitors, his comments both generous and shrewd. He saw people's weaknesses but loved them nonetheless—a compassion he could never extend to himself. "You love another person not because of his virtues—that is infatuation—but in spite of his faults," he said to her. "Love has no place for idealization." Once, when Nehru was staying at the ashram for a day, occupying the guest room in Bapu's hut, Mira had seen Nehru's face light up when the pretty Amtussalam walked past him on her way to Bapu's room. Mira mentioned this to Gandhiji in the evening. He laughed and remarked, "Well, Jawaharlal likes two things: politics and women."

Mira was not particularly fond of the handsome Nehru; she considered herself immune to his fabled charm. She resented the special marks of favor Bapu bestowed on him, going so far as to ask that his own commode be placed in Nehru's room so that the much younger man was not inconvenienced by being forced to use the common lavatories. She did not understand the attraction Nehru held for Bapu and wondered if it was because of the spirited way Nehru disagreed with him. She had observed that Bapu was infinitely more attracted to people who resisted or criticized him than to those who readily concurred with him. He was more grateful for criticism than praise, deriving a secret pleasure from the former, like he would from a reviving and stimulating cold shower.

———

On the day Gandhiji boarded the train to Bombay to attend the meeting called by the Governor, Mira had accompanied Mahadevbhai, Maganlalbhai and Surendrabhai to the station to see him off. Mira was standing on the platform, watching Bapu's serious face peering out from behind the iron bars of the carriage window, his folded hands acknowledging the ovation of the crowd that had quickly gathered on hearing that Gandhiji was traveling on the train, when suddenly she found to her astonishment a stream of tears coursing down her face, its rush unstoppable. The tears seemed to spring from an unknown recess in her heart; they did not belong to her. They were like squatters who had temporarily taken over her tear ducts and eyes.

When the guard blew his whistle and waved his green flag to signal the Gujarat Mail's departure, the sadness underlying the tears, a peculiar heaviness in her heart she had not been aware of, hit her with the force of a blow to the pit of her stomach. Her eyes blurred by tears that had reclaimed their rightful owner, and almost choking with the effort of keeping down a howl of pain pressing up to force a passage through her throat, Mira did not see Gandhiji look worriedly in her direction and wave at her as the train steamed out of the station.

On the way back to the ashram, in the black T-model Ford gifted to Gandhiji by Ahmadabad's leading textile mill owner, Mira was again composed. Her apparent calm, though, was attained at the price of a certain numbness. The men, carrying out a subdued conversation in Gujarati that excluded her, tactfully ignored the signs of overwhelming grief on her face: her large gray eyes now unnaturally small and lifeless, her skin mottled with raw, red patches spreading down her throat.

Back in her hut, Mira made straight for the trunk containing her books. Lifting up its lid, she rummaged in the piles for Romain Rolland's biography of Beethoven, which she had not opened since her arrival. As she took out the book, a dry, mottled leaf fluttered down on the floor. Mira carefully picked up the leaf and put it back from where it had escaped. Sitting on the mattress that also served as her bed, a kerosene lamp throwing a small pool of yellowish light on the pages of the book, Mira immersed herself in Rolland's stirring prose. His sonorous sentences marched anew into her heart, accompanied by a drumroll and the voice of a choir raised in the chant "Through suffering, joy!" Beethoven's motto for his own life. Tonight, she would again walk in the valley and the cool shade of the woods south of Vienna, his spirit her guide.

In the ten days that Gandhiji was absent from Ahmadabad, Mira wrote to him every day. Her letters are brisk accounts of life in the ashram telling him of the admission of an inmate to the hospital with suspected appendicitis, or about her witnessing the birth of a calf and the amount of yarn she had spun, or sharing with him her observations on the books she was reading. Apart from the first letter, which she wrote in Hindi (anticipating his pleasure and pride at the progress she had made in learning the language) and which ended with "I miss you" in English, none of the subsequent letters alluded to their separation and to the excruciating agony it was causing her. The very frequency of her letters conveying a prolonged cry of pain. Gandhiji, too, wrote back almost every day, even if some of his letters were no more than a couple of hurriedly scribbled sentences on a postcard. Except in his reply to her very first letter, written from Deolali on 10 May, he too did not refer to their separation and the feelings it had aroused in her, or in him.

Chi. Mira,

Your Hindi letter is very well written. Not hospital "se chorega" but "chutega." "Chorega" is transitive and so you drop the case ending "se" but keep it before "chutega," which is intransitive.

I knew you were feeling the separation. You will get over it because it has to be got over. The few days' separation is a preparation for the longer one that death brings. In fact the separation is only superficial. Death brings us nearer. Is not the body a bar—if it is also an introduction?

With love,
Yours,
Bapu

A few weeks after Bapu's return however, their relationship again seemed to undergo a subtle shift. I call it "subtle" because most people in the ashram remained unaware of the change. Except Ba though, who unwittingly made me conscious of it (or perhaps not so unwittingly for there was always a shrewd mind at work behind Ba's façade of an artless, traditional Gujarati housewife beginning to run to fat). Ba's comments provided me with an explanation for Mira's recent loss of interest in her Hindi lessons and a general lassitude that I had attributed to the humid heat of July which can be particularly enervating.

Ba was not unusually jealous; certainly her possessiveness was far less than what Bapu's had been in the early years of their marriage. Ever since Bapu had established Phoenix Farm more than twenty years ago, Ba had become used to a procession of women entering his life. The women came charged with feelings that spanned the whole range from a silent doglike devotion to a florid and demanding infatuation. On rare occasions, Ba (who proclaimed "One saint in the family is enough!") was perfectly capable of showing her irritation if she felt Bapu was unduly indulging the foolishness of some woman, or appeared unusually animated by another. Normally, though, she was politely reserved with all women who sought Bapu's proximity. This irrespective of whether the woman, blind to the existence of anyone else except Bapu, ignored her, or whether she fawned over Ba in the belief that she could use her to get closer to Bapu.

With Mira it was different, and Ba had known this from the very first day of her arrival. It was not only a matter of Bapu showing her singular marks of favor which were there for all to see; the Englishwoman had intruded into a space that had never been violated by any other woman before her. Ba's cooking and serving of Bapu's meals, the massage of his feet and legs, the rubbing of ghee on his forehead, were but the outer manifestations of the intermediary space between body and mind that the couple inhabited together. To Ba, these were not just traditional ways of serving her husband but the medium of a vital exchange between Bapu and her, the play of countless subtle antennae seeking one another. Mira had severed this vital connection.

Ba had silently put up with Mira taking over many of her tasks in caring for Bapu's personal needs. She had observed Bapu's unusual animation in the hour Mira spent with them each evening. Whenever he was with Mira, Ba sensed a vivaciousness in his spirit that effectively banished her from his presence, blocked her from his mind, even when her palm was on his forehead, rubbing ghee. But lately, although there was no change in the arrangements—Mira still looked after Bapu's clothes and food, cleaned his room and spent the evening hour with him—Ba had felt her own essential link with Bapu revive.

I had just come out of the kitchen after cutting my daily quota of vegetables when she had asked from her veranda, where she was grinding moong dal, "Where is Mira, Navin? I haven't seen her since the day before yesterday."

"She is not well, Ba. She has also missed her Hindi lessons," I replied. "She says she is feeling very tired."

"Tell her to take plenty of rest for some days." Ba's expression of sympathy was minimal. "She need not worry about Bapu. He is being looked after well. Tell her Bapu's blood pressure has come down in the last two days."

———

Much was to change in Mira's life and in her relationship with Bapu in the next four years. I take the liberty of reconstructing with a novelist's pen the incidents that took place in that time, since I left the ashram in the latter half of July 1926.

In her rising disquiet over Gandhiji's increasingly erratic behavior towards her, Mira once again turned to Rolland. In a letter dated 30 August 1926, she writes:

> . . . I am well, my dear friend, but with less energy than I had hoped for when I arrived in India almost a year ago. Perhaps it is the weather. For more than a fortnight now, ever since the rains were over, the earth has been sweltering under the punishing sun. The August sun in this part of the country can be very strong and as it wrings out the remaining moisture from the ground, the days become very hot and humid indeed. I am writing these lines in the coolest part of the day, by the light of a lamp, while outside a pale movement of dawn begins to climb and outline the dark window frame of my hut.
>
> But more than the lethargy in my limbs, it is my soul

that is troubled. As you can guess, this has to do with Bapu. He has always been serious with me. With others, he used to laugh, laugh heartily, and so much. With me, he never laughed. Now he is often irritated, and scolds me for the smallest mistake. Yesterday, I saw that one of his leather sandals was broken. I took the chappal to the cobbler who sits outside the gate of the ashram. When I came back, I found him looking for the missing chappal. He asked me whether I had seen it. I told him that it was with the cobbler. And had I settled the cobbler's fee or did I expect the man to do it free in the name of the Mahatma, he asked sarcastically. I told him the price was eight annas. He became angry. "Since neither you nor I earn even a paisa, who is going to bear the cost? Get it back," he said. I hastened to get back the unmended chappal from the cobbler and informed him of the situation. Hearing that the chappal belonged to Bapu, the cobbler was delighted and offered to do the work for free. He also refused to give back the broken chappal as he regarded it as a good omen that he could be of service to the Mahatma. I had to take the man back to Bapu, who was sitting with some British visitors, and explain the situation. Bapu's mood had changed. He ignored me but laughingly told the cobbler, "If you really want to be of service to me, why not become my teacher and teach me the art of mending footwear?" The cobbler was delighted. Bapu invited him to share his seat and then and there began to learn the art of repairing chappals while carrying on a conversation with the visitors. He continued to ignore me.

Our evenings together, which I have always longed for during the day, no longer bring me the joy they once did. Something has happened. He seems so withdrawn of late.

In fact, after his return from Bombay I have noticed a certain reserve in him that has progressively increased. When I talk to him, he still listens. But his face is less open, his eyes more opaque. Our conversations become fewer and fewer as his need for silence grows. From one silent day a week, he has gone on to two. I am happy to sit quietly with him, if that is what he wants. As Ba does while she rubs coconut oil on his head. That one hour each evening when we were by ourselves meant so much. I waited for it the whole day, from the moment I woke up at dawn. It was like his laying a cool palm on my fevered brow, draining away all the tension, lifting me into the realm of spirit where he dwelt. But his silence has an edge to it now. I feel it contains messages I cannot decipher but which fill me with deep unease.

I once asked my Hindi teacher the word for silence. (By the way, he still hasn't returned from wherever his wanderings have taken him.) He explained to me that there are two. "Sannata" has the connotation of fear, shock, consternation. "Mauna," on the other hand, is an inner silence, an all-encompassing silence of the inner self that is an attribute of a saint. Bapu's silence had always been "mauna" but it is no longer so. When I am with him in the evening now, I feel his silence is of the "sannata" kind, the silence of that part of the jungle where a tiger is passing by.

Bapu once told me that he senses his deepest convictions in the dark hour before dawn when he is lying on his cot, gazing up at the night sky, when the world's silence is at its most profound. His silence, like Beethoven's music, has been the highest form of prayer. I fear it is now subject to a strong disturbance. I do not know why. Perhaps it has to do with the rise in his blood pressure. Mahadev tells me it has been fluctuating wildly. Yesterday, it was 180/110. He has started taking an Ayurvedic medicine, sarpagandha, and I hope the pressure will soon stabilize.

But, dearest friend, you need not worry about him or me. He continues to be the pole star guiding the ship of my life, my telos. Even more than Beethoven, our European Mahatma, Bapu remains for me the strongest mediator between the life of senses and Eternal Life. I thank you for having led me to him. He was remembering you the other day, wondering if the two of you would ever meet.

Another letter followed the next day.

. . . This morning, I realized with a shock that in my last letter I forgot to enclose the first chapters of Bapu's autobiography that is being serialized in English in *Young India*. Actually, that was the purpose of my letter of 30 August but preoccupied with my own petty concerns, I simply forgot. Forgive me for being so selfish.

I am sure you would want to know how people are reacting to the story of his early life that has appeared so far. Most people outside the ashram marvel at his courage in being so frank. But they do not know the intensity of his devotion to truth. Mahadev tells me that there have been some letters questioning the propriety of devoting so much space to his youthful sexual temptations and failings. But those people do not understand that for him sexual desire is the biggest roadblock for someone who would travel on the spiritual path. They do not realize the depth of his conviction that passions are poisonous to the true, inner self, that sensuality sabotages our deepest purpose. In this respect, he is like St. Augustine, with whose *Confessions* Bapu's autobiography can be compared. I know, since I am involved in the final corrections of the English version after Mahadev has translated it from the original. Whenever I suggest a change that does not magnify his "sins" as much as he does in Gujarati, he is quick to veto the suggestion.

"No, Mira," he says, "I *was* obsessed with sex in the early years of our marriage. I could think of nothing else. I could not leave Ba alone for a single moment after I came home from school. I would have become a physical and emotional wreck if she had not been away so often on frequent visits to her parents. 'Obsessed' and 'wreck' *are* the right words."

I must confess I was amused that Ba, such a staid and dignified old lady now, could arouse such strong cravings in him, be the object of such unbridled passion. But then, I have been told that though small of stature, Ba was a very attractive girl when she was young—with glossy black hair, large, dark eyes set deep in an oval face, a well-formed mouth and a determined chin she has kept to this day.

Curiously, there has been no reaction to the passage I found the most moving in his story. The passage where Bapu talks of his father dying while he was making love to Kasturba in the couple's bedroom upstairs. I think people are respectful of Bapu's agony and his lifelong remorse that his "mind was not free of lust even at that critical moment." They are sympathetic to rather than critical about "the dark stain of shame" he has not been able to wash away till this day, as he says in this chapter.

Mahadev did tell me of a letter in which someone asked him whether it was not disrespectful to call one's own father "oversexed" because he had married for the third time at the age of forty a girl twenty-two years his junior. "Bapu was not upset at all," Mahadev said. "He dictated a reply saying that he had written about his father after long reflection and in greatest filial reverence. That he does not believe baring the faults of our dear ones to public gaze denotes a lack of love or respect."

My dearest friend, I wonder what you will make of his confessions, and how you would compare them to St. Augustine's which I know you regard so highly. In their striving towards the life of spirit, both struggled mightily against the grip of sensuality and both waged a war on their wants. Yet I feel, the austere saint is a very different person from our vivacious Mahatma. I can hardly imagine St. Augustine having Bapu's humour, his vigorous grace of movement or his delight in listening to music. Alas, all these qualities are absent these days. Bapu continues to be weighed down with . . . I don't know what. His blood pressure remains high and he has become uncharacteristically moody of late. I wish we could come to Europe and visit you. I know how fond he is of you and how much he respects you.

Rolland did not respond to the two letters. His diary entry for this period shows a strong concern for what is happening to Gandhiji, and a lesser one for Mira's state of mind.

Two letters from India from my erstwhile "daughter" Madeleine and now friend Mira have reached me. She encloses with the second the first chapters of Gandhi's autobiography. These pages are a proof of what I have said before, that his humility surpasses that of Christ. I am afraid the Mahatma is in the throes of a personal crisis. Reading the autobiography, I remembered (perhaps imperfectly) St. Augustine's words in his *Confessions*—"I become again an enigma to myself, and ask my soul why it disquiets me so sorely." For the sake of India and the world, I pray Gandhi emerges from the disquiet of his soul undiminished and even stronger than before.

As for Mira, she may be stepping into the waters of a lake whose depth she does not fathom. For some Europeans, the call of the Eternal, heard most clearly in India, can make them throw all caution to the wind. Theirs is then a reckless rush toward a merger with the herald, be it a Hindu god or guru. I am afraid Mira may be heading for heartbreak, if not worse. But I shall not warn her. It is perhaps better to foolishly heed this particular call than be wise and close the ears.

twelve

WITH THOSE WHO were close to him—Ba, Mahadevbhai, Maganlalbhai and, of course, Mira—Gandhiji did not hide his feelings although he struggled to control the outbursts of temper Mira had euphemistically termed his "moodiness." Bapu's "moodiness" was apparent only to his close associates. To the rest of the ashram he appeared as calm, patient and good-humored as always. A perceptive observer, though, would have noticed slight changes: a new frown line, a welcoming smile that did not quite reach his eyes, a laugh that was not as hearty as before, that no longer crinkled his eyes into thin slits while fiercely shaking his slight frame. When he was angry, and this was now often, a particular line in his forehead would begin to pulse with a stress born of a barely controllable impulse for violence, which would later upset him as much as it did Mira whenever she happened to be an inadvertent witness.

One such incident occurred with Helen Haussding, a small, thin, middle-aged German woman with a surprisingly large bosom who had come to stay at the ashram for some months. Helen was tiresome, constantly seeking Bapu's nearness, prattling on about how she had given up eating meat and drinking alcohol, even wine, after she learnt of Bapu's objections to both, and how she had persuaded her husband, a retired steelworker, to follow her example. Gandhiji, with his fondness for giving new names to his European followers, called her Sparrow.

On that particular evening, after the prayer meeting was over, Mira had brought the latest installment of the edited pages of the *Autobiography* for Bapu's comments. Helen was already in the hut—she must have followed him from the prayer ground. Bapu sat behind his desk, going through his correspondence, while Helen stood behind him, a blissful expression on her face in spite of a bad case of sunburn along her peeling nose that must have been quite painful. She was fanning him vigorously with a fan made from bamboo and palm leaves. Bapu seemed tense, his welcome perfunctory, as he gestured to Mira to keep the corrected chapter on the desk. And then it happened. Overcome by curiosity, Helen bent over him to look at the papers. Either the fan or a part of her well-filled blouse must have brushed Bapu's shoulders for he swiveled around and slapped the German woman. For a moment, the three of them froze in shock. Helen's jaw dropped, her fair skin turned deep pink. Throwing the fan down on the floor, she ran out of the room, her bosom heaving as she struggled to draw breath. Bapu lowered his head between his arms on the writing desk, the set of his shoulders, encased in an invisible armor, discouraging any gesture at closeness or comfort Mira might have been tempted to make.

The next day, Mira received a short note from Bapu on a piece of paper, cut from the back of a brown envelope, telling her that he would not see her that evening. "Today will be an extra day of silence," it said. "Not as penance but as an antidote to the turbulent anger within myself which I often experience these days. One of the benefits of silence is that it eats away anger."

———

During the latter part of that year, Mira had the feeling that Bapu's magnification of his own lapses resulting from what most people would have considered an unattainable ideal of purity, was making him more unbending towards the failings of others. It was as if his memories, in being retrieved and set free during the process of writing his autobiography, were coloring his perceptions and taking over his moral judgement. Two incidents following close on the heels of each other convinced her of this.

The first involved Lakshmi, Gandhiji's adopted daughter. Everyone in the ashram was expected to spin a minimum quantity of yarn and the amount spun each day was announced during the evening prayer meeting before being entered in a register kept for that purpose. Lakshmi, it transpired, had been stealing yarn from others and passing it off as her own. Along with the ashram manager, Maganlalbhai, Mahadevbhai and Devdas, who was staying at the ashram for a while, Mira was present at the meeting that was called in Bapu's room to discuss what should be done. Bapu looked more sad than angry, though quite composed.

"I can sacrifice everything for this girl," he began in a grave voice. "The game of swaraj is like a ball game. Sometimes one team wins and sometimes the other. That does not disturb me. There is no happiness or sadness in a particular result. But my blood dries up if my child does evil. Lakshmi is my first daughter. I adopted her to atone for Hindu society's sins against the untouchables. That is why I have showered her with so much love. She has kept on disappointing me. I could never imagine she could stoop so low."

"She is only a child, Bapu," Maganlalbhai tried to console him.

"That is what makes it worse! I don't mind if adults behave badly. But children are innocent. I suffer if they betray my trust. Lakshmi! To be so sinful at such a young age!"

No one spoke. They were all looking down at the floor, reluctant to meet the pain in Bapu's eyes.

"At first, I wanted to beat her with a stick," Bapu continued, confessing to the violence in his soul. "Then I thought I should go on a fast. But on reflection I decided that if I went on a fast, the ashram would be further inflamed. The anger against the girl and the attitude towards untouchables will worsen. No, I could not announce a fast."

Then, addressing Devdas, he said, "You have influence with her. Bring her here."

The room was silent while Devdas was away, the atmosphere much too heavy with foreboding to permit small talk. Bapu seemed to have come to a decision. "I have to deal with her myself. As long as she listens to me and does not lie, there is still hope. I am convinced that I can make even the worst child like myself. If Lakshmi cannot become good, then how can I? I must join her thread to mine. If she remains evil then I too will never transcend the evil in my heart. There may be a difference in degree but both of us will remain a kind of untouchable."

Later, Mira heard that Devdas had to almost drag the girl by the arm to Bapu's hut. She was in a state of total panic by the time she was pushed into his room.

"Don't hit me," she cried, throwing herself at Bapu's feet. "I will never do it again."

"Come, stand up," Bapu said, his voice still cold.

"Will you send me back to Doodhabhai?"

"No, I won't send you back to your father," Bapu said, his face softening. "But you must promise never to lie or steal again, and you have to return the stolen threads. Two and half thousand every day."

Mira did not believe the girl would keep her promise. She felt Lakshmi was destined to be a source of many a heartache for Bapu. And Bapu knew this too.

The second incident was even more troubling. For four days in the beginning of October, Mira had sat alone in her room in the evening, fitfully reading or looking wistfully at Bapu's hut no more than fifty yards away, racked by the longing to be with him, to talk to him. She did see him during the day when she cleaned his room or took his blood pressure in the morning, but he was rarely alone at these times—someone from the ashram, usually Mahadev taking a dictation, was always present. On the fifth day, as they were walking out of the prayer ground after the morning prayers, Mira took courage and went up to Bapu to ask him whether they could resume their evening conversations, if he could give her back the hour he had kept for her before he went to sleep. Bapu's nod of assent was hesitant but Mira decided to ignore his lack of enthusiasm.

As she walked up to Bapu's hut that evening, pushing open the wicker gate at the back of the small vegetable garden, Mira felt that tingle of delicious anticipation she had often experienced as a little girl when she set out for her Sunday morning excursions with her mother. But if there was a spring in her step, it was soon flattened by Bapu's raised voice coming from inside Ba's room. Although she could not understand what he was saying in Gujarati, the fury in his voice was unmistakable. It was less an argument than a tirade, relentless, simultaneously accusatory and condemning, recognizing no defense, allowing no mitigating circumstances. Mira could not go any further. She turned back.

Next morning, at the end of the prayer meeting, Bapu did not invite questions but began to speak himself. "All of you who have been reading my autobiography know the unstinted praise I have lavished on Kasturba. She has stood by me through the changes in my life. She has never hindered me in my progress towards my ideals. She has been a tower of strength to me in my self-imposed vow of brahmacharya. Though it is true that her renunciation has not been based on an intelligent appreciation of the fundamentals of life but from blind wifely devotion."

Mira quickly glanced at Ba, sitting on the ground two seats away from her in the front row of the women's section. Her face was without expression, her eyes fixed on Bapu's face.

"But Ba's white surface of virtues is not without dark spots," Bapu said. "Although, impelled by wifely devotion, she has renounced earthly possessions, her longing for them has persisted. As a result, about a year or so ago she laid up a sum of about two hundred rupees for her own use out of the small sums presented to her by various people on different occasions. The rule of the ashram, however, is that even such personal presents may not be kept for private use. Her action therefore amounted to theft. On discovery, her remorse appeared to be genuine. However, events have proved that her remorse was only temporary. Evidently, it did not root out her desire for possession."

Everyone was trying to avoid looking at Ba who sat motionless, her face impassive, her eyes held by the slight figure of her husband on the raised platform.

"Recently some unknown visitors brought her a sum of four rupees. Instead of handing over this sum to the manager, she kept it with her. A trusted and tried inmate of the ashram was present when the donation was made. It was his obvious duty to warn Ba, but impelled by a false sense of courtesy he remained instead a helpless witness of wrong. He has now come forward and yesterday informed Maganlalbhai of the incident. Courageously, though in fear and trembling, Maganlalbhai went to Ba and demanded the money. Ba felt humiliated and quickly returned the four rupees. She promised never to repeat the offense. I talked to her yesterday evening and believe her remorse to be genuine. She has agreed to withdraw from the ashram in case she should lapse into such conduct again.

"I hold the corruption in the ashram to be merely the reflection of the hidden wrongs within me. I have never claimed perfection for myself. Who knows what aberrations in the realm of my thought have reacted on the environment around me? The epithet of 'Mahatma' has always galled me and now it almost sounds to me like a term of abuse.

"Let me once more reiterate my opinion of the ashram. Imperfect as it has always been, full of corruption as it has been discovered to be, this institution is my best creation. I hope to see god through its aid. Revelations put me on my guard. They make me search within me and they humble me, but they do not shake my faith in it."

Many people were crying openly when Bapu finished. Dry-eyed herself, Mira saw Ba dabbing at her eyes with the end of her pallu.

———

The incidents involving Lakshmi and Ba did not dent Mira's idealization of Bapu. The envelope of devotion in which she had encased his image did not rip apart. On the contrary. Not only did she continue to revere Gandhiji as a sacred being, as the highest embodiment of the Eternal Spirit, but now she also marveled at the effort it had taken him to reach these heights. After all, she had been a privileged witness to his struggle against his own inner violence, to his wresting of tolerance from an overweening, moralistic conscience, to his rescue of brahmacharya from the swamp of sensuality. Is not the lotus even more beautiful for having its roots in muck?

Mira's wish to be close to Gandhiji now transformed into a strong need and, when thwarted, an almost unbearable craving. Lying sleepless in bed on the evenings when she had not been able to spend time alone with him, Mira suffered acutely from the pangs of separation. To improve her Hindi penmanship, I had once given her a song by Mirabai to copy. I had thought this would also make her more familiar with the saint after whom Gandhiji had named her. Mira had copied the song, over and over again, till she knew the lament of the Rajput princess by heart, the only piece of Hindi poetry she could recite in an accent that remained stubbornly English.

> I am driven mad with love,
> No one knows my pain.
> Only the wounded knows the agony of the wounded,
> No one else.
> Only the jeweler knows the value of the gem,
> Not the one who has lost it.
> O Lord, Mira's pain will only disappear
> If the Dark One is the healer.

With Lamond, the fire in which she had burnt had conjured in its flames hallucinatory images of entwined bodies that had deeply shamed her, finally pushing her into a guilt-ridden despair. Her agony was different this time, Mira told herself. For, with Bapu, there were no such phantasms, there was no question of an intrusion of the physical. Yet Mira could not understand why, in spite of the absence of guilt, the pain was so familiar, with a hint of the same sweetness that paradoxically made it more unbearable.

thirteen

THE BHAGWADBHAKTI ASHRAM is located outside the small town of Rewari, on the railway route from Delhi to Bombay. One of the poorest parts of the country, it is not far from the deserts of Rajasthan which lie to the southwest. The land is barren here and the town thinly populated. During the day, which gets quite hot even in winter, swirling winds from the desert blow sand through the cracks in the frames of the doors and windows, covering the floors with a thin layer of dust that has to be swept away every few hours. Mira arrived at the ashram in January, when the nights were still very cold, but remained oblivious of the near-freezing temperatures.

For more than a month her eyes refused to see and her limbs to feel. She had barely enough energy to attend her classes and spin for an hour every day. The rest of the time she lay on her mattress, looking out through the open door, beyond the barbed wire fence enclosing a thin strip of lawn that surrounded the simple stone building of the ashram. It could be called a lawn only in comparison with the dusty olive-green scrub that dotted the sandy land of the surrounding countryside. The grass was dark green and coarse, already old though the shoots were fresh. To her English eye, the landscape was singularly unprepossessing, scarred with dried out gullies, narrow ravines and a jagged, rocky outcrop that emerged from the tawny ground like the scaly protrusions on the back of a dinosaur.

At the end of February, Mira wrote to Romain Rolland.

. . . I have been here since the middle of January. In exile, or at least that is how it feels. Before leaving Ahmadabad, Bapu kept on telling me that I should look upon our separation as a preparation for carrying out a sacred task, that what is important is the realization of his ideals, not his person. So I am to carry out his work, but not with him. My mind understands but my heart rebels. You have been banished, Mira, it says. You were found unworthy.

For more than a month after my arrival here, I found it hard to leave my room. I kept lying on a mattress on the floor, awake but utterly listless. I could not even say that I was sad . . . just empty. Dearest friend, the thought of writing to you did come but it was without any impetus, devoid of all energy. I now understand why there are so few suicide notes. And, of these, why most are so short and none a literary creation the momentousness of the occasion would seem to demand.

I am feeling better now, even capable of an occasional jest. Bapu has sent me to this ashram to further my study of Hindi. His hope, and my goal, is that one day I will speak the language like a native, understand the dialect of the simplest villager. My teacher and the head of the ashram, Maharajji, is a middle-aged school inspector who resigned his government job to follow Bapu in the country's freedom struggle. He is an enthusiastic little man whose friendliness can at times become overwhelming.

He keeps on trying to convince me of the superiority of Indian civilization, deaf to my protestations that I need no convincing on that score, that I agree with him.

I will be here for three months and then travel to some other ashrams in northern and eastern India, familiarizing myself with their work and place in Bapu's scheme of things before I decide on the future course of my own work. I keep to myself here, even more so than in Ahmadabad, not only because I have always been solitary, with nature as my preferred refuge, but also because I never know which of their several taboos I might be breaking. Even with Bapu, I have occasionally felt like I was coming up against an invisible barrier. Such moments have been rare, though. Most of the time I feel myself opening up to him in a way I have never done before with any other human being.

Dear friend, Indians are the sweetest, gentlest people but they live their lives in constant fear of transgressing some taboo or the other. Did you know that the Jains, a numerous and influential people in Gujarat and perhaps the most consequent believers in non-violence, claim that millions of organisms are killed in a sexual embrace? Celibacy not as something wonderful and vital in itself but as the essence of non-violence! No wonder that when I argue with Bapu on his notions about celibacy, it often seems that we are talking of completely different things.

He is in Delhi these days. He will be here next week, staying in the ashram for a day before he goes on a long tour of South India. You can imagine the excitement with which I await his arrival, and the dread with which I contemplate the separation that will follow.

P.S. When my teacher here asked if there was any particular book I would like to study for my Hindi class I immediately answered, *The Songs of Mira*. My namesake has bridged the gap of centuries and cultures to enter my heart and make a corner of it her own. I find a resonance and melody in her words that till now was the province of Beethoven's music. With the humility of a bad translator, I send you one of her short verses to Krishna which haunts me these days, like the snatch of a song that plays over and over in one's head, refusing to go away.

My eyes have fashioned
An altar of pearl tears,
And here is my sacrifice:
The body and mind
Of Mira,
The servant who clings to your feet,
Through life after life,
A virginal harvest for you to reap.

I wonder what you will make of it, and whether it moves you . . . a little.

————

Gandhiji was without his usual retinue when he came down from Delhi to Rewari to spend a day with Mira. Only Mahadev and Devdas accompanied him.

It all seemed to begin well. Mira saw how happy he was to see her and how he reveled in her happiness to be with him. But their joy in each other did not outlast the morning of his arrival. Other people in the ashram wanted to meet him and Mira fretted over the time he gave them, which made him edgy. On hearing the news that Gandhiji had come, people from the surrounding villages gathered at the ashram gate in the afternoon for a darshan. He talked to them about the importance of spinning and the need for building lavatories in the villages. Mira had some time alone with him when they went for a walk at sunset. Actually, they walked round and round on the thin strip of grass skirting the building, like monks strolling in the courtyard of a Benedictine monastery. Gandhiji asked Mira about her life in the Bhagwadbhakti Ashram and she poured her heart out. It all came out in a rush; she could not control herself. She told him how she hated to be there without him, that she had nothing in common with the others, that her only connection to them was through him.

"Don't say that," he chided her gently, although, knowing him, she could detect the hidden anger in his voice. "You are connected to them through your common humanity."

He spoke some more in this vein but Mira was not listening, or not as closely as she normally listened to each word he uttered.

"Bapu," she said, drawing on an unsuspected reserve of courage, "I am not as evolved as you are. I cannot relate to large entities like mankind or higher ideals except through a person. My god has to be personal, alive, a palpable presence. He has to permeate my heart, mind and body. He must fill every inch of space in and around me, like Mirabai's Krishna. If I have that then there is no sacrifice I cannot make. There is no river, however turbulent, that I cannot cross, no work, however difficult, that I cannot do."

Mira was well aware that though she did not tell Bapu directly that he was her "god," he knew what her words meant. She could see how perturbed Bapu was at what she was saying, how agitated he became although the disturbance lasted only for a few moments before his iron self-control reasserted itself. With a forced smile he said, "For Mirabai, Krishna was all-pervasive but not in the flesh, not in the body. You still have much to learn and to draw the right conclusions from what you know."

Mira slept badly that night. She was aware of Bapu's presence in the next room and of the fact that he was going away the next morning. She broke down when she went to his room to say goodbye just before he was to leave for the railway station. Perhaps it was the love in the look he gave her, the compassion in his eyes when he motioned her to sit next to him on the floor, that made Mira lose all control. Sobbing helplessly, she clutched his hand between hers. For a fleeting moment she sensed a separate life in his hand. She felt it come alive within hers, even as he quickly pulled it away. His face was now stern, his eyes cold. The frown line on his forehead began to pulse.

"Control yourself, Mira," he said, "you are making a spectacle of yourself." Mira went on crying, fat tears rolling down her face, unable or unwilling to stop, not because of the sting in his words but from a strange and surprising mixture of hurt and exultation. Bapu sat there, unmoving but moved. Mira felt he was struggling with himself not to put a consoling arm around her shoulders. Later, after he left for the station, Mira had an odd thought. She wondered if Bapu envied her a little that she had become free of all restraint in his presence whilst he had to retain his self-control; even more so now, when the responsibility of controlling the situation in which they found themselves was solely his. Could Krishna envy Mirabai?

The letter, in Bapu's spidery handwriting made worse by the jolting of the train where it was written, arrived a day before the telegram.

> *On the train*
> *After Bharatpur*
> 22-3-27

Chi. Mira,

The parting today was sad, because I saw that I pained you. And yet it was inevitable . . . You must not cling to me as in this body. The spirit without the body is ever with you. And that is more than the feeble, embodied, imprisoned spirit with all the limitations that flesh is heir to. The spirit without the flesh is perfect, and that is all we need. This can be felt only when we practise detachment. This you must now try to achieve.

This is how I would grow if I were you. But you should grow along your own lines. You will, therefore, reject all I have said in this, that does not appeal to your heart or head. You must retain your individuality at all cost. Resist me when you must. For I may judge you wrongly in spite of all my love for you. I do not want you to impute infallibility to me.

With love,
Yours
Bapu

The telegram, sent five days after the letter, was from Mahadevbhai informing Mira that Gandhiji had narrowly missed having a severe stroke. His blood pressure was still unacceptably high. Doctors had ascribed it to overwork and nervous exhaustion and had advised complete rest. Gandhiji's tour program in the south was being canceled.

Mira was frantic with worry when she heard the news. Her first impulse was to get on a train and rush to him. But before she could act on that impulse, a letter came from him effectively asking her to stay where she was.

"You must not be perturbed," Bapu wrote. "The crash was bound to come some day. You must forget me in the body. You can't have it forever. You must do the work in front of you. I must not write more for fear of offending the doctor and those around me. I am taking as much rest as I think I need. But I cannot pamper the body overmuch. You must promise not to worry. Merge yourself in your work."

Feeling guilty that she had unwittingly contributed to his breakdown, Mira wrote to Rolland imploring him to help her out of her dilemma over "my desperate need to be with him, which sometimes makes me feel that I would wither away and slowly die in his absence, and my fear that my importuning presence not only disturbs him but can even make him physically sick."

Rolland wrote back that she should not worry. Gandhi's breakdown was understandable. It was not surprising that it happened to someone in whom the spirit burnt so brightly that the body could not stand the heat of its effulgence. Rolland would pray for Gandhi. He was needed for the great tasks that lay ahead and which were vital for the future of humanity. Gandhi was the man who would show mankind the way out of the circle of murderous violence in which it was trapped and which prevented man from realizing his divine potential.

In his diary, Rolland is more frank. "Mira's letter was disquieting and a cause for worry," he writes, "for her as much as for him. I fear she overestimates her importance in the worrying turn of events. Her role in his illness is peripheral. I must confess that I am surprised by the psychological acumen of some of her remarks. I did not suspect she had this particular talent. Like most spiritually inclined people, I thought she either lived her life naïvely on the surface or in depths unfathomable to all but the select few. That the gates of the 'middle heaven' of psychological sensibility were closed to her. I should not be surprised, though, since all our senses—physical, psychological and spiritual—get sharpened in the state she finds herself in, the state of spiritual love. The lives of mystics bear eloquent testimony to such transformations. I shall write to her, a bland letter of concern and encouragement, taking care not to interfere in the working out of her destiny, in the unfolding of her karma as the Hindus would say."

Mira was in a state of vacillating panic throughout the months of April and May which Gandhiji spent in Nandi Hills in Mysore recuperating from his breakdown. She desperately wanted to be with him but was held back by the knowledge that he wanted her to stay where she was. Like a caged wild cat hurling itself, again and again, against the bars in an effort to escape, Mira too struggled against Bapu's firm but gentle prohibition which he kept reinforcing through his frequent, almost daily, letters. On 25 April, Gandhiji writes:

> . . . I have your four letters of which three were received together yesterday.
>
> One of your letters yesterday prompted me to send you a preemptory wire asking you to come to Nandi. But I restrained myself. The other two letters were less gloomy. But even so, if the separation becomes unbearable, you must come without waiting for an answer or any prompting from me. The love of the people around you should really strengthen you and keep you there. Your letter describing the affection of the people there is most touching and it would be a matter of sorrow if you cannot be at peace with yourself there. But no one can suddenly change one's nature, and if your effort to compose yourself there becomes fruitless, you should tell the friends there so plainly and come here without the slightest hesitation. *On no account* should there be a breakdown there. You must not try your nerves to the breaking point.
>
> You must develop iron nerves. It is necessary for our work.

Two days later, in response to a more composed letter from Mira in which she seems to accept their physical separation in the secure knowledge of an abiding spiritual connection, Bapu writes:

> . . . I have your cheerful letter. If you can realize every word of what you have written, all your trouble is over and also my anxiety. We perish through our perishable bodies, if instead of using them as temporary instruments, we identify ourselves with them.
>
> The more I observe and study things, the more convinced I become that sorrow over separation and death is perhaps the greatest delusion. To realize that it is a delusion is to become free. There is no death, no separation of the substance. And yet the tragedy of it is that though we love friends for the substance we recognize in them, we deplore the destruction of the insubstantial that covers the substance for the time being. Whereas real friendship should be used to reach the whole through the fragment. You seem to have got the truth for the moment. Let it abide forever.

Mira's philosophical calm, however, did not last long; the fragile dam she tried to erect against the swirling waters of her emotional turmoil collapsed yet again. Gandhiji was sympathetic and encouraged her efforts, yet his very involvement in her struggle made it more intense for her, increasing both the intensity of the wish to be with him and its simultaneous proscription.

In a letter dated 2 May 1927, he tells her that he will leave it to her to do as she pleases. She should not, on any account, base her decision to travel to Nandi Hills on the state of his health for he is much the same as he was when they last met. However, she should look deep within herself and make up her mind about what she must do, irrespective of his wishes. "I would like you to do what your inner spirit tells you to do," he writes.

He is more firm in another letter that follows on 8 May.

I have your further letter. But I see it will be sometime before you regain your balance. I do not mind the ups and downs so long as you retain the elasticity. My own opinion is this—it will be perfectly natural for you to come to me wherever I am *after* finishing your allotted task, whenever that happens. An ordinary person may not give up a self-imposed programme. But if you become highly emotional and your nerves remain under tension, you should come even though your course may not be finished.

Naturally I am anxious for you to finish your course. I should not like to have to think that it was beyond you. But your health is more precious to me than your studies or any other preparation.

You must not think of coming to me for my health. For it is good and I cannot be looked after better even if you came. If I needed your nursing, I should wire for you. But such an event will not happen, if only because I have got into the habit of taking nursing from anybody and train new nurses to my requirements. There are more nurses than I need here. So if you come in the hope of doing some personal service, you would feel idle and yawning.

Now for the necessity of personal touch. My own opinion is that it is necessary in the preliminary stages. And then the touch comes through joint work. You come in daily touch with me by doing my work as if it was your own. And this can, must and will outlast the existence of this physical body of mine. You are, and will be, in touch whether I am alive or dead. And that is what I want you to be. You have come to me not for me, but for my ideals in so far as I live them. You *now* know how far I live the ideals I set forth. It is now for you to work out those ideals and practise them to greater perfection than has been given to me to do. He or she who does that will be my first heir and representative. I want you to be the first, if only because you studied me from a distance and made your choice. And when, in the course of work, God brings us physically together, it is well, but it is well also when He keeps us apart in pursuance of the common object.

But this is counsel of perfection. Having listened to it and understood it, you are free to do as you choose. If you cannot contain yourself, you must come, and not feel that I shall be displeased. I should be displeased if you did violence to yourself and became prostrate.

Caught in the struggle to rush to him and its equally strong prohibition, Mira found a fevered release in writing her diary.

How I envy Mirabai! How free she was, how much courage she had to abandon all ties to parents and kin, walk away from the stifling luxury of the palace, thumb her nose at convention and wander around the land dancing and singing her love for Krishna. "Nothing is really mine, except my Girdhargopal," she sang.

> Krishna, my lord,
> Take this girl as your slave.
> Loving Thee, I am set free.

Like her, I, too, have

> . . . planted the creeper of love
> Watering it silently with my tears.
> Fully grown now,
> It covers my home.

In this dry, barren land, baked every day in the heat of the summer sun, it is this green creeper in my heart that sustains my sanity and my life in its cool shade. But *my* god forbids me to dance with ankle bells on my feet and with castanets in my hands. Why did he give me her name if he did not want her passion? My head understands his letters one way: he will be angry if I throw up everything and rush to him. My heart reads them differently: Come if you must, obey the call of your heart. I will not be displeased.

Why, why, must I be saddled with the burden of choice?

In the meanwhile, I suffer. I lose weight. I lose sleep. I have no interest in the people I am with or in the work I am doing. Most of the time I feel I am in a daze, desperately trying to summon his presence or to hold it when it is there. Then I am happy and can laugh. Perhaps I even laugh out aloud, for people have begun to give me strange looks. But I cannot help my delight when his presence suddenly takes concrete form and I see him clearly before me . . . my god with the leprechaun ears.

fourteen

UNABLE TO GO TO BAPU, yet too restless to stay in Rewari, Mira decided to go to the Wardha ashram and live there for a month. Bapu and she had stayed there for a week on their way to the Congress session in Kanpur. Her decision to go to Wardha instead of to Ahmadabad had something to do with recapturing the happiness of those days that now seemed to belong to a distant and less troubled past. It also had to do with her reluctance to stay in the Sabarmati ashram; it would be empty without Bapu.

She missed Bapu terribly but was careful not to reveal this in her letters. Hours of heartfelt prayer helped her through the worst of the crisis. She wrote to him every day, mainly reporting her progress on his path, and received regular replies. Her letters do not betray any signs of the struggle between her head and her heart. She often appears impatient with the shortcomings of Gandhiji's followers—the continuing hold of superstition and debilitating custom on their minds, a lack of zeal in leading a simple, ascetic life, their adherence to ashram rules, such as of regular prayer, followed in letter rather than in spirit. She notes

the ongoing conflict between the reform-minded and the orthodox inmates of the Wardha ashram and is incensed at the latter's
insistence on continuing the custom of segregating women at the
time of their monthly period.

Gandhiji's replies to these letters are warm and personal.
He seems pleased with how well she is doing and relieved that
her emotional storm has subsided. His letters inquire about her
health, suggest changes in her diet, dispense advice (she should
be patient and tolerant of the orthodox view on the segregation
of menstruating women even if she does not agree with it), and
encourage her in her efforts to put his ideals into practice.

Chi. Mira,

I have your letter about prayer. The letter is beautiful. I
also like the caution that you have uttered for yourself.
Love means infinite patience, and exactly in the measure
that we become impatient of our own weaknesses, we
have to be patient with regard to the weaknesses of our
neighbours. We easily enough see their weaknesses; but
we have absolutely no knowledge of their striving to overcome them. One thing must not be overlooked. That the
prayer meetings at the Ashram are not what they should
be—full of fragrance and reality—is really due to my own
shortcomings of which neither you nor anybody else can
have any notion whatsoever.

The value of prayer dawned upon me very late in life,
and as I have a fair capacity for imposing discipline upon
myself, I have by patient and painful striving been able
now for some years to conform to the outward form. But
do I conform to the spirit? My answer is: No. Whilst it is
true that life would be insipid for me without prayer, I am
not absorbed in the message of the prayer at the prayer

times. The mind wanders whither it would in spite of incessant striving. If I could but lose myself in the prayer like
the great Ali, you will not have to make the complaint that
you have rightly registered in your letter. You will not now
wonder why I am patient with those who are slack even
in attending to the external form. I therefore tremble to
impose any iron rule upon the people. Knowing my own
weakness, I sympathize with theirs, and hope that if I grow,
they must grow with me. You will now understand more
than ever what I have so often said to so many people: I
must be measured not by what I appear personally, but
by how I appear in the lives of the people at the Ashram.
The Ashram, especially when I am withdrawn from it, is
really the only infallible guide to a knowledge of me.

With superhuman effort, Mira was able to maintain her calm
till the middle of September. Gripped by a restlessness that did
not allow her to stay in any one place for long, she went from
Wardha to Bombay and then to Poona. The storm finally broke
in Poona, geographically the closest she had come to Bapu who
was still traveling in the south. Without informing him, she
simply boarded a train to Bangalore and then took the bus to
where he was staying outside the city.

The meeting was a disaster. At first, Bapu seemed genuinely
happy to see her, a broad smile of welcome lighting up his face.
But within a few hours the clouds began to gather. He appeared
unusually troubled. His intimacy alternated with distance, love
with indifference, even anger, and he began to berate her for her
lack of self-control. Mira sat there in silence, her head bowed,
unable to move, tears running down her face. After a sleepless
night, when she went to his room the next morning, he was

again composed, though his face looked drawn. He handed her a slip of paper on which it was written that this was his day of silence. He then gave her a second piece of paper that asked her to immediately return to the Sabarmati ashram. Seeing the shocked expression on her face, he took the paper from her hand and wrote on it, "You have great courage but you are weak. Courage without calmness is not strength. I am doing this for your good."

Mira's humiliation was complete when Mahadevbhai, who saw her off at the railway station, politely but firmly told her that she was to stay away from Bapu. Her visit had again raised his blood pressure to a dangerously high level.

Back in the Sabarmati ashram, Mira once again wrote to Romain Rolland.

The Ashram,
Sabarmati, Ahmadabad
24 September 1927

Dearest Friend,

This is a letter of my shame. I could not control myself, and frantic with worry about his health went down to the South to be with him. He was furious and sent me back. Like a kicked bitch, with its tail between its legs, I slunk away. How one despises people who cling! I am one of them. I could clearly see that I was getting on his nerves yet could not stop. I hated seeing myself become a barnacle sticking to the hull of a ship, resisting all efforts at prying it loose. I grovelled in the letters I wrote to him from here. I promised I would strive harder to exercise more self-control. I would not let my emotions rule my actions.

I have now thrown myself with renewed vigour into

what I think is going to be my future work in India—serving the poor by improving dairying practices in the villages. I learnt milking when I was a child at my grandfather's farm and have always felt at home with farm animals. Here, too, working in the ashram's dairy after my return has helped mitigate my distress. This time I am determined to be worthy of him.

But, dear friend, you must not think that my love for him is solely the stuff of raw nerves, bleeding wounds and sheer pain. It may be built on a trembling foundation of sadness and feared loss, yet my ache is anything but a void. My love for him, often rejected, sometimes humiliated, does not deplete me but fills me to the brim. It is a source of simultaneous joy and anguish. Even in its worst moments, at its most painful, my adoration of him is a rush of life, divine life. Even in my tears, I feel my love heightening my sense of myself and of the world around me, as if both were being discovered anew. It is true that I do not recognize myself in my bleeding moments of humiliation and self-hate. Yet it is precisely at these moments that I also feel the shock of an uncanny encounter, of recognizing myself *too* well. This degraded creature, abasing itself in an impossible love is who I am in the deepest recesses of my soul, perhaps next only to the core that hides the soul's sacred mystery.

Wish me the courage to keep my love in the face of all the tribulations that seek to test its endurance, and the will to act otherwise in spite of its dictates.

Yours,
Mira

Five days after she mailed the letter to Romain Rolland, Mira received a short note from Gandhiji that made her spirit soar;

she was back on the seesaw of feelings that had lately dipped to despair more often than it had risen to the bliss she had experienced in her first year with Bapu. "I could not restrain myself from sending you a love message on reaching here," the note said. "I felt very sad after letting you go. I have been very severe with you, but I could not do otherwise. I had to perform an operation and I steadied myself for it. Now let us hope all would go on smoothly, and that all the weakness is gone."

Two days later, came a postcard dated 29 September—"This is merely to tell you I can't dismiss you from my mind. Every surgeon has a soothing ointment after a severe operation. This is my ointment." Another arrived on his birthday, 2 October— ". . . I have never been so anxious as this time to hear from you, for I sent you away too quickly after a serious operation. But the sending you away was a part of the operation . . . You haunted me in my sleep last night and were reported by friends to whom you had been sent, to be delirious, but without any danger. They said, 'You need not be anxious. We are doing all that is humanly possible.' And with this I woke up troubled in mind and prayed that you may be free from all harm. And your letter gave me great joy."

In her diary, in the entry for 12 October 1927, Mira writes, "Perhaps I can split myself into two? In his presence and in my letters to him I will be the Mirabehn of Satyagraha Ashram, strong, sensible, loyal to his ideals and his vision. And in my diary, the Mirabai of longing and yearning, dedicated to his person."

———

After Gandhiji's return to Sabarmati, Mira did not protest when he suggested that the time had come for her to strike out on her own. Her resolve to be Mirabehn of the ashram and not Mirabai of longing was still fresh. She was determined to remove all traces of her ego, of an individuality that constantly wanted, wished and demanded, and then sulked when the world refused to fulfil its demands. She was determined to learn the art of letting go, of surrendering. In contrast to the ego, always seeking to scale heights, surrender would expose her to the novel experience of depth. She would have no wishes other than his for her, no activities other than those that served the cause that was larger than both of them. Many years later, she would look back at this time as a period of severe spiritual austerity, her tapasya. She would find it ironic that whereas the tapasya of saints had the goal of uniting them with the divine, her own was dedicated to the attainment of a separation from her "lord."

Mira now decided to put the greatest possible physical distance between Gandhiji and herself. After leaving the Sabarmati ashram, she went to live in Chhatwan, a remote village in the Madhubani district of north Bihar, a five-day journey from Ahmadabad by train, bus and bullock cart. Here, she intended to devote herself to work that was dear to Gandhiji's heart: helping the women in the villages to adopt improved methods of carding and spinning cotton. She set up house in one of the few brick buildings in the village. Her house consisted of a single small hall with pillared arches on one side that opened into the village street in the front, and one tiny room where she kept her meager belongings, mostly books, in a steel trunk. A bamboo-and-thatch hut at the back served as the kitchen. During the first week, she sat in the hall through the day carding cotton in full view of the passing villagers. The women often stopped to watch her, curious about the mem in their midst attaching so much significance to lowly women's work. Having caught their attention, Mira would roll slivers from freshly carded cotton and hand them out, saying in her now passable Hindi, "Here, you take them home and spin with them. If you find they are good, come to me to learn how to use this kind of bow." The women were shy at first. They examined the slivers with keen interest but giggled and stepped back when Mira offered the bow. Soon, though, a couple of them decided to try out the new method and all the women were clamoring to learn new ways of carding and spinning.

On most evenings Mira sat in the darkening hall by the light of a kerosene lamp, as the sounds of barking dogs and crying babies being put to sleep filled the night air, writing letters to Gandhiji describing her experiences. She missed him terribly, but took care to prevent personal references from creeping into her letters, revising them more than once to eliminate any expression of feeling that might have escaped her vigilant eye. Under a self-imposed injunction to avoid words of love, Mira poured out her love in the act of writing itself, secure in the knowledge that in dipping the reed pen into the bottle of ink and putting it to paper to form neutral words, she was expressing a yearning of her soul that would remain her secret alone, safely concealed from Bapu. Seeking a more apt outlet however, the yearning became intolerable at times, especially when she lay alone in bed at night or woke up well before dawn, unable to sleep. She would then lie on her back, looking up at the night sky imagining that he too was gazing at the same sky from his bed on the veranda in front of his hut in the ashram.

Besides the scribbled notes on postcards, Gandhiji was prompt in replying to Mira's letters. At the end of a grueling day of travel, meetings and making speeches, his last act before retiring for the night would often be to write to Mira. He offered solutions to the technical problems that cropped up in the spinning of cotton and was liberal in his advice on her diet. Her health was a matter of continuing concern and he constantly exhorted her to take good care of herself so as to avoid a breakdown. Now that she was far away, he declared his affection for her more easily and even told her how much he missed her.

During this time, Mira wrote but one letter to Romain Rolland. It gives no clue to her emotional state. It is as if she were deliberately eschewing the comfort of communication, of being understood, as if her tapasya demanded not only that she bear her suffering in silence but also that she reach a state where she would not feel the need to either understand it herself or explain it to others.

As I read the letters that Gandhiji and Mira exchanged during this period, the parallels with Mirabai become even more striking. Krishna was the flute player and dancer and Mirabai did his work, wandering around the land singing and dancing to her dark lord. Gandhiji's music and dance was of another kind and Mirabehn followed the way of *her* lord. Can digging latrine trenches not be a song, teaching new methods of spinning a dance?

fifteen

*M*IRA'S EXILE ENDED in the summer of 1929 when Gandhiji asked her to join him on his speaking tour through north India.

Besides Mira and the indispensable Mahadevbhai who looked after his secretarial needs, Gandhiji's entourage consisted of four persons from the ashram and a small number of Congress workers from the province they were touring at the time. The latter organized the public meetings, transport and lodging of the party. Long-distance journeys were made by train in a third-class compartment packed with baggage, files and baskets of fruits, snacks and sweets gifted by people thronging the stations wherever the train halted. A mat was laid out at the back of the compartment where Gandhiji could lie down and rest. Cars were used for short distances when Gandhiji traveled through a series of villages.

They were constantly on the move during these two months, with Gandhiji sometimes addressing four to five public meetings a day. There were two main halts during the day. The first was for lunch and washing clothes and the second, in the evening, for dinner and a night's rest. The feeling of frenetic movement and being surrounded by endless crowds was permanent. People swarmed the platforms of railway stations, blocked the roads when they passed through villages and flocked around the places where they halted, desperate and eager for a darshan of the Mahatma.

In the absence of Ba, who traveled less and less, preferring to look after Sabarmati ashram in Gandhiji's absence, Mira's job was to see that Bapu's personal routine went off punctually and smoothly. She could not conceive of anything else she would rather do. While Bapu was addressing the public meeting at the first main halt of the day, Mira would rush off to inspect the room, generally in a private home, where he would be staying for a couple of hours. She had to see to it that his room was cleared of all furniture, a mattress covered with khadi placed near the door, and that the bathroom was spotlessly clean. She had to also make sure that goat's milk and fresh vegetables were available for cooking his lunch. As part of his unending dietary experiments, Gandhiji was at this time observing the "panch vastu" regimen in which he ate five different things a day. Each vegetable and fruit counted as a separate item and could not be repeated in the evening if it had already been served for the midday meal. To be certain that the milk was fresh and clean, Mira preferred to milk the goat herself, her skill at milking cows, developed as a girl on her grandfather's farm, being put to good use.

When Gandhiji came to the room after the meeting was over, the shouts of "Mahatma Gandhi ki jai" receding behind him as the crowd following him from the venue of the meeting was stopped at the gate of the house where he was staying, he would be hot, tired and covered with dust. Mira would show him to the bathroom where a bucket of water, a tumbler and a fresh towel awaited him. She would prepare his food and serve it immediately after he finished his bath. While he ate and perhaps snatched a few minutes of sleep afterwards, she would wash his clothes as well as her own and take a bath herself. If the clothes did not dry in the two to three hours they had at the midday stop, the damp bundle would be packed with everything else and the whole party would be off again. And this would go on, day after day.

Sometimes Mira found the time to attend one of Bapu's public meetings. Here, her job was to help in the collection of money after Bapu finished his speech. Armed with a cloth bag she, along with other members of the party, moved amidst the tightly-packed crowds squatting on the ground, collecting copper and nickel coins from poor peasants eager to contribute to Gandhiji's cause. Once, Bapu made a stirring appeal to the audience in a women's meeting to donate their ornaments to the cause of combating untouchability. Mira was moved to tears at the way the poor village women began pulling off their rings, earrings, bracelets and anklets, vying with each other to be among the first to put what was possibly the only wealth they possessed into the collection bags. One young woman caught hold of her hand and pointed to her sole ornament, a heavy silver anklet gleaming softly against her dark skin. It was so thick that she needed help to pull it off. Mira pulled at it one way and the woman the other till the anklet was removed from her leg. Her face was beaming with pride when she handed the anklet to Mira. "For Mahatmaji," she said simply. Mira also noticed that it was the rich who were the worst at giving. Most of them would search for a coin rather than hand over a note of high denomination from their bulging wallets. In the evening, the bags were emptied and the thousands of small coins counted. Each item of jewelery was listed and a detailed report on the day's collection was given to Bapu. The sacks of money and jewelery were carried from one village to the next till the party reached a large town where they could be deposited in a bank.

Sweaty and coated with dust, jolting around in an old car with no suspension to speak of on roads no more than dirt tracks, Mira was supremely happy. She could not know that like the approach of the monsoon, still a massive aerial current south of the equator in the Indian Ocean, storm clouds were once again gathering over her life. That, in spite of her best intentions, her feelings toward Bapu, pent up for so long and now further reinforced by their close proximity, were on the verge of overflowing and breaching the dam she had erected in the last eighteen months with such enormous effort.

After their return to Ahmadabad Mira repossessed her hut that had lain vacant in her absence. Bapu had not assigned it to anyone else. She spent the first day cleaning the hut, taking out her books, going through her mail and answering the two letters from her mother and one from Rhona which had not been forwarded to her. Before the evening prayer, when Mira went to pay her respects to Ba she found her surprisingly warm, quite unlike her usual formal self. Ba complimented Mira on the improvement in her Hindi, inquired after Mira's health and asked whether Mira had kept well during her stay in Bihar, an area known for its susceptibility to malarial fever. She did not ask about her travels with Bapu.

After dinner, Mira walked over to Gandhiji's hut. He was already lying on his cot in the veranda. Ba sat beside him, a bowl of warm ghee on the floor, all set to massage his feet. They looked up and then at each other as Mira approached. Gandhiji sat up on the cot and helped Ba to her feet. Without saying a word, Ba went to her room, leaving the two of them alone. Mira felt her body begin to tremble. She knew what was coming: Bapu no longer wanted their hour together. She did not hear his exact words, nor was she aware of what she was saying or doing. Later she could not even recall how she had found her way back to her hut. She only remembered collapsing on her cot, her body racked with sobs that tore her apart, demanding a release which only death could grant.

The next morning, after the prayer which she did not attend, a grave and unsmiling Mahadevbhai brought her a folded note from Bapu.

24-6-29

Chi. Mira,

It is well you do not want me to speak to you on the incident. But I did want, after witnessing the exhibition, to reduce to writing my thoughts. I do that now.

The exhibition is proof of the correctness of my statement. None else would have felt like committing suicide over a simple innocent remark of mine. You want to be with me in my tours occasionally, it is true; you want to come to the Ashram leaving your work at least every four months. You recognize these desires as limitations. I make allowance for them. But why feel disturbed when I tell you what I feel to be the truth: that they are not themselves the disease, but they are symptoms of a deep-seated disease which has not been touched. If you were not what I have described you to be, you would rejoice over my drawing attention to the disease and courageously strive to overcome it. Instead, you simply collapsed, much to my grief and anxiety.

This disease is idolatry. If it is not, why hanker after my company! Why touch or kiss the feet that must one day be dead cold? There is nothing in the body. The truth I represent is before you. Experience and effort will unravel it before you, never my association in the manner you wish. When it comes in the course of business, you will, like others, gain from it and more because of your devotion. Why so helplessly rely on me? Why do everything to please me? Why not independently of me and even in spite of me? I have put no restrictions on your liberty, save those you have welcomed. Break the idol to pieces if you can and will. If you cannot, I am prepared to suffer with you. But you must give me liberty to issue warnings.

My diagnosis may be wrong. If so, it is well. Strive with me cheerfully instead of being nerve-broken. Everyone but you takes my blows without being unstrung.

If your effort has hitherto failed, what does it matter? You have hitherto dealt mechanically with the symptoms. There you have had considerable success. But if I say you have not been able to touch the root, why weep over it? I do not mind your failures. They are but stepping-stones to success. You must rise from this torpor never to fall into it again.

I have done. May God be with you.

Love
Bapu

I am not sure whether the letter I found among her papers was a draft of her reply, or one that she had composed but never sent. I suspect it was the latter.

25 June 1929

Dearest Bapu,

Yes, I kissed your feet, over and over again. Yes, I bathed them in my hot tears. I wept from happiness that I was with you and from agony that you will send me away again. Yes, I pressed my face against your legs even as I hugged them tightly to my breasts. I can still feel the muscle in your calf go taut. I felt your chapped skin against my cheek and even in that flood of feelings that washed over me I blamed myself for not taking care of your body. For not rubbing ghee on your skin to make it soft and supple, as I used to, once. Yes, I did all this and felt no shame. On the contrary.

Bapu, I do not worship an idol but the living God. You incorporate the Eternal and paying homage to the Eternal, to the Divine, is not idolatry. Indeed, sometimes I wish you *were* a stone idol. I could then have bathed you every morning, rubbed you with fragrant pastes and offered flowers and incense at your stony feet. Unable to move, you would have had no choice but to let yourself be adored by me. Why can't you accept my love, bear my devotion? Are you a god who recoils from his most ardent worshipper? Or is your reaction a test that you are setting me, as Hindu gods often do to their devotees and sages to their would-be disciples. Are you testing how much rejection I can bear and still not lose my love?

Oh, my dearest, you will be surprised at how much I *can* bear although I may have my moments of weakness. Yes, there was such a moment last evening when you said those harsh words to me. It was less the words than the coldness with which they were spoken that made me want to end it all, then and there. Your voice was like a sliver of ice boring slowly through my heart, and I wanted to die. My love for you opens me like a flower, but it can also be open like a wound, red, raw and throbbing. My love makes me suffer and most of the time I welcome its suffering. Indeed, I choose it. And if in a weak moment I cease to welcome my pain, when my suffering is not a joy, then it is a failure in my capacity to love, a failure that I must atone for. *That* is the failure I must overcome.

"I must make myself into a zero for God to act through me, take me where He will," you often say. I, too, must reduce myself to zero in relation to *my* god.

And, oh, my beloved physician, how wrong you are in the diagnosis of my disease! My disease is my separation from you. Your absence is my affliction. The only treatment for my disease is your presence, your return when you are away. My doctor is the cause of my disease, as he is also its cure and its sole physician.

Yours,
Mira

P.S. I am ashamed when I re-read this letter. The way to "zero" is arduous and long. I must learn to follow your script for me; not be the character you think I am and strive to be what you want me to become. I am taking another vow. From today, I shall keep down the shouted protests of my heart, strangle the deep dark sobs the moment they are born. This, my destiny, will henceforth be my delight. Only then can I truly call myself

Your Mira.

Gandhiji left for another tour of the United Provinces soon after, and it was only while he was away from the ashram that he returned to what had happened between them that evening.

Chi. Mira,

Our train being two hours late, the whole of the programme was upset. It was somewhat set right by my foregoing the afternoon rest, and putting off the bath for the night station. I finished spinning at 9:30. It is now nearly 10 p.m. But I may not retire before writing this.

The foregoing preface is to show you, I have been think-ing of you the whole day long. Now that you are away from me, my grief over having grieved you is greater. No tyrant has yet lived, who has not paid for the suffering he has caused. No lover has ever given pain without be-ing more pained. Such is my state. What I have done was inevitable. Only I wish I did not lose my temper. But such is my brutality towards those I love most. But now that you are away from me, I can think of nothing but your extraordinary devotion. May God remove what I consider is your moha [infatuation] or may he open the eyes of my understanding, and let me see my error.

You are to keep well.

Love,
Bapu

Away from Mira, Gandhiji could more easily express his love for her and the special place she held in his affections. He could also acknowledge the tempestuous nature of their relationship. Sending her English translations of Indian hymns, translations he had done especially for her, he writes, "In translating the hymns for you I am giving myself much joy. Have I not expressed my love, often in storms than in gentle soothing showers of affec-tion? The memory of these storms adds to the pleasure of this exclusive translation for you."

In another letter that follows soon after, he tries to explain why he could not accept her devotion.

You are on the brain. I look about me, and miss you. I open the charkha and miss you . . . You have left your home, your people and all that people prize most, not to serve me personally but to serve the cause I stand for. All

the time you were squandering your love on me personally, I felt guilty of misappropriation. And I exploded on
the slightest pretext. Now that you are not with me, my
anger turns itself upon me for having given you all those
terrible scoldings. But I was on a bed of hot ashes all the
while I was accepting your service. You will truly serve
me by joyously serving the cause.

sixteen

*I*N STARK CONTRAST to Mira's intimacy and ease of intercourse with Bapu, my own infrequent encounters with him had continued to be mired in feelings of shame and discomfiture that went back to our very first meeting. However, I have imbibed enough courage from Gandhiji's own example of always publicly confessing his private failings, especially in his autobiography which I read avidly while it was being published in *Navajivan,* to take the difficult step of exposing my own transgression. Thus even if I lack the equanimity with which he could reveal the most trying moments of his life, my association with him has put enough steel in my spine to confess to an incident that occurred in the month of July, 1926. It is an incident of my shame which, whenever it comes back to me, can still make my shoulders twitch involuntarily in embarrassment.

The sky had been overcast that morning. Around 11 a.m., when we had just sat down for our daily Hindi lesson, there was a sudden, uneasy stillness all around us, a vast inhalation as the earth drew in its breath. The sky became dark, as if in a solar eclipse. A nervous, uncertain chatter of birds broke the silence. The wind began to rise in gusts with a high-pitched whistling sound, and rotating pillars of dust, following each other, swept across the ashram grounds heralding the storm that was to soon break upon us. The crack of hailstones hitting the corrugated roof of the dining hall and the windowpanes of Mira's hut drowned out all other sounds. We could no longer hear the snapping of branches, or the frightened bleating of Gandhiji's goat and the lowing of cows from the cattleshed. Then came the rain, a short but heavy shower that washed away the thick coat of dust from the leaves. The downpour was of such ferocity that within minutes large parts of the ground that had baked in the heat of the summer months turned into morasses of mud. Potholes, and streamlets of tawny, guttural water, appeared all over the ashram.

The storm passed, giving way to a soft rain. The fine drops of water glinted in the sunlight as the cloud cover thinned. It was a sight that had never failed to enthrall me as a child, that simultaneous presence of sun and rain, the short-lived miracle of the "wedding of frogs."

Mira was reluctant to continue with the day's Hindi lesson. "Can we just sit quietly for a while, Navinbhai? Just for today?"

I nodded my assent, but she had already turned her face away, offering me her profile, her large, gray eyes looking out of the doorway towards Bapu's hut less than fifty yards away. Suddenly, it was as if I was seeing her for the very first time. My eyes held her face gently, reluctant to let it go: the firm chin, the wide, soft mouth, the smooth skin stretched over high cheekbones. As if aware of my stare, made bold by her serenity, she turned towards me with a smile warm as fresh milk, a smile that disappeared as quickly as it had surfaced; it was but an ephemeral wave of the heart. My sight blurred. I continued to sit still, though with some effort, aware of the urgent beating of my heart, awaiting the return of self-possession so I could leave gracefully.

I can truly claim that till that moment I had not broken my vow of celibacy even in thought (there was no question of ever doing it in word or deed) in spite of all the time Mira and I had spent together. I had been alone with her in her hut for the Hindi lessons, in Bapu's kitchen helping her prepare the food, riding in the tonga showing her around Ahmadabad on our several outings to the city. No untoward thought had ever crossed my mind, in spite of the fact that I had never been alone before with a woman who was not a part of my family. Perhaps this was because she was English, a woman so utterly different from the ones I knew—female cousins and aunts, my sister's friends, sisters of my friends—that as far as I was concerned, she could have been from another planet or belonged to a different species altogether. Without my being aware of it though, her lack of all the familiar attributes of womanhood to which I was accustomed, had in fact enhanced her femininity and made me unconsciously experience her as nothing *but* a woman. I am now convinced that knowing what he did about my "difficulty," Bapu had deliberately thrown us together. I imagine he wanted to strengthen my purpose by exposing it to a searching trial, to steel my resolve through an ordeal by fire so to speak.

I failed him that night. Embarking, in a dream, on a journey to the primal forest within, flinging caution to the winds, my heart's curtain parted to expose my shame that was also an inexpressible wish, a wish that manifested itself in a mortifying solitary deed.

I still have that scrap of paper on which Bapu wrote his short answer to the despairing letter I wrote him the next day. The paper has yellowed with age and the ink is so faded that Bapu's handwriting is barely legible. But I do not need to read what is written there. I know the sentences by heart.

Chi. Navin,

I have received your letter. There is no reason why you should leave the ashram. Especially, when your heart is so full of repentance. Come and see me.

> *Bapu's blessings.*

I was nervous when I went to his room in the evening after the prayer meeting. Not that I had any doubt about his capacity for forgiveness or the depth of his compassion; I knew that Bapu's sympathy for a sinner who accepted he was one and wanted to atone for his sin was unlimited. I was only afraid that he might want to inquire more closely into the details of my lapse. Yes, it *had* happened in sleep; it *was* the recurrence of my "difficulty," the disease of svapandosha, "night fall." Yet, on awakening I had found my hand wrapped around my erect organ, making me doubt whether the emission of semen had been really quite as involuntary and without my conscious participation as I so dearly wished to believe. What I feared most were his questions on what could have led to the lapse, and whether the emission was accompanied by any visual images. I had kept that particular detail tightly segregated even from my own awareness.

For a moment, when I entered Bapu's room and as he looked up at me through his glasses from his seat behind the writing desk, his face grave and unsmiling, my heart sank. But my fear was unfounded. When he began to talk, I could feel the empathy in his voice, and I savored the warm sympathy of his words. He was not throwing alms of compassion to a beggar but respecting me as a person who was trying to pick himself up after falling. That day, the generosity of his heart and the vastness of his love that washed away the stains of my self-disgust overwhelmed me. I began to have faith in myself once again.

I have never seen Bapu talk with so much animation as he

did on that hot and damp July evening. The fervor with which he encouraged me not to give up but to walk again on the path of spiritual growth was like a revelation. One after another, he narrated incidents of heartfelt atonement—from his own life and those of others—which had transformed grave transgressions into unexpected blessings. One of these stories was about a young man who was prepared to commit suicide if that was the only way he could rid himself of the affliction of svapandosha. After Bapu dissuaded him from taking this cowardly step, he began to spin for twelve hours a day and to live in another ashram where no woman was permitted entry.

But the story I remember most vividly was from a period of Bapu's life right after his return from South Africa and before he was known as the Mahatma across the country. It was about a judge who, after retirement, went to live with his best friend. His pension was adequate and he spent most of it on his friend's family, which he regarded as his own. Like the judge, the friend too was old, but he had married for the third time, and brought home a young bride. For a while the old judge was completely infatuated with his friend's wife. When he re-turned to his senses, he was stricken by remorse and decided to atone for his sin.

"What an atonement that was, Navin!" Bapu's voice was full of awe. "He openly confessed the sin of his heart to his friend and also to the friend's wife. Then he shut himself up in a small room, never to emerge again. He refused to meet anyone. The friend tried to dissuade him. Others tried to convince him. But the judge refused to let anyone enter his room and took a vow that he would spend the rest of his life in this self-imposed solitary confinement." Bapu fell silent, as if mentally bowing in reverence before the majesty of such austerities.

"Somehow I learnt about this incident. I was astounded.

By this time, the judge had kept himself in isolation for several years. He had not given audience to any man, not even to the sun-god, nor to any kind of light. I felt an intense longing to meet this great man, so I went there and sent in my request in writing. 'I have been astonished by the firmness of your resolve, the single-mindedness of your atonement. I have come for your darshan. I have not come to break your vow. I have come to learn from you. To gain strength from you,' I wrote. He did not meet me, but sent back a note instead, "I am a sinner. I am repenting. How can anyone think of *my* darshan?'"

It was getting dark. The lamp in Bapu's room was yet to be lit. I could barely make out the outline of his face but sensed that Bapu's eyes were moist with unshed tears. I felt understood in a deep, profound way, and forgiven.

"Bapu, I would still like to go away from the ashram for a few weeks. Be by myself for a while, in silence," I said, my voice full of strength and fresh resolve.

"You have my blessings," he said. "Come back whenever you want and, when traveling, remember to sleep in fresh air as much as you can. Sleep early and be up by dawn. Eat light food, enough to maintain the body but not to fill your stomach. Give up spices."

That night, I lay awake for a long time thinking about all that Bapu had told me. Like a song which for a short while so occupies one's mind that one finds it impossible to be rid of either its music or its lyrics, a poem by Bhartrihari I had studied for my Sanskrit literature class went on repeating itself in my head.

My face is graven with wrinkles
my hair is streaked with gray,
my limbs are withered and feeble
my craving alone keeps its youth.

"I must write down this verse for Bapu," I thought. "Not only would he understand Bhartrihari's self-disgust but even acclaim it as deserving the highest honor."

The verse left me after I wrote it down, but the image of the judge sitting alone in his dark room lingered before my eyes till they closed in sleep.

seventeen

W HEN I LEFT THE ASHRAM that summer, I had expected to be back within three months. But I stayed away for more than three years.

Even though I quaked inwardly at the thought of Bapu's disapproval, I had written to him frankly of the restlessness that had begun to claim me and confessed to doubts that had surfaced on my fitness for ashram life. I could have used my sister's marriage, planned for November of that year, as an excuse for delaying my return, but if there was one thing I had learnt from Bapu, it was the adherence to the dictates of truthfulness, irrespective of consequences.

I was not concerned about my vow of celibacy. I had invested too much of myself into *that* struggle to withdraw from it now, especially when I had just emerged victorious. I knew I needed only a modicum of vigilance in the future to keep the enemy in permanent subjugation. My doubts had more to do with the arousing of a general sensuality in my nature that was unrelated to sex. In the few weeks I spent at home, reconciled with my parents who sensed and welcomed the changes taking place in me, I rediscovered my love of good food. I discovered how much I had missed the hot, spicy taste of my mother's cooking, how I longed for the artfully combined flavors of fried onion, ginger, garlic, coriander, cumin, red chillies and garam masala—none of which were tolerated at the ashram. I remained a vegetarian, of course, but, I am ashamed to say, not at heart. At dinnertime, I could feel the unassuaged longings of my mouth, its drooling wetness when my father's favorite mutton curry, cooked Muslim-style in a thick creamy and spicy sauce, was served. I also indulged my sweet tooth, greedily consuming my favorite piping hot jalebis even between meals.

I was also drawn to the pleasures of poetry and fiction. With Bapu's emphasis on useful bodily labor and dismissal of what he regarded as products of idle fancy, literature had never found a home in the ashram. In my letters I confessed to Bapu that in my constitution my taste buds and literary imagination held sway and, worse, that I was not averse to accepting their sovereignty. I wrote to him that I was reluctant to return till I was free of the doubts that had begun to assail me, that I needed more clarity on the goal of my journey before I could reaffirm my commitment to the ashram. My commitment to him, of course, was undying.

I stayed home for two months, eating, reading and thinking over things, the latter more in the nature of an occasional reverie than sustained inquiry. In September, I decided to make a trip to Benares where my literary hero Premchand was living at the time. It was an impulsive decision, inspired by his new novel *Rangabhumi*, which I had just finished reading. This was his masterpiece, an epic about contemporary Indian life and its diverse facets, unmatched in Hindi literature in its sweep and range. I had always admired Premchand, not only for his literary genius but also for his reverence for Gandhiji, which was evident in his writings.

Before I joined the ashram, I had played with the idea of doing my doctoral thesis on the influence of the Gandhian ethos—truth, nonviolence, the purifying power of suffering, individual conscience as the final arbiter of right action, the Gandhian "fourfold" path, so to speak—in Premchand's writings, especially his novels *Sevasadan* and *Premashram*. In his latest work too, the novelist had not wavered from his commitment to Bapu's ideals. He had continued his practice of having at least one of the main characters in the novel represent Gandhiji's view of life. In *Premashram* it had been Premshankar, who believed that Bapu's constructive program for villages would build a happy society; in *Rangabhumi*, it was the calm and detached Surdas who was the spokesman for Bapu's philosophy of nonviolence. Reading *Rangabhumi* had revived my wish to go back to academics and chalk out an alternative route for my life. In contemplating such a move I was not betraying my commitment to Bapu, just taking another path to serve his ideals, albeit one more suitable to my nature.

When I finally located Premchand's house—no one in the neighborhood seemed to know where the writer lived—in a narrow, winding alley that branched off the main bazaar near Vishwanath Ghat, I was surprised to see how small it was. The man who opened the door was of medium height and build. He was clad in a white shirt and dhoti, both of which needed the urgent services of a dhobi. He had a full head of thick, disheveled hair and a large, arched mustache flecked with gray. My first reaction was of disappointment; Premchand looked more like a peasant than a famous writer. I don't know what I had expected, perhaps someone with the thin, aesthetic face of a Ramana Maharishi, or someone with the commanding presence of Tagore. Soon though, the warmth of his welcome and the intelligence in his gentle eyes overwhelmed me.

On that first day, after I told him I had been living in the Sabarmati ashram, we talked mostly about Gandhiji. Premchand was curious to know details of Bapu's personal life—what he ate, what he read, how he behaved with people who were close to him. He especially enjoyed the stories about the examination of Shyam's stool and how Bapu persuaded Bhansalibhai to unstitch his mouth. He then told me of his own initiation as a follower of Gandhiji. It was 1920 and Premchand had been working as a schoolteacher in a government school in Gorakhpur when Gandhiji came for a public meeting. It was the biggest gathering Gorakhpur had ever seen. Since early in the morning, long lines of bullock carts, carrying men, women and children from the surrounding villages had begun to converge on Gorakhpur from all directions, emptying the surrounding countryside. Premchand had gone to the meeting with his wife and two children. He heard Gandhiji speaking about India's need to recover self-respect and struggle for self-rule and was immediately converted. "The man is a miracle-worker," he marveled. "I came home and immediately, without consulting anyone, wrote out my letter of resignation from the education service of the government. After hearing him, it was impossible for me to continue to serve the alien British rulers. Many people, especially the principal of our school who had become fond of me, urged me to take back my letter. How will you live, they said. At least think about the future of your family. But nothing could shake my resolve."

Premchand's monetary situation had been precarious ever since. Saraswati Press, a printing press he had started in Benares was on the verge of bankruptcy. The writer was aware that his financial acumen left much to be desired. He was scrupulous about meeting all his obligations but reluctant to press his debtors to meet theirs. His straitened circumstances worried him but did not affect his writing or diminish his zest for the pleasures of life, especially good food and stimulating company. By the third and last day of our meeting, we had become friends, or rather we partook of as much friendship as the difference in our ages and my admiration for him (which always creates a certain distance) could permit. I had found our conversations stimulating and inspiring and I guess Premchand enjoyed them too, if not for any insights or interesting observations I might have contributed to them but for my open adoration of his person, the unique contribution of the young in their friendship with the old. It was then that he told me of the offer he had recently received to edit the well-regarded Hindi monthly, *Madhuri*. He had decided to accept the offer, he said. It would mean giving up his dream of running a printing press and also involve a shift to Lucknow from where *Madhuri* was published. He wondered if I would be interested in joining him if a position opened up at the magazine. It wouldn't pay much—literature never did—but he was sure that a small monthly salary, a stipend really, could be negotiated with the publishers.

I was scrupulous in informing Bapu about the possibilities that were opening up for my life. I told him of my wish to stay on in Lucknow and pursue a literary career under Premchand's tutelage. I also wrote that I was translating the Gujarati and English songs sung at the ashram's prayer meetings into Hindi, and I added that I intended to do fourteen to fifteen hours of voluntary work a week at the local Congress office on the village khadi program. I realize now that the translations and voluntary work were a kind of offering, as much an attempt at appeasement as a demonstration of my fealty to his ideals and the expression of my need to remain close to him.

Bapu's reply was short but encouraging. I still have it, written in Gujarati in cheap black ink that has faded into an uneven brown. I held on to this letter when I donated his other letters to the Nehru Memorial Library, where his papers are kept.

Chi. Navin,

I have received your letter. The Hindi translation of the bhajans will be very useful. I leave it to you to judge how much time you will devote to the country and its struggle for self-rule. You must discover for yourself what you need. I have never tried to influence any one to live according to my beliefs. Only when a person has decided to do so, do I then humbly offer myself as a guide. Keep writing.

Bapu's blessings.

———

After a hiatus of almost four years, political activity had finally begun to pick up pace. Across the land, there was an unspoken agreement that it was time to resume the freedom struggle against British rule, and people were looking towards Gandhiji to give the struggle its form and shape. Charged with fresh energy after a year of total withdrawal from active politics, Gandhiji was traveling all over the country, crisscrossing it from north to south and east to west, attending important political meetings and conferences while also gathering funds for his khadi movement from visits to places as far away as Burma and Ceylon.

When at the end of 1928, the Viceroy, Lord Irwin, invited Gandhiji to Delhi for talks, there was a flicker of hope that the looming political crisis might be averted, that the British were prepared to discuss some sort of a plan or even a timetable for Indian self-rule. The talks failed. His Majesty's Government, Lord Irwin informed Gandhiji, had decided to appoint a commission under the chairmanship of Sir John Simon to investigate India's constitutional problems and make recommendations to the government on the future constitution of India. This was all His Majesty's Government was prepared to offer at this and any foreseeable time, and the Viceroy would advise Mr. Gandhi personally, and the Indian National Congress through him, to cooperate with the working of the commission when it arrived in India. Gandhiji, who unlike some of his other colleagues in the Congress was under no illusion about British policy towards India, was not particularly disappointed by the outcome of the meeting. He had expected little else. All over the country, the Congress Party began preparations to boycott the Simon Commission and to hold demonstrations against its visit in the major cities, a prelude to the much bigger mobilization of the country and its people that would soon be required.

In 1928 and early 1929 Gandhiji also suffered personal tragedies. Maganlalbhai, Gandhiji's nephew, who had shared his life for almost twenty-five years, died in April 1928 after a brief illness. Maganlal had managed Gandhiji's first attempt at communal living, the Phoenix Ashram in South Africa. Later, after their return to India, he had been indispensable in setting up and running the Satyagraha Ashram in Ahmadabad. Gandhiji was strongly affected by Maganlal's death. Except for attending the prayer meetings, he completely withdrew from ashram life for a week, closeting himself in Maganlal's hut on the riverbank, less than two hundred yards from his own, to mourn silently by himself the death of a close friend and ally. In a moving obituary, penned for *Young India* under the title "My Best Comrade Gone," Gandhiji's grief and the fortitude with which he tried to bear it finds eloquent expression.

> He was my hands, my feet and my eyes. The world knows so little of how much my so-called greatness depends upon the incessant toil and drudgery of silent, devoted, able and pure workers, men as well as women. And among them all Maganlal was to me the greatest, the best and the purest.

As I am penning these lines, I hear the sobs of the widow bewailing the death of her dear husband. Little does she realize that I am more widowed than she. And, but for a living faith in God, I should become a raving maniac for the loss of one who was dearer to me than my own sons, who never deceived me or failed me, who was a personification of industry, who was the watchdog of the Ashram in all its aspects—material, moral and spiritual. His life is an inspiration for me, a standing demonstration of the efficacy and supremacy of the moral law. In his own life he proved visibly for me, not for a few days, not for a few months, but for twenty-four long years—now alas all too short—that service of the country, service of humanity and self-realization or knowledge of God are synonymous terms.

Maganlal is dead, but he lives in his work whose imprints he who runs may tread on every particle of dust in the Ashram.

In contrast, his sadness at the death of his favorite grandson, a seventeen-year-old youth who had lived with Gandhiji since he was a child, is scarcely visible through the cracks in his self-control. So many years later, rereading the piece "Sunset at Morning" still brings tears to my eyes. His effort was to transcend grief through spiritual understanding rather than through a dulling of the sensibility with which such an understanding is sometimes confused.

"It was not my intention to [publicly] notice his death," Gandhiji writes, "but as the news appeared in newspapers and people have written to me, it seems proper for me to take some note of it . . . As for me, the death of friends and relatives does not hurt as much as it used to. All religions forbid fear of death or grief over death. Yet we are afraid of death and grieve over the death of a dear one. And if someone dies in the prime of youth, there is greater grief. Truly speaking, death is God's eternal blessing. The body which is used up falls and the bird within flies away. So long as the bird does not die, the question of grief does not arise.

"When despite this there is grief on the death of a relative, it only shows our selfishness and delusion. For the past many years, I have been trying to rid myself of this delusion. Hence the shock of hearing the news of Rasik's death was not severe. What shock there was, was due to selfishness . . . He met death while cherishing noble sentiments and receiving unsurpassed care. Everyone will envy such a death. And if a grandfather like me feels grieved at this, it is purely selfishness and infatuation."

In spite of the furious pace at which he drove himself during these years, the ashram continued to be a major focus of Gandhiji's concern, through letters when he was on tour and through personal attention to every detail when he was back in Ahmadabad. Indeed, the prospect of an imminent national struggle against British rule spurred Gandhiji to prepare the inmates for the ordeal ahead. After all, they would provide the model for nonviolent resistance, a model that he hoped would inspire and be imitated on a mass scale. Men, women and even the older children from the ashram would, so to speak, form his Praetorian guard when the time to take up arms against the might of the British Empire finally arrived. In case of the nonviolent resisters their weapons could only be fearlessness and a determination to bear violent onslaught without similarly retaliating, even in their hearts.

Friends from Ahmadabad wrote to me of the heightened sense of purpose that was coursing through the ashram and the changes taking place in it: rules were becoming stricter and their infraction being regarded with greater seriousness than ever before. The training of a nonviolent soldier, Gandhiji kept repeating during the prayer meetings, required two components: spiritual purity and hard discipline, both mental and physical. Anyone telling a lie, stealing, cheating or indulging in any other immoral act had no place in the ashram or in a future regiment of nonviolent soldiers. As for discipline, he said, we have no right to break the law, even one made by alien rulers, till we learn to live our lives by the strict rules we have laid down for ourselves. In an army, the punishment for the breaking of a rule is court-martial; the punishment for an erring member of this nonviolent army will be voluntary separation from the community. After some discussion with the inmates, it was decided that the self-imposed banishment was to apply after three violations of the rules relating to discipline but would come into force with immediate effect with even a single breach of the moral code.

Friends further reported that Gandhiji remained extremely busy whenever he was back at the ashram. He slept for fewer hours at night and each moment of his day had become more precious than ever before. His distinctive laugh, earlier heard often and from different parts of the ashram, was now just a memory from the past. The only time one saw him smiling or even laughing out loud was during the evening walk when he was in the company of children, but these moments were also becoming rare. Appointments with people he could not meet during the day were spilling into the hour he kept for the evening walk. Instead of putting his weight on the shoulders of two boys and spurring them to run fast, he would now be striding towards the Sabarmati prison gate involved in earnest discussions with adults hurrying to keep up with him.

In all this time I did not write to him as often as I would have liked to. Knowing how particular he was about attending to his correspondence and answering all his letters personally, I did not want to further presume upon his time that was in such short supply. Moreover, I had got used to writing to him only when I was mired in a crisis of some sort and needed his advice to find my way. This was, however, a time in my life when I was happy with the work I was doing and the future seemed full of hope. I enjoyed working with Premchand. My job involved editing accepted manuscripts and exchanging literary gossip with him over endless cups of tea. Aspiring writers like Jainendra Kumar who looked up to Premchand as a model and a mentor often joined us. The tea and talk sessions in which discussions over the current political tension had begun to figure prominently often stretched late into the evening when Premchand had to be reminded to hurry back to his waiting wife and children. On Fridays and Saturdays, I worked at the local Congress office where I helped the secretary of the United Provinces branch of the All-India Spinners' Association. This work was my direct link to Gandhiji, and the letters I wrote to him were more in the nature of reports on the spread of the khadi movement in the United Provinces. They did not require a reply. Nevertheless, Bapu would always pen a line or two in acknowledgment and add a personal note saying he thought of me every time he took up my translation of the prayer songs and that he hoped I was looking after my health, physical and moral.

———

It was not as if I was completely out of touch with Mira during these three years. One day, when I went to the Congress office at the end of the week, I found a letter lying on my desk. The Hindi letters spelling my name and address were formed in a child's hand, but the writing was familiar. The letter was from Mira, living on her own in Bihar at the time. She wrote that she had heard about my move to Lucknow from Gandhiji and was glad to know that we were once again connected, this time through our common work on Bapu's khadi movement. She wondered if I could help her by arranging to have another spinning and carding teacher sent from UP. The women from the neighboring villages were now enthusiastic about learning new methods of spinning and carding and she found it difficult to cope with the demand. She would also like to write to me occasionally if I didn't mind. It would give her a chance to practice her written Hindi and she would welcome my corrections. At the end of the letter, without any preliminaries, were the lines, "Yesterday I received a telegram from Bapu. It reads, 'Rhona's wire says father died peaceful Friday night. Peace. Love. Bapu.'" That was all. No further words on how her father's death had affected her. No asking for sympathy. Simply, someone had to be told.

I wrote back conveying my condolences. I said I would try to arrange for someone to be sent from the Spinners' Association here but it would be better if she approached their Bihar office in Patna. I also said that I would welcome her letters and that I had found a great improvement in her Hindi.

This exchange started a correspondence that continued fitfully for the next ten years whenever she happened to be living on her own, away from Bapu. Her letters were short, giving glimpses of her life in the village she was working in then. The letters reveal a shy Mira, quite different from the imperious guardian of Bapu's comfort and privacy I had known in Ahmadabad. I would answer similarly, giving her an outline of what was happening in my life, the rest of my letter correcting her Hindi and in effect constituting a long-distance Hindi lesson. Mira's sentences, like Bapu's, were simple and to the point, erring on the side of terseness rather than excess. Although in my youthful exuberance, I was partial to literary ornamentation, to sentences that twisted and curled into strange and unexpected shapes, I nevertheless appreciated the effort it took her to attain a crisp clarity.

eighteen

*T*HE MOUNTING POLITICAL tension in the country came to a head at the end of December, 1929, when the All India Congress Committee, meeting in Lahore, passed a resolution demanding full independence from British rule. They left the "how" of reaching this goal to Gandhiji. He alone would decide the time and tactics of the battle for freedom.

The next two months were a period of tense anticipation all over the country. People anxiously awaited word from the Sabarmati ashram where Gandhiji had secluded himself after his return to Ahmadabad. As days stretched into weeks, rumors began to sprout around his continuing silence. He is retiring from the struggle, one said, the saint who had strayed into politics was returning to the real business of saints, the pursuit of salvation of the spirit. Another—and this was a favorite among college students in Lucknow—had him endorsing a violent movement to drive the British out; he had given up his faith in nonviolence that had not served the country well and would now exhort the youth of the country to join the revolutionaries.

"How little our young people know Gandhiji," Premchand

said to me. "To believe that he could ever endorse violent ways is to be ignorant even of rumors about his philosophy of life."

Caught up in the excitement of those days, in the general mood of exhilaration tinged with foreboding that prevails before an imminent battle, I asked Premchand for a fortnight's leave. I wanted to be present at the ashram, especially now, when it had become the command post for India's battle for freedom. Premchand was supportive.

"Let's just bring out the March issue of *Madhuri*," he said. "Then you can be away for even longer than two weeks. I will somehow manage the next issue by myself, or ask Jainendra for help."

I was almost too late, reaching Ahmadabad on the evening before it all began.

Mira later told me that it took Bapu many weeks to decide on the shape the struggle should take. What he was searching for was a form of collective action that would capture the imagination and rouse the spirit of the poorest of India's masses. Many expected that his proposed movement would follow the time-honored path of civil disobedience: a refusal to pay taxes to the government, for instance, or the boycott of its law courts, something like that. But Gandhiji was looking for something that touched the life of every villager, and he decided on salt.

"Salt!" the Congress leaders were incredulous when he first told them in a hurriedly summoned meeting at the ashram at the end of February. "Are you serious? You expect us to make salt?" But Gandhiji's arguments and the good humor with which they were advanced soon convinced them. Salt was a basic necessity of life. It could easily be made by us, yet the British imposed taxes on it and exercised strict control on its production. Gandhiji decided that India's freedom struggle should begin by breaking British salt laws all over the country and that he would be the first one to break them.

The letter to Lord Irwin informing him of the decision was characteristic of Bapu. "Dear friend," he wrote on 2 March, "I cannot intentionally hurt anything that lives, much less fellow human beings, even though they may do the greatest wrong to me or mine. Whilst, therefore, I hold the British rule to be a curse, I do not intend harm to a single Englishman or to any legitimate interest he may have in India." He then went on to list the evils and inequities of British rule and his intention to launch a civil disobedience movement aimed at winning independence. "I regard this tax [on salt]," he wrote, "to be the most iniquitous of all from the poor man's standpoint. As the independence movement is essentially for the poorest in the land, the beginning will be made with this evil."

It had to be the most ill-assorted company of soldiers that ever assembled. Some were barefoot, others wore old, brown canvas shoes or cheap leather chappals, the soles reinforced by swaths of rubber cut from discarded truck tires. The men's dhotis began at the waist but ended anywhere between the knee and the ankle. A few were bare-chested, most wore long-sleeved kurtas or had thrown a light cotton wrap around their shoulders. The variety of beards and moustaches, almost equal to the number of clean-shaven faces, represented all parts of British India. The only semblance of uniformity I could detect was in the rough material of the cloth. Every dhoti, every kurta, each wrap, was made from hand-spun and hand-woven khadi. In most cases though, the original white color of the cloth was overlaid with other hues because of repeated washing in the muddy waters of the Sabarmati, from the yellowish tinge of discolored teeth to the light gray of a kid goat's belly hair. But, yes, each soldier wore a new cloth cap, the shapeless Gandhi topi that flopped down to cover most of the forehead.

My first thought was that this was less the vanguard of an army than Shiva's wedding procession so wonderfully described by Tulsidas—"Skulls and snakes and streaks of ashes, matted locks and bodies bare, witches, imps, and frightful goblins, and appalling ghosts were there." I doubted, though, that this particular procession would scare the British as much as Shiva's barat had frightened the citizens of Daksha's capital city.

Yet, for all its sartorial disaster, this was the first regiment of soldiers of the truth-force, Satyagrahis, setting out to fight what we all believed was going to be the decisive battle for the country's freedom. Their soldierly calling was not reflected in their clothes or appearance. Their uniform was the determination in their eyes, the spring in their feet, the aura of elation that hovered around each body marching for the sacred cause of winning independence from British rule. The commander, stepping briskly at the head of the column in spite of his sixty-odd years, staff in hand, his rapid strides forcing his close aides to scramble to keep pace with him, was an unlikely Shiva. Thin but wiry, his ribcage prominent against a tightly stretched skin, Gandhiji wore a short dhoti that ended just above his knees. A heavy steel pocket watch, fastened to the dhoti at the waist by a chain, dangled against his thigh. His bald pate, a gray fuzz covering its sides and back, had begun to gleam with a sheen of perspiration even though the sun had just begun its day's climb.

Since midnight, thousands of men and women had begun to gather along the route the march was going to take, starting from the ashram gate. They came from the city just across the river and also from neighboring villages. Now, as the seventy-nine Satyagrahis approached Ellis Bridge, the crowd pressed against the Congress volunteers who lined both sides of the road, forming human chains with tightly linked hands. The crowd pushed forward whenever Gandhiji drew near. The chain bent, threatening to break, but always held, the reverence in which

Gandhiji was held acting as a brake on the surge of adoration that impelled people towards him. Without breaking his stride, Gandhiji sometimes raised his arms, palms folded, as much in benediction as in an acknowledgment of the love showered on him. He smiled as he did so. For those close enough to feel its full impact, his childlike smile, framed by a straggly gray mustache and exposing five missing front teeth, introduced an odd feeling of protectiveness in the affection and reverence they felt for him.

The huge crowd gathered on Ellis Bridge made it impossible for the Satyagrahis to cross the Sabarmati at that point. After a few minutes of deliberation with Mahadevbhai, the spot Gandhiji chose for the crossing was a couple of hundred yards further down the road where the riverbank sloped down gently towards the bed. Here, at dawn, before the rains came and the river started filling up, one could see lines of undersized Kathiawar donkeys trudging up the bank, with bags of river sand slung over their strong backs. At dusk, they could be seen moving in the opposite direction, patiently clambering down the bank, sure-footed in the sand, crossing the river bed on their way home to nearby villages.

It was now the beginning of summer and the Sabarmati had shrunk to a narrow strip of water meandering through a wide sandbed, the water less than knee-deep. Having crossed to the other side of the river the column of marchers soon left the old part of the city behind them to the left and entered the countryside. For a couple of miles, five to six hundred of the more enthusiastic townspeople followed at a respectful distance, the crowd thinning as the day warmed up and the swirling dust took its toll. It had not rained in many months and the topsoil was dry and loose. A cloud of dust, thrown up by trucks racing up and down the length of the column, settled on the marchers like a shroud. Hired by movie companies, the trucks carried camera equipment and newsreel crews trying to film the march from different angles. Gandhiji's odd challenge to the might of the British Empire had aroused a good deal of interest in many parts of the world. Fox Movietone, J. Arthur Rank and Paramount News, were immediately recognizable from the logos pasted on the sides of their trucks. But there were also other, less familiar names: Deutsche Wochenschau from Germany or Cinepathe from France, for instance, names we never saw on our cinema screens. The technicians, even the British ones, waved to us as the trucks finally sped past the column to wait ahead at the village Gandhiji had announced as the first halt for the day. They all looked alike to us, though, these goras. Mopping their red, perspiring faces with irritated jabs of large handkerchiefs and wearing almost identical uniforms of cotton bush shirts, twill pants and wide-brimmed hats, all in khaki, they looked like white hunters in Hollywood movies setting out on their expeditions to the African bush or the Indian jungle.

Around nine in the morning, after covering a distance of seven miles from the ashram and a few minutes after the trucks and the taxis carrying radio and print journalists had disappeared down the road, we reached Chandola Lake. Gandhiji stopped under a large pipal tree next to the lake, no bigger than a small pond in the middle of a vast expanse of mud at this time of the year. By now, the marchers were in some disarray. Their eyes itched and smarted from fine grains of sand lodged under the eyelids. Racking coughs testified to the valiant effort made by their lungs to resist being choked up by the billowing dust. The distance between the marchers and those who had tagged along in support and out of curiosity had disappeared. When Gandhiji turned to address us, I was close enough to marvel at his appearance. From head to toe, he was covered with a thick layer of dust that had congealed on his skin with sweat. When he began to speak, his voice firm, the movement of his eyelids revealing bright eyes shining with purpose, it was as if a clay statue had awakened to startling life.

"Your surpassing love has drawn you thus far," he said to the townspeople who had accompanied the marchers, his voice hoarse from the dust coating his throat. "I value your affection for me. There were rumors of my being arrested last night. But god is great, mysterious indeed are his ways. Go back and resolve to do your share. Be prepared to offer yourselves as Satyagrahis. At present, though, your way lies homeward; mine, straight on to the sea coast. You cannot accompany me now, but you will have the opportunity to do so in a different sense later."

As I turned to walk back to Ahmadabad with the others, I was unaware that this was the last time I would stay at the Sabarmati ashram, and that almost a decade would pass before I saw Bapu again.

That is why the morning of 12 March 1930, the start of what later came to be known as the Dandi March, remains undimmed in my memory even after a passage of fifty odd years whereas other, more recent, historical events have long receded into the realm of vague recollection. They lie there as old newspaper headlines, flotsam bobbing on the surface of my life's flow, meaningless because unattached to any real feelings. Except, that is, for the parade celebrating Allied victory in the Second World War, which I watched with my father from the balcony of our house.

I still remember its every detail as if it were yesterday. The police brass band playing "It's a long way to Tipperary" as it marched through the main bazaar, at the head of a contingent of smartly dressed policemen in starched khakis and red turbans with tassels hanging from the side. Four lancers in scarlet tunics with golden cummerbunds and wearing crimson turbans rode behind the open carriage bearing our British Collector and his wife—he in a dark suit and gray fedora, she in a pink printed floral dress and a wide white hat with a pink ribbon. Behind the lancers on their high-stepping black chargers, were sundry government officials of the district administration, including my father's colleagues from the Collector's office. They walked clumsily in rows of four, looking self-conscious in rarely worn, ill-fitting suits. I could see the expression on my father's face, a mix of longing and pride. I sensed his desire to be a part of the procession, to strut behind the carriage of the Collector Sahib and his mem. I can still feel his thin arm around my shoulder as he leant forward. For a moment, our political differences were swept aside by obscure currents of genetics and karma that bind fathers and sons. His frail body trembled against mine, seeking solidity and support. The tuberculosis that would kill him three months later was already far advanced.

Indeed, it is only the intersection of personal life and national history that provides us with the most vital connection to the times we have lived in. By itself, history is fated for a quick oblivion, to be then interred in tomes that collect mold on dusty library shelves.

I stayed on in the Sabarmati ashram for almost a month. Although we had written to each other, this was the first time I was meeting Mira after a gap of almost three years. She was thin to the point of gauntness, yet softer than the Mira I remembered from the old days. Under the prominent cheekbones, the set of her wide mouth was no longer as uncompromising as before. The cool light of her gray eyes was warmer, yet also more remote, as if she had begun to look at the world in a kindly but detached way. When she spoke, she was poised, self-confident, with even a hint of her earlier imperious self. She greeted me with perceptible warmth; she was no longer as reserved as she had been when I used to teach her Hindi. She now spoke the language with some confidence, the rush of words unimpeded by the pitfalls of grammar. She merrily confused tense and gender and disregarded quite disdainfully the shortcomings of her Hindi vocabulary. In spite of our involvement in the Dandi march, we did get a chance to spend some time together and catch up on the missing years. Her face glowed as she narrated her experiences of traveling with Bapu through the hot, dusty plains of north India. Sometimes, though, she would become thoughtful even while she spoke, her voice fading into silence. At such moments, her eyes would turn inwards, towards sites of memory to which no one was granted access. As we sat there on the bank of the Sabarmati, almost exactly at the spot where, long ago, I had waited that first evening to compose myself before venturing into Bapu's presence, I did not know that an era, personal and historical, was ending. That the ashram would soon be a shell of its old self, a temple deserted by its deity and emptied of devotees; only a cluster of desolate buildings, many with a door or window missing, would remain and its once faultlessly groomed grounds would be covered with withered weeds.

Caught up in the excitement of unfolding events, we did not dwell on the past. The ashram, of course, provided a ringside seat, with bulletins on the progress of the march received daily from the field. Mira was at the center of this flow of information. Bapu's letters to her gave us the commander's view of the battle's progress. We were told about the unimaginable enthusiasm with which Gandhiji and his band of Satyagrahis, our people from the ashram, were being received all along the route to Dandi, a small village on the coast of the Arabian Sea, 241 miles from Ahmadabad. Huge turnouts were reported at all the public meetings held on the way. In Surat, the largest town between Ahmadabad and Dandi, a meeting was held in the open on the bank of the Tapti river. Surat's total population did not exceed a hundred thousand people, yet the attendance at the meeting was easily twice that, with men and women thronging to the site from villages and small towns all around Surat. A high platform had been erected and equipped with a loudspeaker so Gandhiji could address the crowd. But with the loudspeaker functioning erratically, Gandhiji's low voice was hopelessly inadequate for the mammoth gathering. All he could do was stand on the stage, raise his folded hands in greeting in each of the four directions, before sitting down on a chair. Mahadevbhai had been luckier with the loudspeaker. He gave a short speech, appealing for donations for the Gujarat Congress Committee. People were swarming towards the stage even before he finished. Women took off their ornaments, the well-to-do men their wristwatches and rings. Within minutes there were three heaps on the stage, of valuables, currency notes and coins, which grew steadily. The frenzy continued well past midnight till Bapu left.

Early in the morning, when the marchers set out for Dandi, now less than three days away, it was as if Surat had stayed awake the whole night. The main street of the town through which the Satyagrahis had to pass was so crowded that if a person happened to fall down it would have been virtually impossible for him to stand up again. But for the two lines of Congress volunteers on each side of the road keeping a narrow passage in the middle free, the Satyagrahis would have been unable to resume the march. The windows, balconies and verandas of the tall buildings on both sides of the main street, decorated with garlands of flowers and buntings made of ashok and mango leaves, were crammed with women and children. They pressed against railings and sills, precariously leaning forward to catch a glimpse of Gandhiji as he passed below. The marchers were showered with so many flower petals that they felt as if they were walking on a thin carpet of rose petals.

It was a little after dawn on 7 April 1930, the day when the salt laws were to be broken all over the country, when Gandhiji and his party walked up to the beach at Dandi. The sun was just rising, flecking the high gray surf with strands of orange light. Despite the early hour, the beach was crowded; some had traveled from as far as Bombay and Ahmadabad to witness the occasion. A police force, armed with Enfield rifles and long bamboo stocks, and commanded by two British officers on horseback, stood at a distance. Some of the men from the ashram took off their upper garments and waded into the sea in their lungis and dhotis for a refreshing bath. Gandhiji, who was wearing a lungi, took it off and entered the ocean in nothing but his drawstring shorts. Small, thin and with a bald head that appeared shaven, he looked like a Jain monk, often seen walking in this part of the country, naked, "clad in space." He did not wear the earnest mien of those holy men though, as he waded merrily into the water before being buffeted by a powerful wave that made him lose his footing. He came up gasping for breath, and visibly apprehensive. Some of the men immediately formed a protective circle around him, but Gandhiji's slight frame could not bear the shock of the waves. He staggered from one side to the other under their impact, falling down and then standing up, sputtering and laughing as the waves receded.

After a few minutes, Gandhiji came out of the water. Followed by the Satyagrahis, who in turn were followed by the crowd, he walked towards a spot he had selected earlier on the coast where sea water had been collected in a small hollow dug in the sand. At exactly 6:30 a.m., he scooped some of the water in a pan and held it out towards the sun, breaking the salt law. The Satyagrahis picked up some natural salt lying around in the dried puddles of seawater and carried it back with them. And though the horses of the British police officers pawed and snorted, the watching policemen did not receive any order to intervene.

In the afternoon, Gandhiji spoke at a public meeting. He had expected to be arrested and imprisoned well before reaching Dandi, he said. He now believed that his arrest was imminent. However, the struggle was too big to be stopped by his imprisonment and the civil disobedience movement would be extended to other areas besides the breaking of salt laws. He announced that he had taken a vow not to return to the Satyagraha Ashram at Sabarmati, his home for more than a decade, till India was free from British rule. At the end of the meeting, the few grams of salt he had panned in the morning was auctioned. A textile mill owner from Ahmadabad, Seth Ranchodbhai, paid the princely sum of Rs 525 for Gandhiji's salt.

By the time Bapu and his band of Dandi pilgrims were arrested a month later, I had already returned to Lucknow. I had left the Sabarmati ashram with a troubled heart. I had stayed there for a month to test myself, to probe into the deeper recesses of my mind and find out if my decision to lead a more literary life in Lucknow was the right one. Perhaps I still doubted whether a life of the mind (and at least a modicum of the senses) I had envisaged for myself would also provide enough nourishment for my spirit. Fifty years later, I realize that I still do not have an answer. Perhaps this is a question to which there are no answers, or one to which each must find the answer on his own. I still wonder what it would have been like if I had stayed with Bapu, immersed in a cause greater than myself, guided through the journey of life by a man people have likened to the Buddha and Jesus. Instead I chose to strike out on my own, with a road map of happiness that detailed ways of satisfying the needs and longings of my self. Yes, I chose to seek pleasure, however balanced and sensible my pursuit might have been. I did not orient my life towards the possibility of a transcendence of my physical being, move towards that wonderful silent space free of the unending din of I, me and mine where happiness is not a goal, where questions of pleasure and pain are irrelevant. I was a callow youth then, but I have not become better with age. The wish for pleasure remains strong even as I doubt the value of what I want. Like my enduring conflict around the merits of celibacy, this too is one of the legacies of my years with Bapu.

nineteen

*L*OOKING BACK, the three years following Premchand's death in 1936 was truly the worst period of my life. *Madhuri*'s publisher had tolerated my presence in the editorial office only as long as Premchand was alive. After he died, I had to leave the newspaper and eke out a living giving Hindi tuition to schoolchildren. My voluntary work at the All-India Spinners' Association had ended some years earlier, shortly after my return from the Dandi March. The routine work of entering the amounts of cotton and yarn in ledgers had never engaged either my head or my heart and I had planned to replace it with a deeper involvement in the freedom struggle, but caught up in the pleasures of my literary work and spending convivial evenings with friends, I continued to postpone these plans and they finally came to a naught.

After Premchand's unexpected death—he was only fifty-six when he died—something vital seemed to drain out of my life. I began to inhabit a mental landscape of increasing bleakness. Whether it was teaching the children or meeting friends (who soon dropped off from my life, such as it was), everything seemed pointless. I went through the day's routine mechanically, all thought muffled by a sense of futility. Each day seemed cruelly elongated and even its end did not bring relief since the night, swathed in hours of sleeplessness, was not much better. But more insidious than the pervasive pointlessness were the attacks of self-loathing.

After the Dandi March, I was determined to respond to Bapu's call to the youth to make all the personal sacrifices required to fight for the country's freedom. Many young men had done so, playing havoc with the accustomed order of their lives, sacrificing future career prospects, as they went on to fill British prisons, and they did not even have the benefit of a close personal association with Bapu with which I had been blessed. To my eternal shame, I did not let any higher considerations interrupt my life. I continued my literary work, earning a monthly wage that afforded me small luxuries of attire and palate. This went completely against the grain of Gandhiji's philosophy of life and my own vows at the time of joining the Sabarmati ashram. I had betrayed both.

There was also the matter of celibacy. Even before meeting Bapu, I had been influenced by Tolstoy's writings on the subject and had seriously entertained the idea of remaining unmarried for life. The months at the ashram and of being in Bapu's company had converted the thought into a firm resolve. But in Bapu's scheme of things, which I shared at the time, there was no distinction between thought and deed; a sin contemplated in the mind was as much a sin as one committed in action. God knows, during my carefree years in Lucknow and the excitement (also bodily) generated in the freewheeling, sometimes ribald conversations with friends, I had often broken my vow of celibacy, even if I had technically remained celibate. Now, subject to bouts of self-flagellation (at least they made me feel alive, even if painfully so), my sexual transgressions, though they were such only in my mind's eye, filled me with guilt and despair.

I do not know how I finally summoned enough energy, or simply, the will, to write to Bapu, describing my state of hopelessness as honestly as I could. Perhaps it was my good karma watching over me that made me write the letter that I believe saved my life. "It has been nine years since I left your noble presence," I wrote. "Since then I have been struggling with myself, hoping for I know not what. The struggle goes on but each battle ends in my defeat. For years I clung to literature and art in the belief that they would be the means to my salvation. But what did I get from them? Nothing. Neither my body nor my mind are healthy. I cannot see a remedy for my ills and am losing all hope, if I have not lost it already." At the end of the letter, I expressed the wish (most unusual for me since for three years I had not given it any thought) that perhaps coming to live with him for just a few months would again show me the way I seemed to have lost. Being near him would perhaps restore a vision of purity I once had, which now seemed to have vanished. I did not need to add that what I was looking for was a rekindling of my desire to live.

Bapu's reply came within a week.

Chi. Navin,

I have received your anguished letter. Your ideals are somewhat different from mine so what will you achieve by coming here? Your heart draws you to me, but that is out of infatuation. According to me, the cause of your disease is your passion for literature and you need to give up your literary desires. Or at least your artistic side should be secondary. I would like you to be a labourer, serve others with your hands and your body, but you have no taste for service. I also think you should marry. After marriage you may exercise as much self-control as you like. I don't see any other remedy for the kind of person you are.

If you still insist on coming, I won't stop you. The space here is limited as is the food although you will get enough milk and fruits. Bring a plate, two bowls, a tumbler, spoon, knife, sleeping mat, bedsheet, pillow, umbrella and a lantern with you. May God give you peace of mind.

Bapu's blessings.

This is how it came about that in the early part of 1939, after a break of nine years, I again spent two months with Bapu and Mira, and was eyewitness to scenes that were to herald a tragic train of events.

———

There had been many developments in Bapu's and Mira's lives and in the country's political scenario since Gandhiji's arrest after the Dandi March. After serving time for nine months, Gandhiji was released following an understanding with the Viceroy that the British would call a conference in London to negotiate India's demand for independence. The conference was a failure. Although on the surface the Dandi March, and the civil disobedience that followed it, did not yield any concrete political results, it had united and enthused the masses as never before. It also marked the first time the British consented to negotiate directly with the Congress and Lord Irwin received Gandhiji as an equal. Winston Churchill, the man who is now among the most admired Britons and who loathed Gandhi, understood the significance of this achievement. He found it "alarming and also nauseating to see Mr Gandhi, a seditious Middle Temple lawyer, now posing as a fakir of a type well known in the East, striding half-naked up the steps of the viceregal palace, while he is still organizing and conducting a defiant campaign of civil disobedience, to parley on equal terms with the representative of the King-Emperor."

Mira had accompanied Gandhiji to London and then to Europe. She was in her elements there, looking after his personal needs—his clothes, his food, his sleeping arrangements—and protecting him from those who would presume unnecessarily upon his time. She did not see much of her family. In any case Rhona was the only one left. Her mother had died a few months before she sailed from Bombay. Mira missed her terribly all the days she was in England and was thankful that her complete involvement with Bapu's welfare left her no time for grief.

The highlight of her European trip was the five-day visit to Romain Rolland's home at Villeneuve at the beginning of December, 1931. Both Gandhiji and Mira had been keenly looking forward to this meeting. On the last evening of their visit, after prayers, Gandhi asked Rolland to play him a little of Beethoven. He did not know much about Beethoven's music but he knew that the musician was the intermediary between Mira and Rolland, and consequently between Mira and himself. Rolland played him the Andante of the Fifth Symphony.

Mira's joy was tempered by a strange disquiet as she revisited the scenes of her former free and independent life, but now under conditions of the strictest discipline. "In order to maintain that discipline," she writes, "I had, without realizing it, shut myself up in a self-imposed inner prison. It was when I met Romain Rolland again, and felt the influence of his penetrating blue eyes, that I vaguely knew something was wrong; wrong in the sense that I was not my full self. My spirit silently longed to reach out to him, but I could not emerge from that inner prison. It seemed to be a part of the tapasya which Fate had ordained for me, in answer to those prayers of long ago. So the days passed in a haze of inner sadness which I could not, at that time, explain to myself."

Shortly after Gandhiji's return from Europe, the British began a harsh crackdown on the civil disobedience movement. Gandhiji was again imprisoned. Mira was arrested a few weeks later and spent a year in jail, the first of her many imprisonments. For a while, she shared a cell with Ba. The two women, anxious about Bapu who had gone on a hunger strike in another jail, came closer to each other in their shared distress. They never became friends, though, but the wariness with which Ba had approached Mira in the past did seem to abate considerably.

After her release from jail, Mira went to England and the United States as Gandhiji's unofficial ambassador to explain his philosophy and struggle to important public officials and the media. On her return, she traveled with Gandhiji, looking after his personal requirements, before moving to a small village called Seagaon near Wardha in central India to work on rural development programs he had planned out. She was restless, but maintained an iron control on her emotions in relation to him, living out his script for her without complaint or rebellion. There were several breakdowns in her health, though, necessitating frequent returns to wherever Gandhiji was at the time.

For Gandhiji, the period between 1936 and 1938 was full of marked swings of mood, including episodes of severe depression and spiritual despair. This was partly occasioned by his failure to achieve the goals of removing untouchability and reducing Hindu-Muslim conflict, his two essential preconditions for swaraj; his vision of harmony, tolerance and interdependence among different religious and caste groups seemed to be receding further and further away. The more severe disturbances to his inner peace, however, were due to what he considered as shortcomings in his determined efforts to maintain his chastity resulting from incidents of sexual arousal while he was awake which deeply shamed him, plunging him into a "well of despair." This is when he decided to live by himself in Mira's village. Mira thought she finally had a chance to fulfil her cherished desire to live alone with Bapu in the countryside. Gandhiji, however, was adamant. He would stay in Mira's village only if she herself shifted to a neighboring one. "This nearly broke my heart, but somehow I managed to carry on, and when Bapu finally decided to come and live in Seagaon, I buried my sorrow in the joy of preparing for him his cottage and cowshed. For myself I built a little cottage a mile away on the ridge of Varoda village, and within a week of Bapu's coming to live in Seagaon I departed for the hut on the hill where I lived alone with my little horse as my companion."

Gandhiji's cottage soon grew into a new commune. By 1939, almost a hundred people, including Mira, were living in Seva-gram (or Seagaon, as it was called then), the new political capital of India's freedom movement. Gandhiji, too, after a searching meditation on his lapses from the standard of chastity he had set for himself, seemed to have recovered his self-confidence. "Now that I am at peace with myself," he writes, "none of these national problems worry me. I had fallen in my own estimation but that did not upset me—what upset me was not knowing the cause, or how to act."

———

It was one of the last days of spring that is always much too short—barely two to three weeks of gentle warmth before the onset of the dreaded summer heat—when I arrived in Sevagram. With its hard, rocky ground dotted with sandstone boulders that reflect and thus magnify the tremendous heat, Wardha is one of the hottest places in India. By the end of March, a week after my arrival, the temperature had climbed well above 100 degrees Fahrenheit. "This is nothing," Munnalal, who looked after the accommodation for visitors, told me with doleful pride. "The temperatures often climb to 120 degrees in May and June. If you touch a metal object, a door handle or a window latch, you are certain to burn your fingers." Following Gandhiji's example, I kept my head wrapped in a wet cloth as long as I was at Seva-gram. But in my weakened state of health this precaution proved inadequate and I was promptly confined to bed with what was diagnosed as a severe heat stroke.

Compared to the Sabarmati ashram, Sevagram was not only smaller but also had an unfinished look about it, as if the decision on how it should evolve was being held in abeyance. It had not started out as an ashram but as a place where Gandhiji could stay by himself with only Ba as his companion. He had specified that only locally available material be used to build his hut, and that no more than five hundred rupees be spent on its construction. An area covering one acre was marked out and on it, under Mira's supervision, was built a large room, thirty feet long and fifteen feet wide, with thick mud walls and open verandas. Its roof was made out of bamboo struts, center stems of date palm leaves, mud plaster and tiles. But Bapu's wish to live by himself was not to be fulfilled. In fact, I now doubt whether this was ever a serious intention. Perhaps it was just a response to the stress he had been undergoing of late.

Mira, who was living alone in a neighboring village, was the first to join him. Since she repeatedly fell ill, first with malaria and then typhoid, Gandhiji wanted her near him so he could nurse her. A small cottage, with wattle-and-mud plaster walls, even cheaper than the solid mud wall model, was built for her in one corner of the plot. Within a year, others joined Gandhiji, including a few of his old associates from Ahmadabad. The large room gradually became crowded as more and more people shared Gandhiji's living space, spreading their beddings on the floor of the room, and he was pushed into one corner.

On his doctor's insistence that he needed periods of peace and quiet, Gandhiji moved into Mira's cottage while she had another small hut built for her own use. Since Gandhiji could not stay anywhere without becoming actively involved in schemes for the betterment of the poor, other buildings soon came up. By the time I arrived at Sevagram and was assigned a sleeping place in the large room, spinning of khadi and animal husbandry were already a part of the daily activity. A small demonstration unit that made sugar from date palm as well as two more buildings, part of a center to test and propagate Gandhiji's recently expounded theory of educating through craft, which he called "basic education," were also under construction.

I found Sevagram very different from Sabarmati, not least because of the changes in Gandhiji. In Sabarmati Bapu had been the father of the community; in Sevagram, he was clearly the mother. Sevagram was more relaxed in the matter of rules of conduct. Except the ascetic code of eleven vows that the permanent members of the ashram were supposed to observe, there were no other restrictions on behavior. In Sabarmati, the ashram bell had ruled us; in Sevagram there was only a skeletal timetable and a wide latitude on how an inmate spent his day.

Bapu's motherliness was also much more in evidence because of the high incidence of sickness at Sevagram. Malaria, typhoid, enteric fever and dysentry were rampant in Wardha district and the ashram was not spared from their outbreaks. Gandhiji spent a good deal of his time ministering and personally supervising the various diet and nature-cure therapies in which his faith had never wavered.

Sabarmati had had its fair share of eccentrics and misfits but they were much less in number as compared to those who had flocked to Sevagram. "It has become a kind of shambhooshala, consisting of all kinds of people who would be regarded as cranks or mad by society," I had once heard him say resignedly to Jawaharlal Nehru who was visiting. "But then I am a madman myself," he had added with a smile. "The statement that swaraj can be achieved through the spinning wheel can only come from the mouth of a madman."

And, of course, Bhansalibhai was now ensconced in Seva-gram, thriving on his diet of silence and the thin gruel of flour and neem leaves ground to a paste. Once in a while, overwhelmed by guilt over his imagined transgressions, he would threaten to hang himself upside down, to be then gently persuaded by Bapu to forego this particular form of penance.

———

Mira was away with Bapu on his visit to Delhi for a meeting with Congress leaders when I arrived in Sevagram. They returned the day after I fell ill with acute stomach cramps. Around nine in the morning, less than an hour after his return, Bapu walked into the large room that I shared with ten others. He took my wrist between his fingers to feel my pulse, asked me to show my tongue and palpated my stomach with the tips of his fingers.

"You need an enema," he said. "Come with me."

Except for the deepening of the lines around his mouth and the stubble on his head being sparser and noticeably grayer, he had not changed much in the last ten years. His stride was still brisk and purposeful. In my weakened state I staggered a little as I tried to keep up with him. He stopped to steady me. Then, to my embarrassment which was considerably more than any pain I felt, he placed my left arm around his neck and circled my waist with his right hand, supporting me.

"I can walk to the bathroom by myself, Bapu," I said. "I know how to take an enema."

He ignored my protests and called out to Mira to have my enema ready. To my horror, as I lay on my stomach on the table in the bathroom, waiting for Mira, Bapu showed no signs of leaving. He adjusted my legs and told me exactly how he would like me take the enema, watching me closely while I carried out his instructions. I again pleaded that there was no need for him to stay any longer, that I would later walk to the latrine unaided. He paid no attention. From a bottle of oil on the shelf, he poured some on his palm and began to slowly massage my stomach. A mellow warmth spread outwards from my navel conjuring inchoate memories of my mother's massages when I was a small boy. The reverie was broken by Mira calling from outside, reminding Bapu that he had an appointment in Wardha that morning. But Bapu did not leave till he had finished. On his way out, I heard him instructing Mira that my bed should be moved into his cottage.

It took a week for me to recover. I spent most of the time lying on a mattress on the floor of the small room adjacent to Bapu's bedroom. Bapu came in thrice a day to monitor my condition and to prescribe treatment. He was the doctor and Mira the nurse. Gandhiji's favored regimen for any illness, or for that matter, health and well-being in general, was a nutritious diet. For my daily dose of two glasses of tomato juice, I remember how particular he was while explaining to Mira that red and ripe tomatoes were to be picked. They should be first washed and then held under boiling water and squeezed over fine muslin so that not a single seed slipped into the juice. I was to also drink three cups of fresh, raw milk each day and as much tamarind water as I could take. (Bapu was an enthusiastic proponent of tamarind as a cure for most ills at the time.)

Mira and I had been out of touch for four years, yet she welcomed me like an old friend. Her concern about my health was more than a duty imposed upon her by Gandhiji. We would talk a bit when she brought me my meals, consisting of various liquids and the fruit Bapu had prescribed for me for that day. In the last ten years, she said, she had seldom been happier than she was now. The happiness showed on her face, smoothening new lines that had not yet etched themselves firmly into the skin. It showed in the occasional glint of amusement in her eyes that edged towards a smile although it would always fall short of laughter. It showed in the confident way her body moved as she walked, with a step and a swing of the shoulders that was more attuned to the female architecture of her body. There was a softness about her now, an absence of tension that I was hard put to explain. Yes, she was glad to be with Bapu and serve him, although sometimes she sensed that he would like her to go away and work on her own. She had never really enjoyed carding and spinning and had stopped giving lessons. She now worked in the cowshed with a young boy as helper and derived ample satisfaction from looking after and milking the three cows and Bapu's goat.

One thing, however, remained unchanged: she was still ferociously protective of Gandhiji. Bapu's instructions had been that I should be given as much fruit as I wanted. With the return of my strength, and the surge of life that had lain dormant for three years, my weaknesses too resurfaced. A major one, intimately related to my craving for good food, was a tendency towards gluttony. In the absence of cooked food and subsisting mostly on a liquid diet, I began to overindulge myself on fruits. Oranges were not a problem; they were cheap and plentiful in that part of the country. But it was the bananas, sent in parcels to Bapu by well-wishers from other regions where bananas were plentiful, that I craved for. Mira kept the bananas locked in the storeroom. When I expressed my desire to eat some, she was clearly unhappy. "Should we not leave them for Bapu?"

But I was insistent. Reluctantly, she picked out two bananas that were pulpy and discolored with unappetizing black patches. "We shouldn't waste the fruit," she explained.

Each day I would get the two or three bananas that had become ripe overnight and since Gandhiji was off fruits at the time, no one ever got to eat a good banana.

twenty

N EVER INTRODUCE a new character after a novel is half-
way through," Premchand often used to say. But I
am helpless. For the course of a life does not follow the rules
of good fiction.

Prithvi Singh's entry into Mira's life, and heart, may have
been late, but it was nevertheless fateful in its consequences. The
excitement that gripped Sevagram when Prithvi Singh arrived
reminded me of the day Bhansalibhai had returned to the Sabarmati ashram from his Himalayan wanderings. Prithvi, though,
was coming back from a British jail where he had spent the last
sixteen months. No one had counted on an early release, least
of all Prithvi himself. Bapu's pleasure at seeing him was partly
due to the fact that his advocacy with the authorities on Prithvi's
behalf had finally met with success.

Prithvi was a strikingly handsome man who looked much
younger than his forty-seven years. Tall and broad-shouldered,
his physical attractiveness was immeasurably enhanced by the
aura of a legendary revolutionary who had spent most of his

adult years underground, fomenting violent resistance to British rule.

Of Bhatti Rajput stock, Prithvi was the eldest son of a Punjabi subsistence farmer. During the famine of 1898, his father left for Burma where he established a small business selling milk. When Prithvi was nine years old, he joined his father in Burma and started studying in a missionary school while helping him run the business. When he returned to India six years later, he knew neither Hindi nor Urdu and had to start afresh in class four of a school in Ambala, Punjab. Now free of the daily chores of feeding his father's cattle and helping in the cooking of their meals, Prithvi, who was an intelligent lad, studied hard and passed three grades in one year. At the age of seventeen, now a tall and strapping boy, he left for Burma to find that the outbreak of a disease had killed off most of the cows and that his father lay sick in bed. Forced to earn a living, he took a job sorting letters in the post office.

Ever since he was a child, Prithvi had been imbued with a strong conviction that he was destined to achieve great things in life. Sorting letters was clearly not part of a superior destiny and Prithvi Singh decided to seek his fortune in China. He first traveled to Singapore via Penang and then boarded a ship bound for Hong Kong.

His introduction to the world of revolutionary activities makes for an interesting story. In Hong Kong in June 1911, while going to report for duty at the soda water bottling factory where he worked as a security guard, he was surprised to see heaps of pigtails lying at various crossroads across the city. He soon found out that the Chinese were beginning to identify long pigtails as a symbol of slavery, and cutting them off was their first act of revolt against the monarchy and the imperial power. Prithvi did not know the goal of the Chinese revolution, but he was astonished to see the change it wrought in the personality of the Chinese. Whereas earlier an Indian policeman, generally a hefty Sikh, could drag four to five unprotesting Chinese coolies to the police station by their pigtails, the Chinese now often fought back and put the policemen to flight. Prithvi and his friends held long discussions on the growing self-respect among the Chinese, and wondered whether Indians too would one day find in themselves the strength and impetus to throw off the yoke of slavery and walk with their heads held high.

When Prithvi heard that young Indians were being trained for revolutionary activity in the motherland, he decided to go to the United States. On board the ship bound for Seattle, he became the informal leader of a group of forty Sikh peasants who were traveling to the United States in search of work. Since he was the only one in the group who spoke English, the immigration officer appointed him the translator for the group and asked him, "And why have you come here?"

"I have come to learn from you how I can free my country."

The officer just sat there without speaking a word, looking at Prithvi who was by now convinced that all was lost. The American finally stood up, smiled, shook Prithvi's hand and said, "Welcome to the United States."

I suspect that in recounting this particular incident, as in the case of some others, Prithvi had not been strictly truthful. He was not averse to occasionally garnishing his biography as an intrepid revolutionary. For instance, he portrayed himself as a founder member of the Gadar Party along with such luminaries of the Indian freedom struggle as Lala Hardayal and Udham Singh. His name is, however, nowhere to be found in the list of the party's founders. No doubt he regarded his small lies as innocent embellishments, exaggerations necessary to bring out the truth more clearly, like an exquisitely crafted setting that enhances the beauty of the gem.

One of the more quixotic incidents of the Indian freedom struggle is the story of a ship that sailed from San Francisco to Calcutta on 5 August 1914. The ship carried a hundred young men, mostly Punjabi Sikhs who had emigrated from India to work as farm laborers in California. Prithvi, then a youth of twenty-two, was on board this ship. He was one of the hundred men, all members of the revolutionary Gadar Party, who sailed that day to do battle with the mighty British Empire under the erroneous impression that, with the outbreak of the First World War, conditions in India were ripe for a revolution.

When the ship neared Hong Kong, the revolutionaries realized that if they entered a British colony, with their firearms, they would be thrown in prison and the revolution aborted even before they reached Indian shores. The pistols and guns bought in America were therefore thrown overboard. The agents of the British-Indian secret police, the CID, who were also traveling in the same ship, finally acted when the ship reached Calcutta. Some of the Indians, who the police had identified as ringleaders were arrested, while others were put on board a special train for Rawalpindi guarded by the Punjab CID and a contingent of Gurkha soldiers.

In the absence of any evidence that a crime had been committed, most of the men were released at Rawalpindi station. Others, Prithvi among them, were detained for further questioning. Then it started raining and while the CID officers on the railway platform were unfurling their umbrellas, Prithvi climbed out of the window of his compartment and quickly melted into the crowd.

Many members of the Gadar Party had traveled to India singly and by other routes than the public one taken by Prithvi and his shipmates. Since most of them were of Punjabi peasant stock, which also supplied the British-Indian army with some of its finest regiments, the intention of the revolutionaries was to organize soldiers, many of them friends and kin from Punjab's villages, to mutiny against their British officers. Politically naïve, intoxicated by their own rhetoric of patriotism, they were unaware of how little support they could count upon for their cause—the Indian National Congress, the foremost Indian leaders, Gandhi and Tilak, and more importantly the chief organization of the Sikhs in Punjab (the center of their activities), the Khalsa Diwan, were all in sympathy with British war aims. Starved of funds, the revolutionaries turned to armed robbery to finance their activities and were soon wanted by the police. Betrayed by an old school friend, Prithvi, then operating from his home district of Ambala, was captured during an encounter with a subinspector of police who had been sent to arrest him. The policeman was seriously injured and Prithvi, wounded in the struggle, was sentenced to ten years' imprisonment for attempted murder. Here, Prithvi got his first taste of an Indian jail. Every prisoner had to grind forty pounds of wheat in a chakki each day and was beaten if he failed to fulfill his quota. In his memoirs, he writes, "My palms were soft and I first made them callused by rubbing them for twenty days against the iron bars of my cell. I was determined to do everything required of me without complaining. I was kept in a prison block with prisoners waiting to be hanged. No one except warders and scavengers were allowed in this area. The prisoners were let out for a few minutes in the morning. The meals were passed to us through the bars."

Meanwhile, in spite of being constantly on the run from the police, the revolutionaries had met with some success in contacting Indian soldiers in the military cantonments. Their plan was to capture the cantonments of Mian Mir and Ferozepur in Punjab and to engineer mutinies in the cantonments of Delhi and Ambala. The preparations for a revolt, slated to take place on 15 February 1915, were betrayed to the police by an informer who had managed to infiltrate the central committee of the conspirators. Widespread arrests followed.

In the Lahore Conspiracy trial which took place later that year, Prithvi and twenty-four others were sentenced to death by hanging, twenty-five were sentenced to life imprisonment on the Andaman Islands, in the infamous Kala Pani prison, and ten revolutionaries were assigned varying lengths of imprisonment. Of the twenty-five sentenced to death, fifteen were Prithvi's associates from the United States who had been arrested when the ship had docked in Calcutta and had been in jail ever since.

"There could be no appeal against the tribunal's judgement," he writes in his memoirs. "We were all to be hanged the next morning. There was no reason to delay. The prison grapevine had it that we were to be hanged in groups of five. I wanted to be in the first group, to lead the others to death, but the decision was out of our hands.

"At four in the morning, a bucket of water was placed before the door of my cell that I shared with eight others. This meant we were to get ready to face our Maker. We used small cups to take the water through the bars of the cell and bathed. We then washed the floor and finished our prayers. We waited for the policemen to come and take us. We waited and waited. Hours passed. In the afternoon, the British jail superintendent suddenly appeared before the door of our cell. We thought he had come to tell us the time fixed for the hanging. But we were surprised and saddened when he said we could write to the Viceroy asking for a pardon. To ask pardon, to beg for life! In the evening of my short revolutionary life, even to contemplate such a step was despicable. 'I want to die for a free India, not live in an enslaved one,' I said. The others clapped, and although the Englishman did not say anything, I could see the admiration in his eyes."

As it happened, only seven of the original twenty-five were hanged. The death sentence of the others, including Prithvi Singh, was commuted to life imprisonment and banishment to the pestilential Kala Pani. Prithvi spent seven years in the Andaman jail, enduring many hardships that embittered him at the same time as they hardened his resolve to spend his life—whatever remained of it after his sentence was completed—fighting the British. In 1922, he was repatriated to the mainland and while being transported to Nagpur Central Jail, he escaped by jumping off a running train.

Prithvi writes with characteristic flourish of the days following his escape. "When I jumped from a running mail train, there was no knowing what would happen. Would I meet instant death or live to bring freedom to the country? Life might have been extinguished just as I fell out of the train. I could have been shot down as I stuck my head out. There was a strong likelihood of my getting disabled. This adventure was a touch-and-go affair. Similarly, last year, after sixteen years of underground life when I surrendered to the British Government at Gandhiji's behest, it was a leap in the dark. I knew that those whom I had treated as my enemies would not trust me. A government that was making all-out efforts to track me down could not let me off so lightly once I surrendered. I could have been hanged on any flimsy charge or I may have been left to languish in prison for the rest of my life or killed in an encounter, real or fictitious. Despite this I surrendered because I wanted to blaze a new trail for the youth of the country."

———

Although I could now sit up and even go for a short walk, I had continued to stay on in Bapu's cottage. Sitting on the floor in the doorway between the two rooms, leaning back against the doorjamb, I was content to be in Bapu's presence as he worked at his desk, dictated letters or met his visitors. This is how I came to be privy to his discussions with Prithvi Singh during his evening visits before Bapu retired for the night. The only other person present during these meetings was Mira, who took notes instead of Mahadevbhai who was away in Gujarat on a family matter.

While Prithvi believed that Gandhiji was one of the greatest men of all times, he remained unconvinced about Bapu's philosophy of nonviolent resistance. "Bapu, you must admit that you have failed. The best men in the land took up your program under your direct guidance and inspiration. Thousands of young men, the flower of youth of our country, embraced it with all the enthusiasm they could muster. Sacrifice and sincerity on the part of your followers was not lacking by any means. Yet, so many years of nonviolent resistance has brought India no nearer to freedom."

"I don't agree," Bapu responded. "My program has awakened the masses. It has increased their capacity for nonviolent resistance. The nonviolence I teach is active nonviolence of the strongest, but the weakest can partake in it without becoming weaker. They will only be stronger for having been in it. The masses are far bolder today than they ever were. I hold that the world is sick of armed rebellions. I hold, too, that a bloody revolution will not succeed in India. The masses will not respond. A movement in which masses have no active part can be of no good."

But Prithvi was adamant. "How can you still believe that England will be just and generous out of her free will? The England which believes in Jallianwala Bagh massacres as a legitimate means of self-defense? The England that sent scores of innocent peasants to the gallows in the Lahore Conspiracy trials in which I—I proudly admit *my* guilt—was sentenced to death for the love of my motherland?"

"My appeal is to the virtue, not the vices that are also present in all men. Armed conspiracies against something satanic are like matching satans against satan, and since even a single satan is one too many for me, I would not multiply him. An eye for an eye will surely make the whole world blind."

"Bapu, I can never agree with you in your intolerance of the revolutionaries. I know them. They are my comrades. Indians were miserably afraid of death, it was our revolutionary party that made them realize the grandeur and beauty that lie in dying for a noble cause. How can you condemn a revolutionary who does not shrink from death, who does good and dies, who believes that ideas ripen quickly when nourished by the blood of martyrs?"

"That is precisely what I question, Prithvi. In my opinion, he does evil and dies. I do not regard killing or assassination or terrorism as good in any circumstance whatsoever. I do believe that ideas ripen quickly when nourished by the blood of martyrs. But a man who bleeds slowly of jungle fever in service of others bleeds as certainly as the one on the gallows, and if the one who dies on the gallows was guilty of another's blood, he never had ideas that deserved to ripen.

"I do not deny the revolutionary's heroism and sacrifice. But heroism and sacrifice in a bad cause are so much waste of splendid energy, and thus hurt the good cause by drawing attention away from it. Self-sacrifice of one innocent man is a million times more potent than the sacrifice of a million men who die in the act of killing others. The willing sacrifice of the innocent is the most powerful retort to insolent tyranny."

"Would you then condemn Guru Gobind Singh as a misguided patriot because he believed in warfare for a noble cause?" Prithvi asked. "Would you say the same about other heroes of our history, Shivaji or Rana Pratap? Or for that matter heroic revolutionaries of other countries, Washington, Lenin, Garibaldi?"

"I do not hesitate to say that it is highly likely that had I lived as their contemporary and in the respective countries, I would have called every one of them a misguided patriot, even though a brave and successful warrior. As it is, I must not judge them. I disbelieve history so far as the details of acts of heroes are concerned. I accept broad facts of history and draw my own lessons for my conduct as long as they do not contradict the highest laws of life, but I positively refuse to judge men from the scanty material furnished to us by history."

Here, using Mira's notes and from my own recollections, I have condensed those evening conversations on violence and nonviolence into a single, running dialogue. Although Gandhiji's words are his own in Mira's notes, I notice that she has considerably edited Prithvi's interlocutions. She has taken a great deal of trouble to improve his English. She has even cut out repetitions, replaced words and added sentences of her own, to give Prithvi's part of the conversations a coherence and consistence that is lacking in the original record. Her concern that in the event of publication Prithvi Singh should make a good impression is touching.

These discussions, however, were not limited to the role of violence in a just cause. Actually, such conversations were few and far between. Prithvi Singh's rhetorical and intellectual gifts were far inferior to the courage of his convictions. What Bapu liked was to hear Prithvi Singh talk about his life. In fact, we would all be enthralled as we listened to him narrate incidents from his life crammed so full with adventure. Uneducated in a formal, academic sense, he was both shrewd and naïve, with that mixture of sincerity and innocent vanity (he *was* somewhat of a peacock) which makes for a gifted raconteur. He was consequently in great demand as a speaker in the Gandhian institutions that had come up around Wardha. Laughingly, he once told Bapu that Kaka Kalelkar, who was in charge of the Mahila Ashram for the training of young village women, had come up to him that morning and said, "Look, Prithvi Singh, don't take it personally, but could you be less intense when you talk to our girls? Don't look into their eyes when you speak. They become very attracted to you."

I could sympathize with poor Kaka Kalelkar. Adventurous without being an adventurer, Prithvi Singh was the kind of handsome idealist who, even without trying, was more irresistible to women than a good-looking rake with all his seductive arts. Bapu, too, had joined in the laughter.

"Yes, Prithvi, virility and manliness are very prominent in you," he said. "If you can absorb the young girls' love for you and kindle in their hearts the fire of love for the country, then you can rise high and make them rise high too. But if you yield to sexual passion, then both will fall."

Prithvi was not one to be overawed by Bapu, perhaps one of the reasons why Gandhiji devoted so much time and effort trying to convince him of his ideas on sex and violence. I don't think the rustic Punjabi, so full of animal vitality, ever understood that for Bapu sex and violence were infinitely more than biological promptings of the body. They were pathways to the highest truths of human life, their connection with the realm of the spirit obscure yet essential. Bapu had ceaselessly explored this connection in the course of his own life, an exploration that had been accompanied by considerable inner turmoil.

"Forgive me, Bapu, but in your ashram is there place for anything other than sex? During their leisure time, the people here constantly discuss the subject. It seems to me that in obedience to your wishes and in an emotional mood, people may take a vow to lead a celibate life but they have not the slightest idea how passions rock the mind and how to control them. I shall remain celibate in the ashram not because I don't want to marry someday—I do—but because I believe in the value of military discipline. As long as I stay here, which can be quite some years since the government has released me in your care, you may be assured that I shall be more zealous than anyone in following the ashram rules. Irrespective of whether I agree or disagree with a particular rule."

I don't remember what Gandhiji said in reply. I did, however, steal a glance at Mira, thinking she would be horrified, not only by what Prithvi said but also by the way he talked to Bapu, man to man, respectfully, yes, but utterly without reverence. She was looking at him in a strange way; I could not quite decipher at the time what was going through her mind. In retrospect, I was a fool not to have understood right away. The expression on her face was unmistakably Desdemona's, as she devours "with a greedy ear" Othello's discourse on his battles, sieges and fortunes, and his story being done, gives him for his pains "a world of sighs." Of course, since life lacks the symmetry of literature, Mira might have fallen in love with Prithvi for the dangers he had overcome but he could not claim that he "loved her that she did pity them."

twenty-one

SOMETIMES MIRA had a suspicion that Bapu was intentionally trying to throw Prithvi and her together. There were other, better carders of cotton and spinners of yarn in the ashram, but it was Mira who was appointed as Prithvi's teacher. When Bapu asked Prithvi to pen his memoirs, which he thought would be an inspiration to the younger generation, it was Mira who was asked to edit the chapters and polish his English as he wrote them down.

Later, much later, as Mira tossed in her bed at night, unable to sleep, far away in the remote settlements that she, in her restlessness, had sought out for her work, she would wonder what Bapu had intended. Had he seen how attracted she was to Prithvi much before she admitted the attraction to herself? Had he known, with his sometimes uncanny prescience, that any chance of happiness in her future lay in being with this man, and thus encouraged their budding intimacy? Was he testing the strength of the vows she had taken when she had come to him that evening in the Sabarmati ashram and he had cropped her hair? Or was this a test, not of her vow of celibacy but of her commitment to him, a testing of her heart when presented with a choice?

At first, she fought against her growing attraction to Prithvi. She concealed the real nature of her feelings by convincing herself that it was admiration for his frank and fearless nature. One evening, she went for a walk with Prithvi after they had worked on the chapter of his fight with the police inspector sent to arrest him. He had told the story before but had skipped its details to spare Bapu's sensibilities. Now, sitting on a hillock outside the village, looking down at the peaceful scene of cattle returning after feeding in the scrub during the day, Mira thrilled to the images her mind conjured up of the struggle that could have easily ended in the death of one of the men. In the dim light of Prithvi's room, she could see the two men grappling in the dark. She saw Prithvi grabbing the inspector's revolver and throwing it away and the policeman taking out a knife from his pocket and burying it in Prithvi's arm. She heard him roar like a wounded lion but, unmindful of the pain, grab a fistful of the policeman's hair and repeatedly dash his head against the wall till he slumped down, unconscious. She blushed furiously when Prithvi caught her staring at the thick puckered scar left behind by the knife wound. It stretched from the wrist to the elbow of his left forearm, a menacing dark crimson against Prithvi's smooth, light brown skin.

On their way back to the ashram along the narrow, muddy path pitted with deep imprints of hooves Mira and Prithvi stood to one side to let the cattle pass. Suddenly, an ox with large horns swerved and rushed towards them. Without a moment's hesitation, Prithvi pulled Mira back. Placing himself in front of her, he grabbed the ox by the horns and forced it to one side. Mira had not been afraid but she felt oddly shaken. As they walked back in silence, Mira seemed to be deep in thought.

"Are you all right?" Prithvi asked.

Mira gave him a wan smile. "You know, Prithvi, I have never

wished for the protection of a man. I have never wanted a man to consider me weak and to come to my aid because I am a woman. Why did you do this?"

The question she had asked was a lie, her first untruth. The real question raging in her mind was, "Why did I like what you did?"

Honorable to a fault, honed to the highest standards of truth by her nature, background and years with Gandhiji, Mira admitted her true feelings to herself as soon as she was aware of them. Spending so many hours together every day yet longing to see him again a few minutes after they had parted was incompatible with the fiction of mere admiration, as were the trembling in her legs and the lurching of her heart if his hand happened to touch hers during the spinning lessons. His touch had become a caress that did not disappear with the lapse of time. It lingered at the tip of her fingers or on the back of her hand with a persistent tenderness, like a long-awaited guest in the house of her flesh.

Mira's attraction had not yet become the helpless passion that was to consume her later when being with him would no longer feel like bliss but a curse from which she would hate to be freed, when their every meeting would be full of pain and yet she would long for the next meeting, when she would close her eyes to the truth about what they meant to each other and be grateful for everything that kept her illusions intact.

Her letters to him when he was away from the ashram on short trips (and these became increasingly frequent), reflect the change. At first, she writes only about the manuscript—". . . I shall start reading it properly tonight. In it I see you striving to express your real self and yet finding it difficult. Because of the language difficulty you even give a wrong impression of yourself at times. But it is a precious and remarkable book which must see the light of the day. When you come here we must go through it together and if I can help you to give full expression to your thoughts, the joy will be mine." But in the very next letter three days later, dated 5 November 1939, there are the first shy overtures towards the author. ". . . A week is over but instead of your coming back, I have only received one letter . . . I won't say anything more than this: don't stay away too long . . . My hut is more than half-done. You will have a corner there. I take the responsibility that no one will disturb your peace there if you want to be by yourself."

I remember how cheerful Mira was during the three days that Prithvi Singh was back at the ashram. They worked on his spinning and his manuscript, and took long walks in the evening. I met her only once as she was coming out of Bapu's hut one morning after cleaning it. She was full of plans for her future work, of leaving Sevagram soon and starting an ashram of her own, dedicated to Bapu's vision of improving the condition of Indian villages. Nothing was concrete yet, she said, and then tenderly inquired after my health. I could have sworn that there was a glint of mischief in her eyes when she asked if I would like to have more bananas.

I also remember that we rarely saw her during the days Prithvi was away from the ashram. She carried out her allotted chores, attended the prayer meetings, but was otherwise confined to her cottage. She would emerge in the afternoon when the postman came from Wardha to deliver the ashram's mail. In the secretary's office she would rummage through the pile to see if there was a letter for her. Wordlessly, she would then hand the postman a letter to be mailed from Wardha and walk back to her hut, her face impassive.

On 11 November, a day after Prithvi left, she wrote two letters to him. One says, ". . . God has changed the vague pain of all these years into a burning fire. But the great difference is that now I know why that pain and why this fire. I have found you at last! . . ."

In the second, she writes about Gandhiji's reaction to her proposal that Prithvi and she would work together.

> I will not overburden you with letters in the days to come, but this morning you must let me write . . . God is giving me strength and understanding and turning my pain into joy, deep joy.
>
> Yesterday I was overwhelmed. You were to go away, and at the same moment I realized for the first time that perhaps in the future we may not see very much of each other. I had no time to gather myself and if I clung to you for a moment, it was because the pain was unbearable. That is past.
>
> Yesterday evening on the walk I talked with Bapu. I told him about what you and I had discussed about taking up his work. He said, "I should now like you to be guided entirely by Prithvi Singh. You have understood one another, you need that guidance and he can give it to you." So there we are! Do not feel burdened by this change. Simply look upon me as a further means of serving the country.

I know from Prithvi Singh's memoirs that he felt flattered, overwhelmed and deeply uneasy, all at the same time. Mira had traveled too far on a path he had no intention of taking. Her letters were becoming the importunate beseeching of a woman hopelessly in love. They were cries from her heart to which he needed to close his ears.

twenty-two

THE FIRST TIME Mira told Gandhiji about her feelings for Prithvi was on the day she went to him with Prithvi's letter. "It is a very good letter," he said after he read it. And it *was* good, full of noble sentiments of service to the nation that the two of them were destined for, of the similarity of their ideals for life and his admiration for her. If Gandhiji noticed the impersonal tone of the letter, he did not comment on it. Mira told Gandhiji she felt that at last she had met someone with whom she could work outside Sevagram.

"With him, I can become independent of you, as you have always wanted," she said.

Gandhiji looked at her, his face grave, and said, "If you feel like that it means to my mind that you should marry him." Then he added, as if thinking aloud, "Perhaps marriage has been the unspoken word in your life."

Mira was speechless. "My mind and emotions were in a whirl," she writes. "For him to say that after all these years! The years of restlessness and anguish, the holding fast to ideals and the effort to attain them—could they be reduced to my lacking what every housewife has without even particularly valuing it? No, Bapu could not have meant that! He could never be so unkind! He could not hand me the ashes of my life in such a tawdry bag."

Bapu saw the confusion on her face and gave a wan smile. "To my mind, your former resolve not to marry should not stand in the way. If you are concerned about me and the vow you took when you joined the ashram, then I absolve you from that vow."

The whole conversation barely took five minutes. Bapu looked more weary and resigned than sad as he watched her go. Mira's own feelings were so strong and conflicting that when she walked out of his room she felt dizzy, as if the breath had been knocked out of her. And then, for a little while, she felt extraordinarily happy.

To Prithvi she wrote, "Your precious letter has come. As soon as I had read it, I went straight to Bapu. He was alone. I gave it to him. He read it through, then looking up into my eyes he said, 'It is a very good letter.' I had not dared to hope you would write. I even feared that I might have displeased you for I feel so utterly unworthy. This very morning, as I was walking upon the hill, the anguish in my heart forced tears into my eyes.

"Oh! Prithvi, you do not know what you have been to me. I have strived and strived to serve Bapu and his cause, but have been weak and wanting in all my endeavours. I have been but half a being. You have made me whole . . . Bapu understands everything and he will guide us. With his blessing the true path will open up before us one day . . . ."

The fearless Prithvi Singh, renowned for his courage and daring in the fight against the British, fled. His thoughts about Mira, her passion for him and her devotion to Bapu are recorded in his memoirs.

Just like the way Mirabai was absorbed in God, I saw this English lady absorbed in Bapu. Yet I never saw the lines of satisfaction on her face. I was troubled by the question why persons living so close to Bapu did not use Bapu's mantra of life to make their own lives happier? There were many who served Bapu but Mirabehn's service to him was marked by singular feelings of love and dedication. But still, I did not believe what I saw. I used to think, "Why is an Englishwoman doing such a difficult tapasya?" My brain refused to believe that any English person could be loyal, honest, devoted and truthful. I had not forgotten the nets of deceit spun by the British in India. I had not forgotten their betrayals of trust and their atrocities. How could I then trust an English lady to be truthful? . . . I had lost faith in the English race. I was convinced that no one with the heart of a human being could take birth in that race. A race that condemns a youth to death for the love of his motherland, that cold-bloodedly murders hundreds of this youth's comrades, was not a race where a person with a human heart could be born. But Mira's dedication changed my view . . .

Bapu had directed that I acquire the skills of spinning, weaving, carding and rolling thread on a pin. He entrusted this task to Mirabehn who began to teach me with a loving tenderness that sometimes irritated me. I tried to learn but could not tolerate the pull of her love. I tried to be distant. She took that as a shortcoming in her love and increased its expression even more. I could not endure the punishment of her love. I have not written a word to Mirabehn about this. I am very proud of her. As a brother I am prepared to even sacrifice my life for her. I regarded the expression of her love towards me as a weakness in her character. I did not want that this weakness of hers should become public . . .

Till today I have not been able to decide whether I did right or wrong in rejecting Mira's love. Its memory still troubles me . . .

I could not withstand Mira's love. I did not know what to do. I was not an adherent of truth and non-violence and could not place the truth in front of Bapu. How could I tell him that Mira loves me but I cannot accept her love? If I had said so, would she have admitted this kind of weakness in herself? What would I say if she did? Finally, I did not know what else to do except sneak out and run away under the pretext of visiting my brother and his family in Burma. It was my firm resolve that a woman's weakness should never come out in the open.

———

Before he left for Burma, Mira found Prithvi becoming more and more uncomfortable when they were alone together. He was always restless, his eyes darting from side to side when they went for a walk, as if he was afraid of being seen with her or was anxious to escape. So strong and fearless yet so frightened of women and their feelings, Mira thought. In so many ways he was just a young lad, innocent under the mantle of knowingness he wore with a swagger. Friends in the ashram had told her how he sometimes boasted about his chastity *and* his attractiveness to women, and broadly hinted that Mira was infatuated with him. Mira did not condemn him for this. She found his preening rather endearing, a young man's hesitant steps into the world of love.

Mira was therefore shocked when Prithvi suddenly left for Burma without saying a word to her. He had informed Bapu the evening before of his intention to visit his brother's family there, and left a short note for Mira that was pitiful in its evasions and fear of causing her offense. It said that he greatly admired her, that he was sorry he could not respond to her feelings for him and formally asked her to forgive him for causing her pain. Mira wrote back, ". . . Do not speak of having wronged me. It is not that you should wrong me but that you should wrong yourself that pained me so much. God has cast you in pure gold and I would find it unbearable if anything would tarnish its glitter . . . Only tell me what you feel and think, that I may understand your wishes. I know you are innocent of all bad intentions. You meant everything for the best. So did I. But somehow everything went wrong. And I have paid for it with my heart's blood."

To describe Mira's pain in the days that followed would be an exercise in futility. The unending tears of all forsaken lovers, the heartbroken cry of those abandoned by their love, are much too familiar from poetry and song. Suffice it to say that Mira could not stay on in Sevagram and went off alone to Punjab and Haryana on a pilgrimage. It was a pilgrimage to the sites of Prithvi's life: the village where he was born, the schools in Ambala and Rajpur where he studied, the Ambala Central Jail where he was incarcerated when he was first imprisoned. She stayed for a week in a village near Hoshiarpur with Pandit Jagat Ram, his best friend since the days of the Gadar Party and his co-prisoner in the Andamans. A small, thin man, but with an iron will, Jagat Ram had been recently released after serving twenty-one years in jail and was in a broken state of health. Mira loved listening to Jagat Ram reminisce about their revolutionary activities, especially the stories about Prithvi's courage and devotion to the cause of India's freedom. These talks comforted her, restoring her belief in Prithvi and reassuring her of the correctness of her choice.

When Mira returned from the Punjab, a terrible anguish took possession of her. "Each morning I awoke nauseated, as if I had spent the whole night in swallowing the foam of my despair. Out of the depths of this mental anguish and physical nausea came the decision to take a vow of silence and devote myself entirely to meditation and prayer till God gave me light. To sit for long periods in motionless meditation being unnatural to me, I decided I would spin a thousand yards of yarn daily. I felt that during this spinning the mind would work in a healthy way, and I would run no risk of hallucinations that seemed to be hovering at the edge of my consciousness."

This silence, with a few days' break for traveling, lasted fifteen months. For part of the time, her rule was to speak once a day for half an hour, if necessary. The rest of the time, when she was in Sevagram, she spoke twice a week in the evening when she went to see Bapu. She read only the Vedas and the Puranas, and the letters from Bapu, and wrote only to him. This was to be her tapasya.

The Puranas are full of stories about people carrying out the severest of tapasyas. These austerities are always for a purpose: to become immortal, obtain knowledge that is otherwise the province of the gods and, for most women, to win the love of the man or god they have set their hearts on. To win Shiva as her husband Parvati practiced severe austerities for 1,000 years surrounded by five fires in summer and sitting in cold water through winter. Arundhati, desired by her father, the creator Brahma, and by her brothers, and desiring them in turn, did penance for hundreds of years till Vishnu granted her the boon that she would not look upon any other man but her husband with desire; Tulasi did tapasya for 24,000 years, eating only fruit and drinking only water, to get Vishnu as her husband. Mira's tapasya to win Prithvi as her husband could thus look back at a venerable tradition in Hindu mythology.

Unable to remain any longer in Sevagram, its innumerable associations with Prithvi constantly threatening to turn his memory into hallucinations, Mira went to stay alone in a hut on a tea estate in Kangra district, 4,000 feet above sea level. The tea estate was owned by Lala Kanhayialal, one of Bapu's many devotees. This was on 2 October, Bapu's birthday, shortly after the outbreak of the Second World War.

The hut stood at the end of a wooded ridge, just before it dipped down into a ravine where a stream flowed, its waters cold and clear. Except for a cowshed at the upper end of the ridge about a furlong away, there was no habitation around the hut; the main house of the tea estate was about a mile away. To the north, from between the trees, Mira had a fine view of the steep, rocky Dhaula Dhar range, its peaks rising up to 15,000 feet. In winter, which soon set in, the peaks glistened with snow against a clear, pale blue sky. To the right, below the pine trees, was a little glade of rice fields, and in the southeast, the forest dropped down into the ravine. The solitude and the picturesque surroundings began to ease her heart. The great boulders of gray rock, covered with lichen, and the sweet, gentle music of the stream in the ravine were a perpetual joy. It was from direct contact with the glory of the elements, from this pure and mighty source, that she began to regain her strength.

Part of her strength also came from Gandhiji's letters, which he wrote regularly, his concern for her palpable in every line, reassuring her that she was always in his thoughts, though out of sight, and expressing the hope that time was healing her pain.

Chi. Mira,

I have your long letter. It enables me to follow the struggle that is going on within you. You have not yet acquired the art of looking within for everything. Carding should soothe as much as spinning once you connect the process with God. Farhad saw his God through breaking a mountain. He is represented as one incessantly delivering heavy blows with God-given strength. He broke the mountain and found his God who is represented as a fair bride . . . What is essential is the spirit of dedication to God. Whatever your outward activity, it must be all for God . . .

God be with you.

Love, Bapu

Mira's tapasya did not involve a struggle against thoughts of Prithvi, her love. On the contrary. She was convinced that her relationship with him was a continuation of one they had shared in their earlier lives, a bond Prithvi had forgotten in this birth. She would wait till he remembered, as he must some time. All she asked for now was to be free of the anguish that each moment of thinking about him caused in her. This boon was soon granted. "At night, when I closed my eyes and imagined the dark hills I would have to cross to reach him in far away Burma, the pain was now soaked in sweetness. Gradually, I could imagine him without crying. I could make him up, his brown body, his strong clear movements, and not dissolve into a puddle of tears. I could think of him as being somewhere on the other side of the wide night, of the great distance between us, and not be overtaken by panic. When I came out of silence, God had given me the strength that I had up to then sought in vain. My way forward into life . . . and love, lay before me, lighted by His beacon."

Gandhiji's concern for Mira did not end with the letters of consolation and reassurance he sent her regularly. He partly blamed himself for what had happened. He felt responsible for Prithvi Singh looking upon Mira as his sister rather than as a possible wife for, when Prithvi had come to Sevagram, Gandhiji had told him that the women in the ashram should be looked upon as sisters. He wondered whether Prithvi was only following his wishes in his behavior towards Mira. Under these circumstances, he felt it was his duty to persuade Prithvi to accept Mira as his wife. He also wrote to Prithvi's friends inquiring about his whereabouts and seeking to enlist their aid in his undertaking. Like the anxious father of a still unmarried daughter, he recommended Mira to them as "a perfect being" who "will be of great help to Prithvi."

twenty-three

$\mathcal{B}$Y THE TIME Prithvi Singh returned from Burma, I had left Sevagram, my sense of agency fully restored. For that I cannot be grateful enough to Bapu, my healer. After recovering from my stomach ailment, I had formulated stringent rules for my conduct which I was determined to follow during my stay at the ashram. The two main rules related to food ("to eat only what is good for health and not fall into the trap of taste") and women ("to control my awareness of women, for instance, by walking with my eyes lowered so as to avoid the temptation to look at a woman when one walks past"). I kept a daily record of my observance of these rules which I handed over to Bapu at the end of the week. Bapu received these pages with a smile but without comment, except once, when he wrote at the back of one page, "Regard these rules only as the means to an end, which is the turning of your mind towards God" and, in English, "Seek ye first the kingdom of God and his righteousness and everything will be added to you."

My diary entry of 7 May, following Bapu's response, shows

my enthusiasm in following the regimen I had set for myself. "In the last four days I have achieved great success in stopping the capricious play of my eyes. If the eyes involuntarily look up, I do not discern in them the wish to look at a woman. On espying a woman, the eyes realize their error by themselves and look down, leaving no trace of curiosity or desire in the heart."

The next entry, three days later, shows that my initial enthusiasm has dissipated. "My wish to leave the ashram and go back to my earlier life is becoming stronger by the day. I find no interest in the dull, routine work I do here. Thoughts of a literary life in Lucknow beckon me. Bapu is right; I don't have the spirit of service that can infuse the most boring task with life. How long can I continue to depend on Bapu? How long will it take me to stand on my own feet?"

Bapu called me on the Sunday after he had read my diary entry and spoke to me with great tenderness. I do not remember his exact words—our talks stretched over three evenings—but their tenor was that he had realized I was forcing myself to change my nature. He was convinced that my nature demanded the normal life of a householder—marriage and children.

"Never do violence to your nature," he told me. "If you forcibly cut off a part of yourself, at sometime or the other it will take revenge. It will come back to haunt you like a ghost, demanding to live the unfulfilled part of its life. Go back to Lucknow, marry, have children and serve the country as best you can. I release you from all your vows."

I went back to Lucknow, eased in mind and spirit. For Bapu had not abandoned, but freed me. No longer an eyewitness to the events after Prithvi's return, I mainly rely on his memoirs for their reconstruction.

Prithvi had written to Gandhiji from Burma inquiring about Mira's state of mind, and he had been reassured by Bapu's reply telling him that he need not worry about her. Though she was still convinced about their connection in an earlier life, which he seemed to have forgotten about, she was nevertheless happy. She was treating the affair as a spiritual problem and doing penance, studying the Puranas and spending hours and hours in spinning.

Thus, when Prithvi returned to Sevagram hoping to resume his earlier life, he was not unduly worried. He thought his dilemma over how to respond to Mira's love had come to a natural end with all the time that had passed while he was away in Burma.

On his arrival, Prithvi went straight to Gandhiji's hut. Bapu was away in some other part of the ashram and Prithvi waited outside in the veranda. It was around eleven in the morning on a crisp and sunny day in February. People were walking around the ashram grounds, not in any hurry to enter the cold buildings to carry out their allotted tasks. The news that Prithvi Singh was back spread fast and Mira ran out to meet him.

"Prithvi!" she cried, happy to see him back.

It all happened so fast that Prithvi could not help his reaction. Her movement toward him was too impetuous, her outstretched hand seeking to take his too eager. He recoiled as if she was the carrier of an infectious disease, raising his folded hands in a polite namaste before stepping back hastily, almost tripping against the doorstep of Bapu's room.

The two years he had been away had added ten to her face. Her once thick hair, now more gray than brown, had thinned; at the height of her anguish, clumps of it had come out with every brushing. She had tied it back tightly in an old woman's knot. Recurrent bouts of malaria had left her skin permanently tinged sallow. The natural oils of her skin, never enough to begin with in a person of her race, had almost been sucked out by the persistent Indian sun, prematurely aging it. She looked frail and vulnerable and Prithvi was determined not to hurt her. At the same time, he did not want to give her a wrong impression about what he felt for her: respect, admiration and the fierce protectiveness of a brother.

In the three days Prithvi spent at Sevagram, he tried to avoid being alone with Mira. On the last day of his stay, after the evening prayer, Mira came up to him in full view of a group of curious ashram inmates and asked him to accompany her for a walk; she needed to talk to him. Prithvi followed her meekly, dreading what was to come, raising a wall around him even as they walked towards the hillock outside the village.

"Are you not cold?" he asked solicitously as they sat down on the flat surface of a rock, the dust left by passing cattle now settling on the path below them and the first glow-worms beginning to appear in the surrounding scrub.

Mira ignored the proffered politeness. You are avoiding me, she told Prithvi, her voice filled with an anguish that left no room for recrimination. She talked to him of her tapasya during the time he had been away and of its goal—their union as man and wife working together to fulfil Bapu's dreams for a free and independent India. In her tapasya she had at last found God's purpose for her life. Did he still not realize that their connection to each other went back a long time, much before this lifetime, to many earlier births?

Prithvi was upset, as much by her words as the intensity of love that filled them, a love that seemed to set her free but which he found unbearably oppressive. Perhaps we'll have to wait for our next birth then, he said, trying to give the conversation a lighthearted turn but aware that he was not successful in lifting its weight. He was going to Saurashtra to visit the places where he had spent his years in the underground, he said to Mira. He did not know where he was going to settle down next. All he was sure of at this moment was his commitment to the cause. He was quite clear that he needed to travel alone on his path, at least in the foreseeable future—the last words were added hastily in response to the expression of pain that flitted across Mira's face. At least we can be companions on that path, Mira said, comrades who can work together. Let us talk it over with Bapu when you return. Prithvi quickly agreed, anxious to escape, knowing he would never come back to Sevagram.

Three days after he arrived in Bhavnagar, a letter came from Mira.

. . . Seventeen years ago, when I came to Bapu, I put myself in his hands, and he, with the fullness of his love, took complete possession of me, guiding not only my actions, but even my thoughts and feelings. It was a great disciplining and training out of which I learnt a tremendous amount, but it also undermined my self-reliance and self-expression, and I became incapable of doing any sustained or independent work. Before I came to Bapu I was a person of free energy, enterprise and self-reliance. All this I somehow lost. Only when you came into my life did my natural strength reawaken. When I went into the tapasya I was conscious of my real self coming back to life. I feel a new strength and freedom added to it during those fifteen months of silent prayers and reading. I gained spiritual riches which were unknown to me before. Having realized all this, what should I do? If I tried to work again under Bapu's personal guidance I knew I should fail . . . So I went to Bapu, put my difficulty to him and asked him to grant me "purna swaraj." Bapu, with that greatness of heart which is his alone, gave it to me straight away . . . I explained to Bapu that my desire was to start a centre for training women somewhere in the UP . . . I am anxious to find a fine and healthy site in the UP towards the Himalayas, if possible on the bank of one of the great rivers, within hundred miles or so, of Delhi . . .

If you have any suggestions or ideas, how glad I shall be to have them. The same inspiration drew us forth from our homes and sent us out into the unknown—the same ideal for India's freedom fills our hearts today. The only difference of opinion between us is that I believe with all my heart and soul that our strength for fullest service lies in our union and you believe otherwise. So long as you feel like that I will accept without further argument your wish and I will strive with all the strength in me to serve alone. But if, in my solitary service, I can have your comradeship of heart, it will enrich my work as nothing else could. To know that he in whom and through whom I live and find my strength is there in my life, a friend, a comrade, oh how that will sustain and strengthen me!

A week later, another letter followed.

. . . I said to you that I knew from the bottom of my soul that if I gave up the hope of winning you and came out of my tapasya, God would withdraw Himself from me. I said that I believed it to be my dharma to dedicate my life energy to God in prayer for you as my husband.

Yet on account of outer pressure and because of the pain that I saw on your face and heard in your voice, I yielded. No sooner did I come out of my tapasya than I felt something had gone wrong. But I sought happiness in the fact that I could see you, and turn to you as a friend. The comradeship which I longed for and the fulfillment of my life seemed to be there; yet it was not. I hid the emptiness of my heart from the world and from you. But

I could not hide it from God. Day by day He drew from me burning, silent tears. I could not pray to Him as in the past and yet I did not admit to myself the cause—that I had departed from the path of truth. In these few weeks my health and spirit became broken and crushed and my only longing was to die . . .

God had mercy on me and gave me the strength to face the truth. I saw that I must go back into my tapasya. Most truly it had been a sin for me to give up hope which is faith. Even the hope you held out to me for the next birth I could not expect to gain if I did not fulfil that which I believed to be my duty towards you in my present birth.

This time my tapasya shall take the form of national service. The only change in my present activities will be from within. Instead of putting away Hope, I shall dedicate my every action to God in prayer for winning you, like I did in my silence.

I tell you this, because it would be a lie for me to hide from you the change . . . Even if you wish to have nothing to do with me, I think you will agree that you should at least acknowledge the reciept of this letter so that I may know that you are not in ignorance of my tapasya.

Personally, I do not feel that truth demands that we should cut off all communication with one another. So long as you know what is in my heart there is no untruth.

Whatever you do, you remain for me that which you have been from the beginning.

Finally Prithvi wrote back, taking care to address her as "My dear sister, Mira."

Received yours. It has given me a great shock. In these stormy days the duty of every lover of India must be to work with a single-minded devotion for the liberation of the country. I do not want to have any other thought upon my brain but the realization of the dreams of my life for which I have lived and suffered. Can't you appreciate the delicate situation in the country? How can any idea other than the service of the Indian people take possession of you and make you mad? Circumstances demand that you should work with all the vigour that you command and be an example to the sisters in India. How can you allow your health to be shattered and thus reduce yourself to a dead weight on India which requires the help of brave persons to rescue her from the chains of slavery? Mira, the Almighty have bestowed upon you so many gifts. Do not be selfish. Please give me your helping hand and be a source of inspiration and guiding light to the aspirants for freedom. Your services will be recorded in history. Do rise to the occasion. Accumulate all the physical and mental energy that you can and devote it to the cause that stands dearer to my heart. At this juncture ordinary citizens are called upon to make the utmost sacrifice that they are capable of making. Won't you rise above the ordinary citizens in the street and make a supreme sacrifice of renouncing your love? This will give me a thrill and I will be inspired to play the part that destiny have called upon me to play. Make a firm stand wherever you are. Do not shirk your national duty. Make up a resolute determination and give me mental peace so that I may die in peace if occasion demands.

With brotherly regards,
Prithvi Singh

For all her self-control, Mira could not prevent her anguish (and resignation) from seeping into her response. As I read her letter,

I feel she has left it to me to feel outraged, even disgusted, by the sanctimonious tone of Prithvi's last letter to her.

23 March 1942

Dearest Friend,

I am deeply touched by your letter and would have answered it at once were it not for the rush of work here, which left no time.

How can I help you to understand what is in my heart? Once God enables me to do that, all your suffering on my account will go and you will come to realize that you have in me, not a hindrance, but added strength for fulfilling your ideal.

Your letter shows me that, up to now, you have wholly misunderstood my love. I can appreciate your difficulty. You are cent per cent a man, with your whole being devoted to your ideal. In spite of all that you have suffered and experienced in life, you have remained the same as you were thirty years ago—strong, relentless, fearless—that is your glory and your power. But along with that strength you also sometimes have difficulty in understanding new things and situations that come across your path. My entry in your life is one such case.

You ask me to renounce my love, as if it were some sort of self-indulgence. You do not realize that *real love*, the love that rises from the depths of the soul, increases the power of service and is as sacred as religion. For women, love and faith become one; to ask me to renounce my love is like asking me to renounce my faith in God and my strength to serve. What good can that do for you or India? Why should you think that my love for you is impure or selfish? A woman's fullest strength comes to her only after she has found her beloved. From that day she becomes a new being, with redoubled strength, patience and understanding. But if her beloved turns on her and says "renounce your love for my sake," he stabs to death the new being and all the sources of endurance and service that had sprung to life in her are dried up.

What I tried to explain to you in my last letter was that I had endeavoured to deny my love in order to please you. But no sooner had I done it than I knew in my soul that I had sinned against God. I had denied the light He had given me. When a person who has faith in the Almighty is conscious of having denied His guidance, then the strength of body and mind are both shattered. I saw that this was no service to you, but a direct disservice to you, to God and to the country. And so I wrote to you the letter telling you that I must no longer try to deny the love and light that guide me. At the same time I tried to make it clear to you that I was not going to retire into silence and solitude but was going to make national service my tapasya. The change is all from within. I have removed from my heart that false denial and put back in its place the light and inspiration of love that you have awakened in me. Outwardly the only change is that my health and energy are coming back to me . . .

In your letter you tell me to use the gifts that the Almighty has given me, and to lend you a helping hand and be an inspiration to those who seek India's freedom. That is what I am striving to do with all my heart and soul. You think, because I love you, I am possessed by a mad and selfish passion. Such a notion is totally wrong and a cruel libel on a woman's love. I seek your love and cooperation, not for my personal pleasure, but for greater strength in service for us both.

Prithvi, why do you turn from me as if my love were poison? Nobody in the world can long more ardently than I do that your great ideals should be fulfilled. From the first days of our coming together I have been conscious of the feeling that my ambitions for you are even greater than your own. I long that your heart should turn towards me and fill me with unfettered strength for work, instead of being left, as I am at present, to struggle under the heart-breaking load of your cold aloofness. You have no need to fear what would happen if you were kind to me. I am not urging you all of a sudden to marry me. I am only asking you, in the beginning, to accept the truth of my love and faith, and not to shun me because I am honest with you. Let us be generous and fearless in our dealings with one another. The rest is in God's hands.

At this moment, when the whole world is torn by cruel war and hate and India is tossed on the waves of the storm, like a ship in peril on the sea, let us pull together like sailors pulling at one rope.

May God guide us to be true to Him, to India, and to one another.

All we have after this is Prithvi's silence and Mira's last despairing attempt to reach him.

I am sending you this letter through Asha, so as to be sure that it reaches you safely . . . I am being true with you, nothing else. I can never really inspire you or make you happy by being false. Do not shun me because I am honest. Alas that you can so little understand me! One kind word from you would lift a deadly burden from my heart . . .

Where and when we shall meet again I do not know. When the storm rises, prison and even death may be in store for us. But I do not fear. If God wills it we shall meet again in this life. If He wills otherwise we shall meet in the next birth to serve with fresh strength the India of our dreams.

May God bless you in every way—ever yours,

Mira

————

The political storm of the Quit India movement, which Gandhiji called his last "do or die" effort to win India's freedom, broke on 9 August 1942 with mass-scale arrests of Congress leaders. In the next six to seven weeks mass demonstrations and public meetings were held throughout the country. Students in schools and colleges went on strike and marched on the streets. Many wrote and distributed illegal news-sheets calling for revolt against British rule and went into the villages to organize resistance. The authorities reacted with teargassing, baton charges and wide-spread arrests. With all its leaders behind bars, the movement began to lose its nonviolent character. Crowds attacked courts, police stations, post offices, railway stations and other symbols of British administration. At a time when the war was going badly for Britain, its armies in retreat before the Japanese in Southeast Asia, the British reacted with harsh repression. There were police firings on demonstrators in the cities and towns. Villagers were whipped, made to pay collective fines and taken as hostages. Entire villages were burnt if found empty of their inhabitants who had fled to escape arrest.

The movement now went underground, focusing on disruption of communications and transport, so essential for the British war effort. Prithvi Singh's young revolutionary friends who cut telegraph wires and derailed goods trains by removing fish plates from railway tracks carried out many of these acts.

Gandhiji was arrested on the night of 8 August immediately after he announced his intention to launch the Quit India campaign at a public meeting in Bombay. Mirabehn, Ba and Mahadev were arrested along with him and went on to share his long imprisonment in Poona. In a later wave of arrests in October 1942, Prithvi Singh, who after leaving Sevagram had been training young men in physical fitness and martial arts all over Saurashtra, was also put behind bars. I, too, served fifteen months in Lucknow jail for helping to publish a one-page newspaper on behalf of the Congress Party in the United Provinces. I regard my imprisonment as a badge of honor, an insignia of the spirit of service that Bapu always believed I lacked, and remain inordinately proud of it to this day.

———

I have often wondered why Prithvi rejected Mira's love. His diary entry on his misgivings about Mira's English origins or his letters to her pleading idealistic reasons—his single-minded devotion to the cause of India's freedom that left room for little else—are difficult to believe. In them Prithvi is once again giving a positive gloss to his actions, fitting his response to a woman in love with him to his image of himself as a revolutionary prepared to sacrifice all chances of personal happiness for a larger cause. It is clear from the memoirs he published when he was an old man that he had never been disinclined towards marriage or women.

I have never tried to lead the life of a puritan. If in my younger days strong urges of intense patriotism to free the country from the shackles of slavery had not taken such strong hold of me, I might have ended enjoying the pleasures of the world . . .

During my wanderings in Burma, Japan, Philippines, Afghanistan, Russia and the Caucasus, I saw many figures of ravishing beauty, enough to steal one's heart, but I never let my heart go after them. In youth I had heard a lovely exhortation: Fallen ideas, fallen words, fall in viewpoint and fall of semen—if a man can save himself from these four falls, then he can safely travel on the road of life, however slippery the way.

The pretty regions of Gujarat and Saurashtra are quite well known for the heart-gripping beauty of its womanhood. I lived in that region for full eight years and yet I stayed whole. In that land, I came across wondrous beauties, each surpassing the other. In that garden of beauties, my heart often felt attracted like a honeybee. But before the bee could spread its wings to alight on a fair flower noble thoughts pinioned it . . . But times changed, my ideology changed . . .

The sum-total of all these happenings [in the ashram] was that it set me thinking that it would be most suitable and correct for me to bind myself in a marriage-tie to a woman who would be full of strength, have sturdy health, and be free of ailment . . . Soon after I left the Ashram, I made up my mind that as soon as a young girl after my heart made an offer of love, I would frankly tell her that I would agree to marry and would ask her if she is agreeable. On getting her consent, I would have no hesitation in going for the wedding.

I believe Prithvi was simply not attracted to Mira as a woman. She was too old, and not someone who could bear him children. Another reason could lie in his Rajput origins and in his being a peasant from Haryana. Both of these predispose a man towards exaggerated notions of masculinity, male honor, and a rigid differentiation between men and women—Prithvi could not let his manliness be degraded to a feminine state by what would appear to him as Mira's mannish courting. He would rather have been the arrow than the target of desire. But these are speculations on my part, not free of my dislike for that charming poseur who was also a brave and courageous man.

After his release, Prithvi eloped with a woman twenty-five years younger than him who shared his passion for physical education. They had a son and a daughter. After Independence, he settled down to a life of comfort and honor in Punjab as a revolutionary icon of India's struggle for independence.

Prithvi Singh and Mira never met again, at least not in this life.

Epilogue

ON THE AFTERNOON my conference in Vienna ended, I drove out to Baden to see Mirabehn. The young diplomat I had spoken to at the Indian embassy had kindly offered to call her and make the necessary arrangements for my travel.

Mira lived in an isolated cottage at the edge of the forest above Baden. Whatever else had changed in the thirty years since we last saw each other, her need for solitude had remained intact. She must have been waiting for me near the door, for it opened even before I finished knocking.

"How well you look!" we lied at the same time, and then laughed with pleasure at seeing each other again.

Mira had become thinner, the planes of her face sharply angled, the prominent nose now a pronounced beak. Her hair was completely white. Cropped by an indifferent hand, it hung in uneven strands down to her shoulder blades. She wore a crumpled khadi kurta and a baggy salwar, both faded to an indeterminate dun hue from many washes. Limping slightly from arthritis in her left knee, she led me into the living room of her two-room cottage.

The room was dominated by a Bechstein grand piano in one corner, musical scores piled on top of it, and a large teak desk facing the French window that opened into a small, unkempt garden. Beyond the garden was a gently sloping meadow that ended at a line of pine trees marking the beginning of the Baden forest. The desk was littered with pencils, notebooks of various sizes, and loose sheets of paper kept down by rocks used as paperweights. A crudely made bookcase, no more than planks nailed together, lined one wall of the room, its shelves crammed with books. A large portrait of a brooding Beethoven, a copy of the famous drawing in the Bonn museum, hung on another wall.

We sat in large, overstuffed sofa chairs that sagged in the middle, their cushions dusty and liberally sprinkled with dog hair. Between the sofas was a round table on which were kept framed photographs that had not been dusted for a while. Besides the photographs of her family, there was one of Romain Rolland, inscribed to Mira in French by the writer and, almost hidden by the photograph of Mira's father in his admiral's uniform, one of Mira with Gandhiji. The photograph had been taken in 1931 when they had sailed to London for the Round Table Conference—Gandhiji, on the deck of the passenger liner, wearing a short dhoti and a wrap around his shoulders, is leaning forward against the ship's railing; a much larger Mira, clad in a rough, white khadi saree, its pallu covering her head, hovers protectively behind him.

Mira's servant, an Indian man in his forties who looked twenty years older, served tea and biscuits. Mira had brought him with her from Rishikesh where he had helped her look after the cows in her ashram. Inordinately pleased to see an Indian face, he began to talk to me in rapid-fire Hindi, pouring out the travails of living in a foreign land, before Mira told him sharply to return to the kitchen and feed the dog. I never saw the dog, though his odor hung in the room.

Mira had chosen to live in Baden because of its connection to Beethoven. He had been her first passion as a girl and a young woman and now she had returned to him. Every morning she walked the trail the composer had taken for his walks during the summers he spent in Baden. Each day she played his music on the piano and listened to it on the records she purchased on her rare trips to Vienna. Books on Beethoven were scattered all over the cottage and she was making good progress in learning German. She was writing a book, she told me, a book on Beethoven as an unrecognized mystic.

When she talked of Beethoven, which was most of the afternoon, the old woman facing me in the chair seemed to dissolve in the passion and vibrancy of a young girl recounting the qualities of her beloved. "Navin, you cannot imagine how happy I am living here, surrounded by his spirit, going for walks in the woods where he composed his music. Oh, Navin, the Eternal has never expressed itself as clearly!"

Almost at the end of my visit I brought up Bapu, a topic she had not avoided but also not really welcomed, into the conversation. I told her I had heard that she refused to talk about Gandhiji to her visitors.

"Yes," she said, her voice fiercely protective. "They write such lies about him. The Westerners I can forgive. They have always been arrogant enough to believe that anyone living differently from their middle-class lives has to be a crank. But even the Indians are now aping them. I wonder sometimes if India deserved him. Navin, no one knew him! No one!"

Her gray eyes under the still dark and thick eyebrows were flashing with an old fire, burning away the wrinkles on her face.

"No one!" she repeated. She did not need to add "except me."

I knew it was pointless to probe further. Mira would never

reveal what she knew, if indeed there were any secrets to be revealed.

As she walked me to the door, she said, "How lucky I have been, Navin, to hear the call of the Eternal, loudly and clearly. Not once but twice in my life. In Beethoven's music and in Bapu's person. Most people never hear the call at all. To others it is so indistinct that all it does is cause a lifelong feeling of vague dissatisfaction. I have been singularly blessed."

Was she really, I wondered. Had she lived a life that had fulfilled her as a woman and a person? Or was hers a tragic story whose heroine insisted on seeing it as a romantic quest in which, after withstanding the perils of the road, she had been rewarded by an exaltation beyond normal human experience? Fortunately, I did not have to answer my own questions. For who can ever judge the success or failure of someone else's life?

When I reached the car, so thoughtfully provided by the Indian embassy, parked a couple of hundred yards from the cottage, Mira's servant came running up to me, his lined face distraught.

"Sahib, I don't want to live here. I want to go home. Please, take me home."

I mumbled an apology for being unable to help and left him standing in the grassy meadow peering after me in the late afternoon sun as the car pulled away.

ACKNOWLEDGMENTS

The following literature was especially useful in the writing of this book:

The Mirabehn Papers, Nehru Memorial Museum, New Delhi

Mirabehn, *The Spirit's Pilgrimage*, Arlington: Great Ocean Publishers, 1960

The Mirabehn Centenary Volume, New Delhi: Himalaya Seva Sangh, 1992

Gitta Sereny, "A Life with Gandhi," NY *Times Magazine*, 14 November 1982

Bapu's Letters to Mira, 1924–1948, Ahmadabad: Navajivan Press, 1949

Romain Rolland Gandhi Correspondence, Delhi: Publications Division, 1976

M. K. Gandhi, *Collected Works*, vols. 32–49, 72–81, Delhi: Publications Division, 1958

M. K. Gandhi, *The Story of My Experiments with Truth*, Ahmadabad: Navajivan Press, 1927

Judith Brown, *Gandhi: Prisoner of Hope*, New Haven: Yale University Press, 1989

Kanu and Abha Gandhi, *Bapu Ke Saath*, New Delhi: Publications Division, 1990

Manubehn Gandhi, *My Memorable Moments with Bapu*, Ahmadabad: Navajivan Press, 1960

Millie Polak, *Mr Gandhi: The Man*, Bombay: Vora, 1949

Narayan Desai, *Gandhi through a Child's Eyes,* Santa Fe: Ocean Tree Publishers, 1992

The Diary of Mahadev Desai, vols. 5–7, Ahmadabad: Navajivan Press, 1953

Mark Thomson, *Gandhi and His Ashrams*, Bombay: Popular Prakashan, 1993

Baba Prithvi Singh Azad Papers, Nehru Memorial Museum, New Delhi

Baba Prithvi Singh Azad: The Legendary Crusader, Bombay: Bharati Vidya Bhavan, 1987

Rahul Sankrityayana, *Sardar Prithvi Singh*, Delhi

Sumangal Prakash, *Bapu Ke Saath*, New Delhi: Purvodya Prakashak, 1976

V. S. Naravane, *Premchand: His Life and Work*, New Delhi: Vikas, 1980

I am grateful to Vaiju Naravane, Christine Zeile, David Davidar, Ravi Singh and my wife Katha for their helpful comments on the first draft of the novel. It is a pleasure to acknowledge the contribution of Poulomi Chatterjee at Penguin India. I also wish to thank the Center for Study of World Religions at Harvard University where I spent a year as its Fortieth Anniversary Fellow, and where I began writing this novel, for their generous hospitality.